D1351890

John Eagles worked as a psychiatrist for 30 years, becoming a consultant in General Adult Psychiatry and an Honorary Professor at Aberdeen University. He published more than 100 papers in medical journals.

Following retirement, he joined the MLitt in Creative Writing course at Dundee University, and now splits his time between Aberdeen and Fife. 'Starting to Shrink' is his first novel.

John Eagles

STARTING TO SHRINK

AUSTIN MACAULEY PUBLISHERS™

LONDON • CAMBRIDGE • NEW YORK • SHARJAH

Copyright © John Eagles (2017)

The right of John Eagles to be identified as author of this work has been asserted by him in accordance with section 77 and 78 of the Copyright, Designs and Patents Act 1988.

All rights reserved. No part of this publication may be reproduced, stored in a retrieval system, or transmitted in any form or by any means, electronic, mechanical, photocopying, recording, or otherwise, without the prior permission of the publishers.

Any person who commits any unauthorised act in relation to this publication may be liable to criminal prosecution and civil claims for damages.

A CIP catalogue record for this title is available from the British Library.

ISBN 9781786938541 (Paperback)
ISBN 9781786938558 (E-Book)
www.austinmacauley.com

First Published (2017)
Austin Macauley Publishers Ltd.
25 Canada Square
Canary Wharf
London
E14 5LQ

Dedication

To my daughters, Katie and Jane.

Acknowledgements

I would like to thank all the patients and colleagues who shaped my experiences during my career in psychiatry. The book could not exist without you. Any specific resemblance between characters in the book and patients or colleagues, however, is coincidental.

In the early stages of the book's inception, Jill Hinnrichs was a huge support. Abi Strachan and Sheila Calder gave useful feedback on the first draft. Later on, Glynis Cook and Sam Robson provided invaluable critiques. Comments from my family—Katie Eagles, Jane Eagles, Chris Eagles—and from my book group—Lana Hadden, Angie Baxter, Ann Pritchard, Helen Simonsen and Paul Sclare—were also very helpful.

Staff on the Dundee University MLitt in Creative Writing course were often helpful, sometimes inspirational. I am thinking particularly of Kirsty Gunn, the late Jim Stewart and Eddie Small.

Jennie Erdal went through my early manuscript with a fine-tooth comb and a discerning eye, and I am very grateful to her.

To: Dr Douglas Barker
Senior House Officer in Psychiatry
Hillend Hospital

842-6 Holborn Crescent
London
28th April 1982

Dear Dr Barker,

General Medical Council Complaint

On behalf of the General Medical Council, notice is hereby given that in consequence of a complaint made against you to the Council, an Inquiry is to be held into the following charges:

"That, as a registered medical practitioner, while providing psychiatric care to Ms Lucy Campbell:

(a) You expressed sexual feelings towards Ms Campbell and suggested that you and she might engage together in sexual activities,
(b) You conducted an unnecessary and inappropriately intimate physical examination upon Ms Campbell in your hospital office,

(c) You visited Ms Campbell's flat where you and she engaged in full sexual intercourse,

(d) Through the above actions, you abused your position during the care of a vulnerable patient with a psychiatric disorder and that, in relation to these alleged facts, you have been guilty of Serious Professional Misconduct."

Notice is further given to you that on Monday the 26th day of July 1982, a meeting of the Professional Conduct Committee will commence at the London premises of the Council at 10 a.m. in order to consider these charges against you, and to determine whether to erase your name from the Medical Register or to suspend your registration, therein. In the meantime, you may continue to practise.

You may appear in person, or be represented by any counsel or solicitor of your choosing, or by any member of your family. If you choose not to appear in person, the Committee have the power to hear and decide upon the said charge in your absence.

Yours sincerely,
Cowdrey, Frost and Johnston
Solicitors to the General Medical Council

10

August 1981

The first day of Dr Douglas Barker's career as a psychiatrist was nearing its end. He was trying to make eye contact with the young woman who was turned slightly away from him. She was staring into space, apparently lost in thought, her long dark hair obscuring his view of her face. She turned towards him.

"A pint of lager," he said.

Once he had a place of his own, this would almost certainly not be his local pub. But, with a barmaid as attractive as this, perhaps he should look for a flat nearby.

There was a lot of eye contact as she placed his drink on the bar.

"To you, fifty pence," she said.

He took his drink over to the barstool in the corner of the quiet pub, intending to take stock of his first day as a psychiatrist. Before doing that, he took stock of the bar. It was not the sort of place he was used to. It had character and gravitas. It had been done up to look old, with slightly battered furniture and grainy black and white photographs on the walls. The photo closest to him could have been taken during a curling match, with four men wearing striped jackets and dressed for the cold. They looked pleased with themselves and perhaps they had won. It occurred to him that maybe the pub was genuinely old, but he didn't know how he could tell. His mother had once described him as 'proud to be a philistine'.

Lots of things in this city were old. Even to his untutored eye, the buildings and the cobbled streets gave the place a solid, classy feel. All around were reminders that people had lived here long before the 1980s. In this city, it might be necessary to take more interest in history; perhaps try to become a little more cultured.

This thought had first occurred to him over coffee that morning with two psychiatrists on his ward. One of them, a senior registrar, was his immediate boss and the other was (like him) a new senior house officer. He tried in vain to recall the senior registrar's name, but all he could remember was that it reminded him of an animal. He resolved to get better at recognising people and remembering their names. He recollected his fellow senior house officer's name—Dick—since almost immediately after the effete handshake, Douglas had decided that it was entirely apposite.

Since it was their first day, he thought that the senior registrar—did his name *start* with an animal, *Hen*derson maybe—would give them an idea of what they would be doing day to day, tell them about rotas, on-call duties and so on. Douglas tried to raise these issues, about which he was feeling rather anxious, but Dick was having none of it. He had already done a year of psychiatry elsewhere, and was intent upon taking this new post entirely in his stride. He wanted to talk about subjects he seemed sure they would find more interesting, such as art, literature and the theatre. The senior registrar (was it *Cow*an?) chimed in, and unfortunately it turned out that they had seen the same play, during which naked people emerged from boxes and delivered soliloquies. Douglas was sure that they would quickly agree

12

what a lot of nonsense it had been but, quite the reverse, they got into a debate about the 'meaning of the piece'.

"I felt it was a clever *trapdoors of the mind* analogy. The boxes being the boundaries of our subconscious, maybe even elements of the collective unconscious."

"I saw it more as a birth metaphor. We come naked into the world, emerging from a *dark box* as it were, and then being bemused, all at sea—the actors seemed to me to be portraying *newborn-ness.*"

His name could well have been *Rat*tray.

"I'm not sure about that," Dick had continued, fingering his wispy beard. "They came in and out of the boxes, not like birth, more like thoughts emerging from the unconscious into the conscious mind."

"Some of them put their heads out and stayed out, perhaps content to be born. Others may have wished to return to the womb."

"The other thought I had was that it was a dream world we were being invited to enter."

Douglas was experiencing a feeling of profound unreality, but Dick regarded him expectantly, apparently waiting for his contribution.

"Didn't see it. Can't comment. Is it still on?"

"No, it was just on for three days last week. I believe it made way for Chekhov."

"Right, I'll look out for that then," said Douglas.

He had spent most of the rest of the morning doing paperwork—his contract, his library card, his name badge application—and skimming through a document entitled 'An Outline of Your Post' that seemed to have been produced by a previous incumbent with some obsessional traits. There were details about everything from history taking techniques to the location of tubes for blood tests.

After lunch he met the two senior nurses on the ward, Tam and Sami. He was reassured to think that he would get on well with both of them. Tam was the Charge Nurse, in overall control of nursing matters and directly supervising one of the shifts, while Sami, his deputy, supervised the other. The shifts overlapped for a few hours in the middle of the day, and the nurses had made a point of seeking him out.

Tam was about fifty, a ginger man going grey. He had various shades of orange, brown and grey in his hair and in his beard, so he resembled a spaniel. He had a twinkle in his eye, and it was quickly apparent that he was experienced and kind. Sami was originally from Sri Lanka. He was small and wiry with dense curly hair, and he wore a sharp suit. He had an infectious giggle and announced that he and Douglas had played cricket against each other.

"Last year in the cup, you hit me for six then next ball you were stumped by a mile!"

Douglas tried to remember and then tried to look as if he had remembered.

"More run out than stumped, wasn't it?" he suggested, happy to be working with a fellow cricketer.

The nurses soon told him that they had met Dr Dick.

"He came up last week—before he had even started—wanting to be shown round," said Tam with raised eyebrows.

"He used to work in Oxford, apparently," said Sami, affecting a posh accent.

The nurses seemed to share his own first impressions of Dick. Douglas described his brief medical career, and they discussed some of the patients he would be looking after.

"And your consultant is to be Dr Burlington?" asked Sami, clearly already knowing this, and looking towards Tam with half a smile.

"Yes, I'm meeting him tomorrow morning. Apparently, he's at a conference today. Is there something I should know?"

Douglas's reflections on his day had been regularly interrupted by the barmaid. Not that these intrusions were unwelcome, especially when they coincided with his need for another drink. She was chatty, perhaps because the bar was quiet.

"And what sort of work do you do?" she asked.

He paused, feeling quite pleased with himself.

"I'm a psychiatrist, actually."

She gazed at him appraisingly.

"Aye, sure, you're a psychiatrist and I'm a bloody acrobat," she said.

"No, I am. It was my very first day today."

"And I'll show you my backward somersault off the bar in just a minute."

Douglas wondered if it was good or bad that the notion of his being a psychiatrist seemed implausible. He smiled and shrugged, and did not pursue attempts to convince her.

"I'll look forward to that so long as you don't knock my pint over," he said.

When he asked the nurses about Dr Burlington, they exchanged a look that communicated 'where do we start?'

They told him Dr Burlington was 'particular, old school' and that he 'sets high standards'.

"And he speaks strangely. I'm still trying to get used to it," said Sami.

"A fair smattering of big words," added Tam. "I gather it impresses the ladies in his book group. He is one of a kind. No doubt you'll soon form your own impressions."

Douglas did not feel reassured by this conversation, but they moved on to discuss an elderly depressed lady who was not progressing. Tam had told her he hoped Douglas would see her that afternoon.

The patient's name was Ina, short for Williamina, named after her father William. He had been a fisherman, lost at sea when Ina was a baby, the case notes informed him. She was the youngest of five children. One brother had hanged himself, another died from alcoholism and a sister had suffered from depression. Since her husband died a year ago she had been living alone in a small village. There was a daughter who lived quite close to her. Ina had come into hospital three weeks previously with depression. Douglas did not read through all the notes about her admission, but decided he would go and see her first and try to form his own view. He felt excited as he went to find his first patient in his new career.

She was sitting beside her bed. He wondered if someone had tried to make her more cheerful by making her look more cheerful. She seemed to have had a recent perm, giving the appearance of a white, curly clown's wig. This look was enhanced by her rouged cheeks, a bright pink dressing gown and matching fluffy slippers. She shuffled uncertainly towards the interview room, causing Douglas to take her arm, and sat in an upright chair near the door.

"High seat—for my back," she said.

"I'm the new doctor on the ward."

"Instead of Dr Cousins."

"Yes, Dr Douglas Barker."

"I heard you were coming."

Her speech was flat and ponderous. She gazed at the cord of her dressing gown as she wound it round her fingers.

One of the pieces of reading Douglas had done before starting his psychiatry post was a refresher on the symptoms of depression, and he tried to run through these with Ina. This became a lengthy process, since she was slow and vague about symptoms and timescales. She apologised frequently for her difficulties in responding rapidly and clearly to his questions. After about thirty minutes he knew that her mood had been low ('dark') for about six months, and that she had been tired but 'cannae sleep'. She had lost her taste for food and found it hard to swallow. She had lost a 'fair bit of weight'. She had contemplated suicide briefly but decided that she could not 'do that to Mavis and the grandchildren'. She felt that her body was 'not workin' right', her insides were rotting away and that this was going to cause her to die. He asked if she had ever been like this before, and she paused at length.

"After I had Mavis I wasn't good."

"In what way? Post-natal depression?"

"I was in my bed for nearly a year.

"Did you get treatment?"

"No. It was the end of the war. My sister moved in."

Ina was clearly tiring, and Douglas took her back to her bedside chair where she sat down and closed her eyes. On her locker was a packet of unopened jammy dodger biscuits and a photograph of two young boys in school uniforms.

"Are you needing another pint, Dr Freud?" the barmaid inquired. "It's last orders."

"Yeah, why not, one for the road. Is there a chip shop nearby, do you know?"

"The best chippie is down the hill. You'll see it across the street at the traffic lights. You're new around here."

"Like I said, it's been my first day as a psychiatrist."

"Aye, sure," she said, as she gave him his drink, holding on to it as she looked him up and down. "You've done well, but you've not drunk quite enough to convince me you could make it as a psychiatrist."

"Maybe I'll need to practise."

Douglas went back to her notes after seeing Ina. She had been admitted the week after first seeing his consultant, Dr Burlington, following a referral from her general practitioner who wrote that she was a 'profoundly depressed old lady'. In his reply Dr Burlington laid stress on the importance of her husband's death, and his diagnosis was one of 'morbid grief reaction'. He described her as 'disengaged emotionally' and as 'morbidly neurotic'. He concluded that she needed to come in to hospital for 'grief work and re-socialisation'. She was on a small dose of antidepressants at night, but Dr Burlington had written that grief work should be Ina's main therapy. This surprised Douglas and he looked forward to discussing her with Dr Burlington.

Douglas was continuing to muse about Ina as he came back up the hill towards his flat, starting to consume his large bag of chips. He jumped as he passed the door of the bar.

"I was hoping to share those chips."

It was the barmaid, now in her coat, emerging from the shadows of the pub doorway.

"My flat's just up there" she said, pointing at the top of a tenement building across the road. "I've got a bottle of wine to barter."

Douglas looked at his watch.

"I do have work in the morning," he said, "but the night is yet young."

****

The next morning, Douglas got in to his office only a few minutes before his 9.30 meeting with Dr Burlington. Douglas' office was small and somewhat dilapidated. The walls, perhaps once white, were tar stained from cigarette smoke, and the paint was peeling. Drawing pins and holes in the walls presumably reflected the previous doctor's attempts at decoration. Above his desk were several larger holes that had cascaded plaster dust on to his notes. He had a reasonably comfortable upholstered chair, but there was space for only two other plastic stacking chairs on the other side of his desk. His office was situated on the inside of a quadrangle and, in the morning sunshine, he could see into the offices across from his window. He thought he could make out an attractive blonde lady, perhaps another new psychiatrist, sitting at her desk in the room immediately opposite his own.

Dr Burlington's office was located just outside the main door to the ward. Douglas' knock was answered by a small, dapper man with a ruddy complexion. Dr Burlington wore a bow tie and a patterned waistcoat. Spectacles perched at the end of his nose. He shook Douglas' hand and guided him into a seat. He flitted rapidly back round the table and propelled himself into a deep, leather armchair. He reminded Douglas of a canary. Following a brief exchange of pleasantries, he said:

"I am a great one for good timekeeping, Douglas. I noted your arrival today sometime after 9 o'clock."

Dr Burlington's window overlooked the hospital's main entrance.

"I regard 9 a.m." he continued, "to be the *very latest* time at which it is appropriate to commence a day's work in my team. I shall expect you to be *robustly* punctual. Furthermore, while I accept, of course, that you may be *en route* to sporting a beard, if you are not—and my preference is for doctors without beards—then I would expect you, as you have not done today, to shave on the morning of each working day."

Dr Burlington addressed a point several feet above Douglas' left shoulder.

"We now have fifteen minutes," he went on, "before we leave my office and go together to the weekly ward round. So please summarise, rapidly and concisely if you would, the *quintessential elements* of your career to date."

As he cleared his throat to reply, Douglas detected a slight taste of stale beer and wine. He described his undergraduate career in Newcastle and being put off psychiatry during an elective period in Cambridge. At this point, Dr Burlington interjected.

"Backtrack, Douglas. Which school did you attend?"

When he named a secondary comprehensive in Fife, Dr Burlington looked puzzled and disappointed.

"I did my resident jobs in Newcastle," Douglas continued. "First it was Gynaecology and then I did General Medicine, with lots of endocrinology, under Dr Blanchard. Apparently he used to work up here."

"Ah, Dr Blanchard, yes, he used to work in this very city, down at the infirmary. And how did that post go?"

Douglas had found Dr Blanchard to be a narrow minded, reactionary bigot.

"It was a solid grounding," he said.

"Yes, it would have been. A bit obsessive compulsive, Harry Blanchard, but a sound chap. And thereafter?"

Douglas described starting a training in hospital medicine but then finding that he was more interested in the patients with psychiatric problems.

"So you jumped ship after the first year and came up to us. What made you feel that you have the makings of a good psychiatrist?" asked Dr Burlington.

Douglas was finding this interrogation to be tiresomely like a job interview, but tried to respond as sunnily as he could.

"I think I'm a good listener, and I like having time to talk with the patients. It's fascinating trying to work out the causes of their problems and how best to help them. I like the sort of detective work involved in that. And I've liked most of the psychiatrists I've met. So I thought I'd be happier in psychiatry than doing anything else."

Dr Burlington had risen while Douglas was speaking, apparently to observe someone from his window. He turned and marched back to his seat, saying:

"In my experience, happiness in a doctor is directly correlated to how hard he works, Douglas. Are you a hard worker?"

This was a difficult question. While he did not always push himself hard at work, when a subject interested him he could become pretty industrious.

"Well," he said, "as a student I was sometimes a bit of a last-minute crammer, I would have to admit, but I never had to resit any exams and I did manage to get a couple of distinctions. I think you'll find me to be a pretty hard grafter."

"Right, well, we'll see. *We shall see*. And have you ever been ill yourself?"

Douglas found this a very odd question.

"I was in hospital with appendicitis when I was thirteen."

"No, no, Douglas, have you ever been ill *psychiatrically*?"

"*Psychiatrically*!? No, never!"

"Lots of psychiatrists have, you know," said Dr Burlington, now addressing a point even higher above Douglas' shoulder. "Some wear it like a badge of honour, in fact. Or they talk about all the illness in their family, of course. Any illness in yours?"

Douglas felt constrained to respond.

"My mother was treated for depression—but she had thyroid problems and then cancer around the same time, so it was very hard to know what might have caused what," he said.

"Your mother, aha, your *mother*," Dr Burlington said, now addressing a point on the ceiling, "I see, I *see*."

Quite what he saw was mysterious to Douglas, and he was about to ask when Dr Burlington stood up abruptly.

"Ward round. We have to go. Keep me posted about your mother," he said as he ushered Douglas out of the door.

Douglas hoped that he might grow to like his consultant.

The ward round took place in a large room that was also the patients' sitting room. They gathered there to smoke, to watch television, to talk or to read. Two rows of chairs were positioned in front of the TV and the rest were around the periphery of the room. Above those chairs, the walls were filled with art work, some of it oddly menacing. Douglas presumed it had been done by the patients.

As instructed by Dr Burlington, Douglas arranged chairs in a circle while a nurse herded the patients towards their bed areas. They seemed familiar with this routine and left the room uncomplainingly.

"He likes ten chairs," said the nurse, "and the coffee table in the middle,"

She repositioned the two chairs nearest the door, so that they inclined towards each other a little.

"For Dr B and the patients who come in to be seen," she said. "You'll get used to it."

Dr Burlington came in with the senior registrar and said:

"Douglas, you no doubt encountered Jim Horsefall yesterday. We need the case records."

Note fetching was obviously one of Douglas' other tasks. By the time he returned, several of the chairs were occupied. Dr Horsefall—he had known it was an animal name—sat beside Dr Burlington. Charge nurse Tam was there, talking to a pretty blond woman, an occupational therapist whom Douglas had met briefly. Two smartly dressed young men, looking a little apprehensive, sat together—medical students, Douglas assumed. He sat down next to another of the ward nurses whom Dr Burlington then addressed.

"Pauline, let us commence with Williamina—your update if you please."

Pauline referred to notes as she gave her report. She was petite and dark, and she flushed progressively as she spoke.

"Ina has not had a very good week. She would stay in her bed if we didn't get her up, and then she would sit by her bed all day if we left her to herself. We have to take her through for meals and she's not eating much. Her daughter brings in biscuits and stuff, but she doesn't eat much of that either. She brightens up a bit when Mavis and the grandsons come in. Night staff say she's restless. Ina says her sore back makes her uncomfortable and she's not used to the hard mattress."

"And is she talking about her husband?" asked Dr Burlington.

"She did a bit at the weekend, when it would have been his birthday, but not generally, no," said Pauline.

"And in the ward therapy group, Anne, is she talking there?" Dr Burlington asked the occupational therapist.

"Not much," she said, "and I haven't managed to get her doing any other activities. Like Pauline said, on Friday she mentioned her husband's birthday. Said she would have baked him a carrot cake if he'd still been alive. But she doesn't interact much with the others."

"I was in the group a couple of times last week" said Tam. "Billy and young Jean were both talking about their losses—Jean's mother finally died on Tuesday—and we tried to bring Ina in. But she didn't bite, did she, Anne? She said she was lucky to have what she has."

"Let us invite her to join us," said Dr Burlington.

Douglas had not fully appreciated that she was to be interviewed and, as Pauline opened the door of the group room, he saw that Dr Burlington's patients were sitting in a row outside. Pauline helped Ina into the 'interview chair' next to Dr Burlington.

"Here we are again, Ina. And what progress have you to report?"

"I'm much the same."

"The same being?"

"No change really. Just the same."

"Yes, but I am asking you how you *feel*, how you *are*", said Dr Burlington.

"Sorry," said Ina. "I'm stiff. And tired."

"And would you perceive yourself as being tired of *anything in particular?*" Dr Burlington asked, leaning towards her.

"No," she said.

Dr Burlington gazed into the distance with his fingertips together, his hands below his chin.

"When we first met," he said, "at your home if you recall, it was clear to me that you were tired, *tired of your life*, as it had become. I shall not forget you sitting there, in the window, beside the photograph of your late husband."

He broke off to look closely at Ina, who gazed straight ahead blankly.

"We talked about your life, your *married* life, the life *that was no more*. No doubt you recall that conversation."

"I'm lucky to have Mavis and the boys," said Ina flatly.

"I do not suspect that you perceive yourself to be lucky, deep down within yourself. Is it lucky to be here, would you say, a patient in a hospital?"

Ina gave Pauline a puzzled glance.

"The nurses are nice," she said.

"Indeed they are, and our therapeutic efforts will endure, Ina, they will endure. Thank you for coming in to see us."

At this cue, Pauline helped Ina from her chair and she shuffled towards the door. Dr Burlington looked in the direction of the medical students.

"Denial and dissociation persist, I am afraid. This bereaved elderly lady remains distant from accessing her grief. Indubitably, we shall need to persist in our attempts to enable her to experience and address her suffering."

"She does seem quite depressed," said Jim Horsefall.

"Grief and depression—so often co-existent demons, Jim," said Dr Burlington.

"She's still on just a small dose of antidepressants," said Jim.

"Increase it, by all means, if you so wish. It may assist with her insomnia, although I suspect that any benefit may prove to be somatically transient. Her underlying grief remains our primary target."

The ward round moved on to discussion of the team's other three patients: a man with an alcohol problem, a depressed mother with overwhelming social and marital difficulties, and a young man who seemed to be presenting with his first episode of schizophrenia. He did not know these patients, and Douglas stayed as quiet as the medical students. As he observed the meeting he decided that his early opinion about Jim Horsefall may have been wide of the mark. He seemed to know the patients well and he made insightful comments about them. He did look slightly odd, with a large head out of proportion with his narrow shoulders, unruly grey hair and wire spectacles that he persistently pushed up his nose, but he also seemed solid and trustworthy. He made a point of listening respectfully to Dr Burlington's pronouncements, and then he might make an observation or a suggestion in a tentative manner. Tam seemed to adopt a similar approach with Dr Burlington, and Douglas wondered if this 'consultant management' technique might be one he could deploy himself. He decided that he would try, but worried that he might struggle. He sometimes had a problem holding his tongue. The relationship with a previous consultant had suffered after Douglas spoke his mind too readily when he felt that a patient dying from cancer was undergoing pointless and painful investigations. He would try to watch and learn, from Tam and Jim Horsefall, the skills of surviving and managing medical hierarchies.

****

Perhaps due to his inefficient speed reading of 'An Outline of Your Post', Douglas missed the first session, but was pleased to hear from Jim Horsefall that he had academic teaching on two afternoons each week. He had no clinical duties on these afternoons, and Jim would cover him 'for emergencies and everything else, in the interests of your education'.

When he asked if she knew about the academic sessions, his secretary Morag, a middle aged lady from the north of Scotland, sighed. She crossed her office to Douglas's pigeon hole, retrieved a document and handed it pointedly to him. He saw that it was the timetable for his academic course.

"You will need to look in here," she said, tapping his pigeon hole with her finger nail, "*very regularly.* As you can see, you have items of unopened mail."

Douglas knew better than to fall foul of his secretary. She was likely to be a pivotal person in the smooth running of things. Charming fallibility felt like his best option.

"Yes, thank you very much. All this is a bit new to me. I'm hoping people will keep me right," he said.

He saw from Morag's maternal smile that he had chosen a good approach.

"I shall do my best. You are not the first of Dr Burlington's young doctors I have looked after and, God willing, you will not be the last," she said.

"That's reassuring," said Douglas. "I've heard that the psychiatry secretaries are pretty good compared to what I've been used to down south."

"Indeed we are," Morag confirmed. "Secretaries are not much more than components of a typing pool in most places these days. I like to think that we still help to run the team, and that my doctors leave here as excellent dictators of notes and letters. If it would prove welcome, I shall be happy to provide you with regular feedback."

"Yes, right, I'm sure that will be helpful."

"Feedback it will be! Good!" said Morag, before asking, in more mellow tones, how he was settling in.

Douglas told her about his hospital flat, confiding that he felt rather lonely and temporary there, and listened to Morag's views on where he might seek to rent or buy somewhere of his own.

****

Douglas was not inspired by the lecture topics for his first academic afternoon, but it was a good opportunity to meet his new junior doctor colleagues. There were three semi-circles of seats facing the lecturer, and he sat at the back, next to the attractive blonde doctor in the office opposite his own. She seemed friendly and vivacious, and she had sexy dimples when she smiled. She spoke in a slightly breathless manner that Douglas found interesting. She—Mandy Morrison—was not a psychiatrist, but was training in general practice, so she would be in a psychiatry post for only the next six months.

"You really are awfully tall," she said as a new arrival sat down noisily on Douglas's other side.

"Up the back again, eh, Mandy? The rebels together," he said across Douglas, while looking him up and down.

"Hullo, I'm Chris Dunn, ye weren't here on Tuesday," he said to Douglas as he shook his hand.

"Hi, Douglas Barker. I didn't hear about these sessions until yesterday."

"Great things, eh? Skives! Two afternoons of no' workin' every week," said Chris Dunn.

Douglas noted from his accent that Chris was from the west of Scotland. He was compact and athletically built. Douglas wondered if his protuberant ears were acquired on the rugby field.

"Are ye a real psychiatrist, or just passin' through—like Mandy?" asked Chris, raising his voice for her benefit.

"Fairly real. I've signed up for three years—if I last the pace."

"Me too," said Chris, "and it's a fine pace too, if ye're here for the beer and the easy life. Mandy'll soon see the error of her ways and she'll be beggin' to join up."

By this time about fifteen people had gathered. The only one Douglas knew was Dick, who sat at the end of the front row, holding court to a man of middle-eastern appearance who looked rather dazed. The lecturers, a neuroanatomist and a neurophysiologist arrived together, and they chipped in with comments on each other's talks, in an apparent attempt to enliven the topics. The strategy did not work for

Douglas, but several of the other doctors seemed to become engaged. Dick was one of them, and asked a long question about the neurophysiology of noradrenalin, the point of which seemed to be to demonstrate his knowledge rather than to seek information. Douglas exchanged a glance with Chris Dunn, leading him to suspect that the two of them might get on well.

At the end of the afternoon, as they were leaving the lecture room, Chris announced:

"It's Friday night, I believe. A good reason for a pint or two?"

Mandy said that her mother was coming to visit, but Douglas agreed readily. A tubby man in a shiny green suit joined them and introduced himself as Harry Cameron. He was also from the west of Scotland and had known Chris when they were students.

They strolled together towards a bar that was out at the back of the hospital. Chris said that he had been before and had heard that it was 'where the psychiatrists go to get pissed'. It was a warm evening and Douglas felt good, walking to the pub in the sunshine with his new colleagues.

Chris led them to a small hotel that had two adjoining bars, the smaller of which was the psychiatrists' drinking place. It was cosy and intimate. The walls, the seats and the carpets were red, matched even by the beer mats on the tables. Douglas felt at home and was pleased to think that he might come here quite regularly after work.

Harry bought the first round of drinks, saying he would be going soon to 'meet up with an old flame from school'. They settled together at a table in an alcove.

"That's it then—one week as a psychiatrist gone, just forty years to go!" said Chris.

Douglas and Harry Cameron disputed this statement light-heartedly, telling him they intended to work for a mere thirty-five years, and this led into a conversation about their career aspirations and motivations. Unlike Douglas, Chris and Harry had graduated in medicine just a year earlier, coming straight into psychiatry after doing their resident house officer posts. They had both decided to become psychiatrists early in their undergraduate years, albeit for different reasons. Harry had always been 'fascinated by the human brain' he told them. He wanted to know 'everything about how it works, why it makes people do what they do, what goes wrong with it when people get ill'. He said he could not understand why other doctors would prefer to study simple things, like the heart or the intestines. Chris agreed, saying he did not wish to spend his professional life 'gazin' up folks' arses and askin' them how much they fart', and it seemed that his selection of psychiatry had been a process of excluding other specialties. He said he was "no' enough o' a bastard to be a surgeon" and that he had little interest in hospital medicine and "investigatin' people within an inch o' their lives for weird illnesses they don't have in the hope ye can write a paper about it." He had dismissed the possibility of general practice—"send in the next hypochondriac with a sore throat"—he said he did not like children and that he thought childbirth was 'hellish messy'. So he had concluded that psychiatry was his best bet from the few remaining options.

"OK, there's a lot o' bampots—and that might help me fit in—but I think most of them are likeable bampots."

Douglas said he was less of a scientist than Harry and less of a cynic than Chris. He was fascinated by the areas in psychiatry that spanned science, psychology and sociology.

31

He wanted to 'understand what makes people tick'. When they were on to their second pint, the discussion moved to qualities they thought might be important in a psychiatrist. Harry thought that an understanding of human brain function was paramount, while Chris talked about 'bein' sensible, seein' the wood from the trees, workin' out what ye can change and what ye cannae change'. Douglas talked about kindness and empathy, and the need to form good relationships with their patients.

After Harry had departed, Douglas and Chris continued to drink through until closing time at 10 p.m. While Douglas had always felt he could hold his drink pretty well, he struggled to keep up with Chris, who drank his pints of export rapidly. It became apparent that they shared a similar sense of humour and a passion for sport. Chris' main sport was football.

"When I first saw you, I had you down as a rugby player," said Douglas.

"Aye, the sticky oot lugs," said Chris, pushing his ears forward to make them even more protuberant. "I wis the victim of parental neglect. They should have taken me tae get them fixed when I wis wee, but they never did. Nah, fir me football will always be the beautiful game. Rugby's fir big folk wi' nae brains."

When Douglas said that his first sporting love was cricket, Chris was even more disparaging—'snails' pace crap'—but they agreed on a shared enthusiasm for golf. Both had played a lot at university, and they planned to have a few rounds together.

Chris had been staying with his cousin since starting his post, but was not finding this easy. He needed two buses to get to work, and he was not hitting it off with his cousin's girlfriend.

"She scrubs that flat like she's a theatre nurse and then she looks doon her massive nose at me like I'm a livin', talkin' germ mysel'," he said.

They resolved to rent a flat together. They agreed to move quickly, since there would be a wider choice before students arrived for the new university term.

****

Douglas was into the third week of his job when Ina's daughter approached him one afternoon. Dr Burlington had instructed him to 'focus on Williamina's grief' but he had found this hard. When he asked about her husband, she did not become tearful or any sadder; indeed, she seemed stoically sad to an unvarying degree. He tried to engage her in reminiscences about her marriage, but she was not keen, deflecting his promptings with 'that was a long time ago' and similar statements.

Ina's daughter, Mavis, had come to visit with her sons. She wanted to talk to Douglas, conveying with a glance that she would prefer to do this without the boys. He asked secretary Morag to look after them, adding:

"They look pretty angelic to me."

"Boys? Angelic? This I have yet to see, Douglas," said Morag, doing her best to sound gruff. "Very well, bring them in, but I shall come to find you should they prove to be *un*-angelic."

Mavis was concerned that Ina had been in the ward for over a month and had made no apparent progress. Douglas said he wondered if she sometimes seemed a little brighter.

33

"Maybe a wee bit, occasionally," said Mavis, "but I'm thinking she does it to try to please me. She might be the same with you."

He explained that they had increased the dose of Ina's antidepressants, that the effect of this was likely to be delayed, and that they were trying hard to get her to talk about her bereavement since it was felt that the death of Mavis' father had been a major factor.

"The consultant told me that," Mavis said, "but I'm not sure. To be honest with you, my dad was a bit of a bastard. Especially over the last five years or so, he was drinking far too much. He worked off-shore—two weeks there, two weeks at home—and he was hardly sober the whole fortnight he was back. Even before that, he wasn't good to her. She got a few hidings from him over the years—one time we're pretty sure he broke her arm, though she never said—and I left home when I was sixteen, after he started his violence on me. Over the years she shut herself off from him. She stayed with him, because she thought that was what you did, but they didn't speak much. She had long ago moved to the back bedroom to be on her own."

Mavis was warmly credible, and Douglas liked her.

"So what was she like when your father died?" he asked.

"It must have been a big shock, of course," she said. "It was the first morning after he'd come back from off shore, and she found him dead in his bed. So she was anxious, very shaken up—even when I first saw her three days later. We had to come back from our holiday in America. But then, by the time of the funeral, it sounds bad, but she seemed almost *pleased*, like a weight had lifted from her."

"So she wasn't generally too bad at all after he died?" Douglas asked.

"No, that's what I'm saying. You wouldn't have called her a merry widow but she got a couple of new interests. She took up painting again, joined a class at the village hall. And she started going into town to meet up with her pal for a blether and some shopping."

"She didn't seem to be missing your dad, then?"

"No!" said Mavis. "It seemed more like a new lease of life. It wasn't until the spring that I saw a change for the worse in her."

"What did you see?"

"She'd lost weight, and she was quieter. I got there at eleven one morning and she was still in her bed. That was in May and it wasn't like her at all. She'd always been on the go. It was then a wee while until her own doctor saw her, and you know the rest."

"And had you seen her like this before?" asked Douglas.

"No, never. She was a cheery person despite everything with dad."

Morag opened the interview room door.

"You were right, Dr Barker, these boys are angelic. But young Calum here is badly needing to visit a toilet, and I thought his mother should take him."

Mavis got up.

"Thank you very much for looking after them. You'll keep in touch, Dr Barker? It's not fine seeing Mum like this."

****

"Committees, Douglas, committees," said Dr Burlington one morning as he hurried along the corridor. "Sadly, the health service does not run itself."

Douglas mentioned to Sami in the ward office that Dr Burlington seemed to be very busy away from the hospital.

"*Busy*?" said Sami. "It depends what you call busy. He's got more private patients than anyone, they say. And the rest of the time he's schmoozing around in boardrooms, chatting to anyone who might further his career."

Douglas knew from the other new psychiatrists that they saw more of their consultants than he saw of Dr Burlington. He found Jim Horsefall and the nurses to be good sounding boards about patients on the ward, but at this early stage in his psychiatric career he sometimes felt he was floundering out of his depth. He had inherited around twenty out-patients from his predecessor, Dr Cousins. The majority of these people had not been admitted to hospital and were not known to Jim or to the nurses, so when he struggled with his out-patients there was often nobody he could talk to. Quite a few of these patients were known to Dr Burlington, however.

Colleagues told Douglas that the Royal College of Psychiatrists prescribed one hour per week of 'supervision' for each trainee psychiatrist from their consultant. But what would they talk about, he asked Jim.

"Patients, obviously," said Jim, "although I think the College assumes that you would get clinical supervision about them at other times. It's really to chat about your career—exams, your education—and how your skills as a psychiatrist are developing. And then of course there's all the personal stuff—your difficulties, relationships with colleagues and all that—I'm sure you'll benefit from discussing those sorts of things with Dr Burlington, don't you think?" Jim concluded with raised eyebrows.

When Douglas arrived for his first formal supervision session, Dr Burlington was sporting a lurid red waistcoat and he appeared to be slightly flustered. His briefcase was open on the desk, which was strewn with piles of papers topped by paperweights in an array of shapes and colours.

"Yes, Douglas, come in," he said. "I see you admiring my paperweight collection, but do not be distracted. What is it today?"

"You gave me this time for a supervision session," said Douglas.

"Yes indeed," said Dr Burlington, consulting his watch. "Educational facilitation, as the Royal College is fond of reminding us. It will be of indubitable educational value to you today, Douglas, if I inform you in outline of an issue ascribed to me for scrutiny, contemplation and advice."

His gaze swept meaningfully across the papers on his desk.

"I take it that you know of Professor Harold Cowdrey, O.B.E., physician and cancer specialist at the Infirmary?" he asked.

"Eh, no," said Douglas, "I don't think I do."

"Come, come, he is a *national figure*, a physician to the Royal Family, a man of influence and of standing. Anyway, his physician's committee, which he has chaired for a lengthy period, has advocated the appointment of a psychiatrist down there to work *in situ* and to facilitate assessment and management of the mentally unwell admitted to their establishment. Professor Cowdrey has had *a word* and hopes that I shall lobby here for the introduction of such a post."

"It seemed to work pretty well in Newcastle. The physicians liked it."

"New notions from the south do not necessarily translate successfully, Douglas. It is difficult not to feel almost *denigrated*, that the opinions I have provided over many years have been", Dr Burlington stood up and gazed out of the window, "*devalued*. And while, of course, one venerates Professor Cowdrey's professional judgement, one worries that he has been influenced to become unwittingly venturesome in making this proposal."

As he turned back from the window, Dr Burlington seemed startled to see Douglas.

"It is a *cleft stick*, Douglas, and I am no lover of cleft sticks," he said, again studying his watch. "But perhaps you have your own concerns."

"There were a couple of patients I wanted to discuss," he said. "I have an out-patient with obsessive compulsive disorder. He thinks about germs and cats all the time, and I'm not making much headway. And then there's Ina on the ward."

"Ina will keep, Douglas, and ask the man about his mother. Cats and dogs are very often mother symbols."

"He lives with his mother, but she—"

"Perhaps he needs to move out," Dr Burlington interrupted, as he gathered up some of the piles of papers and put them in his brief case.

"I have a lunchtime meeting at the Infirmary," he said, opening the door for Douglas to depart. "I am pleased to note that you are finding your feet and I shall see you, no doubt, before too very long."

September 1981

"Sorry, Mandy, I've forgotten it again," said Douglas one lunch time.

He had promised to lend her a music tape.

"Ye've still no' recorded it?" asked Chris. "Backin' group lettin' ye down?"

"I nearly remembered to hunt for it last night but I got distracted. It must be somewhere in my extensive bedsit," said Douglas.

It was during his preparations to move into a flat with Chris that he came across the tape—an early Bob Dylan concert—and Mandy had come to his office to collect it. As they drank coffee, she looked round at his bare walls.

"You need a woman's touch," she said.

"Anywhere in particular that you would suggest, doctor?"

"*On your walls*! You bring patients in here. What must they think? It's about as welcoming as a prison cell."

"I like to work with as few distractions as possible," said Douglas.

"Male nonsense," said Mandy. "I'll bring in some stuff to brighten it up a bit."

Next day she arrived at his door with a cardboard box. She started above his desk, covering the holes in the plaster with abstract art postcards. She then fixed a drape of brightly patterned material to the wall near his window.

"That's good there—it was left over from my curtains."

"It does look good," Douglas agreed.

"My flatmate's ex-boyfriend was another cricket fan and he left this when he scarpered," she said as she unrolled a large poster.

"Ian Botham!" Douglas exclaimed. "Excellent!"

She clambered on to a chair, holding the poster, and told Douglas to pass up the drawing pins. While he did this, his eye line was very close to the hem of her mini-kilt. As Douglas helped her down from the chair, their hand and eye contact was slightly protracted.

"Perhaps I could buy you a drink to thank you? After work tonight?" he suggested.

"Fine," said Mandy. "Knock on my door when you're ready to go."

****

Billy Franks was one of Dick's patients. He was a ruddy faced man, bald but for a sparse comb over. His eyes were bloodshot beneath white eyebrows. He was in his early fifties, but he looked older. When Douglas first arrived on the ward, Billy had been quiet and reclusive, but he was no longer keeping a low profile. As Douglas was leaving the ward with Dick one evening, Billy came to the door of his dormitory and shouted.

"Bye, bye, have a nice night, Doctor Dick. Doc Dick. Dick Doc. Tick tock, Doc Dick," followed by a loud "Hah!" as he went back into his room.

Douglas was quietly pleased to identify the speech pattern—rhyming, flight of ideas—of someone with hypomania.

Dick walked on, quickening his pace and with his nose slightly in the air.

"He's changed," said Douglas, catching up with Dick as they reached the front door of the ward.

"Yes, he'd been stuck for a while, almost psychotically depressed, until I gave him ECT and you see the result."

"He's gone the other way—high, hypomanic?"

"Perhaps a little," said Dick dismissively, "and we may contemplate lithium in due course."

It was clear over the next few days that Billy's hypomania was not abating. He was a fervent football fan, and he liked to go about the ward singing, or whistling, football songs. His most favoured tune was 'Ally's Tartan Army', the anthem during Scotland's ill-fated football world cup campaign three years previously. He was singing when he approached Dick outside the ward office.

"We're representing Britain,

And we're gonnae do or die,

For England cannae do it,

'Cos they didnae qualify."

To Douglas's amusement, the last two lines were sung challengingly, about six inches from Dick's nose.

Later that afternoon, Douglas was walking past an alcove in the old part of the building, close to the small hospital shop, where patients often congregated. Billy sat there alone, shaking his transistor radio.

"Hey, Doc, big man, what's your name?"

"Barker. Douglas Barker."

"Come here. Sit down."

He took the seat next to Billy.

"Radio's fucked, so I need someone to talk to. You a football fan, son?" said Billy.

"I follow it a bit," said Douglas.

"You follow it a bit, do you, so you'll have a team? What's that then?"

"Dundee United—but I'm pretty much an armchair fan these days."

"Give them up, Dundee United—they'll go nowhere, son. I'm goin' nowhere. I've got nowhere to go. Football's kinda my life if you follow me. Follow, follow, that's what I've done for years, and you know I was fine until '78—until the fiasco."

"Ally's Tartan Army?" asked Douglas.

"Exactly. Ex-fuckin'-xactly!"

Douglas smelled beer on Billy's breath. His eyes were glazed, but this perhaps related more to emotion than to alcohol. Billy continued at even higher volume.

"Before that, I was fine. We were all fine until that. 'The Demise of a Once Proud Nation'—that's what it said last week in the paper. It was certainly the demise o' me and many more like me."

He stopped to follow the progress down the corridor of a pretty young nurse.

"I had a woman then," he said. "I called her my wife even if she wasn't. Football fan, son, Douglas, she was a *football fan*—even if it was Rangers she liked—she was still a fan! What more could you want? A woman that liked goin' to the football, mixed wi' the boys, took a good drink."

He looked round before continuing.

"Enjoyed a good shag too, son, I'll tell you, man to man."

42

"Nice that she liked football," said Douglas.

"She did that, and if there was one man on the planet she wanted to shag more than me, then it was Ally MacLeod himself. She worshipped the ground he walked on. She would have eaten his shit, son. Lots of us took '78 hard but she took it worse. Most lassies fancy the players, but she was in love wi' the manager. Aye, so when Ally became a figure of fun, it was no fun for her at all and she plummeted. She hit the drink—and the drink hit her back—and the drink won the fight, and that was us buggered and the start of all this for me. She took off for London, down to the smoke to smoke and drink."

At this point Billy saw Dr Burlington walking past and he broke off to shout:

"Hey pal, doc, how's it goin'? Come here and have a chat with me and Douglas."

Dr Burlington walked on, looking studiously ahead, and went into the hospital shop.

"Gettin' yir fags, are you? Ha!" Billy shouted.

Douglas started to rise from his seat, but Billy's strong grip on his arm restrained him.

"You're a nice young fella," Billy said. "Don't get the same way as that stuck up arsehole."

"I'll have to go," said Douglas, freeing himself. "I'm the duty doctor. I've got a lady to see in one of the old age wards."

"You should have said, son, but thanks for your chat. You better go if there's a life to be saved," said Billy.

****

Douglas and Chris Dunn stood, looking at each other, in the kitchen of their new flat. They had failed to grasp the definition of 'unfurnished'. In vain, they had hunted in cupboards for plates, cutlery, a kettle, pots and pans.

"The bastard even took the light bulb out o' the wee bedroom," said Chris.

"*Your* wee bedroom," said Douglas.

"Just because ye're a big bastard, I'm no' sure ye automatically get the big bedroom," said Chris.

"There's more light in the wee one. You folk from the west are stunted because you're starved of sunlight. I'm just thinking about your welfare."

"Well we might need tae swap when I start bringin' back loads o' gorgeous women."

"Fair enough," said Douglas. "If that happens, we can think again. But from what I've heard about your track record, I'll go ahead and settle into the big room."

When Douglas and Chris had viewed the flat on the preceding Saturday, following a late night, they had not been at their sharpest.

"The man did say he was takin' everything up tae his son's new flat in Aberdeen," said Chris, "but I didnae think he meant *everything!*"

"It is a nice part of town, though," said Douglas.

"Handy fir some good pubs, aye. But where do we start wi' this place?"

"I could give Mandy a phone? She's domesticated."

"Great idea," said Chris.

****

In his interviews with Ina, Douglas raised some of what her daughter had told him. Ina agreed that sometimes her husband had been 'quick to raise his hand' and that her marriage had not been a happy one, 'but a lot of folk have it worse'. Douglas felt that her accounts of the marriage were more upsetting to him than they were to Ina. She confirmed that she had felt well in the months after his death and had enjoyed her new activities.

"Mavis thinks your illness doesn't have much to do with losing your husband," said Douglas.

"That's what I thought myself," she said.

When Douglas updated the ward round on his talks with Ina, Dr Burlington smiled.

"Ah, Douglas," he said, "it seems that you have much to learn about the vagaries and complexities of human relationships and feelings. Go back to your Freud. It is a starting point that I am confident you will find to be definitively enlightening."

He looked round at the doctors, nurses and medical students.

"This is a *most important teaching point,*" he continued, clapping his hands against his thighs. "This lady has lost an *ambivalently regarded object.* Losing any loved one, any loved object, is of course difficult for all of us. But when one's love is essentially fulsome—uncomplicated and unambiguous—then the loss is easier to bear. When feelings of love are *mixed*—let us say, as in this case, with those of anger, resentment and repressed hatred—then the loss is more complex and grievous. Through one's ambivalence, one is forced to battle with complicated and conflicting emotions which may prove to be irreconcilable. And naturally, it

45

would attract opprobrium were one to speak ill of the recently departed, and so one is over something of an emotional barrel with one's feelings. These cannot be expressed and sometimes, as in this case, cannot even be consciously acknowledged by the lady herself. So how does she respond, Douglas? What do we see? We see the common clinical picture of *denial* and *depression*. When anger has no outlet, it turns inwards upon the self, and depression is the inevitable consequence. Williamina is a textbook case.

Tackle this lady's *denial*, everybody. It is through this that she will begin to address her emotional conflicts and will resolve her symptoms of depression."

Dr Burlington looked round the group. His educational speech had clearly been well received. The group's silence confirmed it.

Later, when Douglas recounted Dr Burlington's exposition to Chris, he dismissed it as 'stupid psychobabble'. Douglas didn't know what to think. He felt he understood Dr Burlington's theory, and he was the consultant; but to Douglas, Ina was a seriously depressed old lady, not someone who was riddled with psychological conflicts.

****

"It's just like Australia," said Mandy. "There's even a big freckle below it that looks like Tasmania."

They were in her flat on a Sunday morning and she had been massaging Douglas's lower back. She was peering at the birthmark on his buttock.

"So I've been told," he said sleepily. "I'm not so sure myself, but I suppose I see it back to front in the mirror."

"I'll borrow a polaroid camera to show you."

46

"Great," said Douglas. "You been to Australia?"

"I've never been further than France. I've led a sheltered life."

"A sheltered life? I didn't get that impression last night."

Mandy smacked him on his birthmark.

"Are you offering to take me to Australia, then?" she asked.

"No. It's too far. You would need three or four weeks. How about Greece?"

"OK, I'll go and get packed."

"Ha, ha," said Douglas. "I was thinking of next month. We've both got holidays due and it would still be hot in October. We could fly to Athens and grab a boat to the islands."

"Are you serious?" asked Mandy, as she massaged his neck.

"You're in a strong bargaining position," he said.

"It seems a bit of a gamble. We don't know each other all that well yet."

"Life's a gamble," said Douglas.

"Well, OK, if the practicalities can be fixed—getting the same holiday dates, the flights and so on. Let's do it."

Mandy looked very pleased as she jumped off his back and wrapped herself in a towel.

"I'll cook us some breakfast," she said.

Douglas lay on in her bed, still sleepy, agreeing with her that they did not yet know each other all that well, and wondering if his suggestion might have been made too hastily.

****

It was Monday lunch time in the ward office, and Sami was recounting recent events to Tam.

47

"You saw Billy on Friday, so you know he was on the up and up again. We had a young woman, Bridget, admitted at the weekend. She's got an alcohol problem and she's been shaky and sick. It's been hard keeping Billy away from her. He wants to give her lots of advice. Perhaps he fancies her. Last night Bridget's boyfriend came in and it looked like he could be part of her problem. He was drunk himself and pretty uncouth. So Billy started lecturing him and then they were standing nose to nose in the corridor and we had to drag them apart. We managed to persuade Billy to take extra sedation."

"But then he hardly slept last night," Sami continued, "and there were fireworks between him and Dr Dick this morning. Dick says he was counselling Billy and suggesting different treatments. Billy says Dick was giving him a row like he was two years old. Anyway, you could hear Billy shouting from here and we had to go into Dick's office and rescue him. Billy was furious and shouting all the way to his room. 'Arrogant little arsehole' was about the politest thing he called Dick".

"A completely unreasonable view," said Douglas.

The nurses smiled.

"So what happened then?" asked Tam.

"He got sedation—chlorpromazine—again and this time he has been sleeping," Sami went on. "But Dick thinks he's dangerous and needs to be locked up in the forensic unit. He said he was going to phone them and discuss it."

"Ho, hum—get aggressive with a doctor and you're dangerous," said Tam. "When does Dick go on holiday?"

"So we're waiting to hear about a possible move to forensic," said Sami.

He turned to Douglas.

"What are you grinning at? You've got work to do too. We've been worried about Ina. She's still not been eating. We weighed her yesterday and she was down another three pounds. She's awfully constipated and her back's no better."

"A doctor's medical skills are required, it would seem," said Tam.

Douglas found the notes from her first day in the ward when she had been examined physically, written by a senior medical student. Her constipation was mentioned and her blood tests, apart from a mild anaemia, had been normal.

When Douglas went to see her, she was propped up on her pillows, wearing her usual pink dressing gown and slippers. She looked gaunt and ashen. She told him she had no appetite and that her back pain was no better despite pain killers.

When Douglas palpated her thin abdomen he thought he could detect, in addition to her constipated bowel, a harder lump.

"It could easily just be wear and tear in your back," he said, "and it's maybe the antidepressants causing constipation—hopefully we can give you something to help with that—but I think we should do X-rays and repeat some blood tests."

"If you think so, doctor, but I don't want to cause you trouble."

"It's no trouble, Ina. Routine tests," said Douglas.

The following Friday morning, Tam updated Douglas on Ina's progress. There had not been much. The therapy for her constipation had proved 'a bit too effective' and the dosage had been reduced. She had continued to eat poorly and she remained quiet and withdrawn. Just then, Morag came into the ward office.

"Mail for Dr Douglas Barker," she said brusquely, handing him several envelopes. "I would not usually act as a postwoman, but you did not collect your mail yesterday and you will note that one is marked for your urgent attention."

"We're trying to organise him through here as well," said Tam. "It's an uphill task, isn't it?"

"That puts it very politely," said Morag as she left the office.

The urgent letter was Ina's X-ray report. There appeared to be an ill-defined abdominal mass, a constipated bowel and two lesions in her spine which were described as "consistent with secondary carcinomatous spread". While this was not a complete surprise to him, Douglas felt shocked. He sat down.

"Bloody hell!" said Tam. "Maybe we should have guessed. Poor Ina."

"Her anaemia's worse but her liver function tests are OK," said Douglas.

"Poor Mavis," said Tam.

"I should have thought," said Douglas.

"The depression and the bereavement were red herrings," said Tam. "They maybe threw us off the scent. It's certainly not your fault."

They caught each other's gaze, and it did not help Douglas to see that Tam was upset. Tears came to his own eyes. He stood up.

"I'll get her transferred to the infirmary," he said, "after I've spoken to her."

"I'll try to get Mavis on the phone," said Tam. "And we'd better keep Dr Burlington in the picture. He likes to know."

He's in London," said Douglas. "Back on Monday."

He walked slowly round to Ina's room. He had broken bad news to patients before, but this was different. He felt closer to Ina than he had to his non-psychiatric patients, and he also felt culpable. He could have examined her sooner, requested earlier X-rays.

She was sitting on the chair beside her bed with her eyes shut. She opened them as he approached.

"I wasn't asleep," she said, trying to smile.

There was no-one else in the room and Douglas sat on her bed, her case records open on his knees.

"The test results came back," he said.

"That was quick."

"The X-rays showed that there could be a lump in your tummy. And perhaps there are lumps in your spine causing the pain in your back. We would need to transfer you to the infirmary to get things checked out further."

"I've got used to being here," said Ina.

"I know, but we do need to get things thoroughly checked physically. We can't do that here."

"That makes it sound quite serious," said Ina.

"It could be, yes, but of course we hope it isn't," said Douglas. "I was going to phone the doctors there and arrange for you to be transferred."

"You make me sound like a footballer," said Ina, with another little smile.

Douglas stood up, closed Ina's case records, and returned to the ward office to make the arrangements for Ina's admission to the infirmary. Tam came in to find him sitting with his head in his hands.

"I should have thought," said Douglas, as Tam sat down beside him.

"We all might have thought," said Tam, "but none of us did. Not just you."

"It makes sense now when you put things together. Now that we know. But I should have thought earlier."

"I think the whole depression and bereavement issues might have thrown us off course. You weren't here when Ina came in, Doug. And then it was you who diagnosed her in the end of the day. I don't know why you're taking it so hard, so personally."

Tam was the kind fatherly figure Douglas had been hoping for in his consultant.

"I do take it personally, Tam. I did tell you my mother had died when I was a student? I didn't tell you it was cancer. I thought it was smoking and a bad diet and getting older that was causing her big belly and her gut ache. I never considered it then, but I did think it was a lesson I wouldn't forget. And I have. I did. You have to catch these things early."

Tam sat nodding for a while.

"I can see why Ina might ring bells, Doug, but really, why the self-blame and the guilt? You were a student. My parents are both long gone, but I thought they were indestructible. You do think that, you don't expect them to get ill. Your mum and Ina are two very different situations."

"Not really, Tam—actually pretty similar."

Tam thumped him gently on the arm.

"Patients strike chords with lots of things, Doug. We'd be brain dead if they didn't. And who wouldn't like Ina and want to do their best for her? As far as I can see, you have done your best. I understand why you're upset—some of it to do with her and some of it to do with your mum—but we're not infallible, we're not magicians. It seems like you expect a lot of yourself, and I'm not saying that's a bad thing, but maybe try not to expect too much, eh?"

****

Dr Burlington answered the knock on his door.

"It can't be supervision, Douglas, surely? This is a Monday morning," he said.

"No, it isn't supervision. There was something I wanted to tell you."

"Very well. But currently I am conversing on the telephone with a colleague. Wait there," said Dr Burlington as he shut his office door.

Douglas stood in the corridor, trying not to look conspicuous. He squinted at the abstract art that was hanging on the walls. He could not make sense of it, and wondered about the effects it might have upon the more disturbed patients, before moving to gaze through the window at the hospital gardens. Ten minutes later, he was summoned by Dr Burlington.

"Nice for you to start your working week with some contemplative thoughts as you peruse the world outside, Douglas. But what can I do for you? Sit, sit."

"I've come to see you about Ina," said Douglas.

"We did discuss her, in some depth as I recall, at a recent ward round," said Dr Burlington.

"Yes, we did, but things have moved on. I transferred her down to the infirmary on Friday."

"The infirmary! The *infirmary*? Why on earth did you do that?"

Douglas described his physical examination and Ina's test results.

"Bowel cancer is their working diagnosis," he said.

"This is grievous, forlornly grievous news, Douglas."

"Yes, it has been upsetting."

"You are no doubt feeling responsible, feeling that you could have done better," said Dr Burlington, as he stared over Douglas's head. "You are perhaps blaming yourself, feeling that earlier attention to detail may have benefitted your patient. It is essential that you *amalgamate* and *integrate* your medical and your psychiatric practice."

"Yes, but the bereavement issue was..."

"*Integrate* your holistic medical care! Do not abandon your stethoscope, Douglas!"

"Yes but—"

"Do not be too upset. You will learn more from your mistakes than from your successes."

Dr Burlington's telephone rang.

"Thank you for telling me, Douglas. You can go now. But think about it and learn from it."

October 1981

Chris returned from a week with his family saying, "Now I'm needin' another holiday." He deduced that Mandy had helped again to make the flat more habitable during his absence. Having acquired a cooker, beds, chairs, cutlery, crockery, pots and a table before his holiday, there were now also a refrigerator, rugs on the floor and a sofa to sit on. Chris was less impressed by the two red bean bags.

"That's what dope smokers lie around on."

He was touched that they had painted his bedroom in the colours of his football team.

"This is grand," he said. "The place is lookin' homely. No doubt Mandy did most of it."

"I directed operations," said Douglas.

As they sat together on the sofa, drinking a beer, Douglas described events surrounding Ina's transfer to the infirmary and his subsequent meeting with Dr Burlington.

"I cannae believe what I'm hearin'! Wait while I get another beer," said Chris as he strode angrily across the room, "and let's see if I've got this right. The old woman got admitted through her own doctor and she's been in the ward fir a few weeks before ye started. And all that time there's been *no mention* o' physical illness—far less any mention o' cancer. She gets examined, right, when she comes in tae the ward, and she gets blood tests? And that a' seems to be fine?"

"She was a bit anaemic. They thought it was from not eating well."

"Right. So most folk think she's depressed and meanwhile Dr Arsehole Burlington waffles his psychobabble about ambivalent bereavements, or some such crap. The lady gets no better, and then *you* twig that she might be ill, *you* do the investigations and *you* discover what the rest o' them had missed? Aye? Is that it? Am I gettin' it right?"

"That's probably a fair summary."

"You seem awful calm, Doug, because this is makin' me mad," said Chris. "See my consultant, Robertson, he's one o' the good guys. He's hands on. He's sensible. But you, ye get landed wi' idiot Burlington. And what did he say tae ye? It's all your fault Ina's cancer wasn't diagnosed earlier? That it was *you* that didnae 'integrate your medical and psychiatric knowledge?' What about *him*?! And then he told ye tae go away and learn from yir mistakes? I think I woulda thumped him!"

"I just felt dazed," said Douglas. "Upset for Ina and her family. And maybe I could have spotted it sooner. It was only when I thought about it later that I got more pissed off with Burlington."

"So what are ye gonnae do?"

"I'm not sure. I think I'll just try to keep my head down and avoid him for a while."

"Christ! But ye'll be with him for a whole year!"

"Apparently they do sometimes move you after six months," said Douglas.

"That's still a long sentence fir doin' nothing, apart from yir job. Let's go tae the pub," said Chris.

****

Douglas was talking with Sami in the ward office when an exotic woman came in. She was tall and slim and black. She wore a white mini-skirt and a blue beret tilted to a jaunty angle.

"Hiya, Sami, baby!" she said. "Did you hear the birds this morning? Ooh, it was lovely. I took off my shoes and walked about in the dew. What a great way to start the day!"

"Yes, I heard about that, Carol. You might try to stay in bed longer, at least until after dawn. It wakens the others in your dormitory."

"When you're awake, you need to get up, Sami, dontcha think?"

Her accent was from the English midlands. She perched on the edge of the desk, turned away from Douglas, and spoke from the side of her mouth.

"And who's the big fella, Sami? We've yet to be introduced."

She turned towards Douglas and extended her hand.

"Dr Douglas Barker, one of the psychiatrists."

"I'm Carol. You want to be my psychiatrist, Douglas Barker?"

"You already have one," said Sami.

"I think I'd rather have big Dr Barker. Any messages come in for me, Sami?"

"No-one has called from your family."

"That's not what I mean. *Messages!* Any messages, any appointments?"

"I told you that we don't take that kind of message," said Sami, trying not to laugh. "And you'll have to leave the office now. Dr Barker and I are talking about a patient."

"OK, OK, Sami, keep your hair on. I only asked. Lovely meeting you, Douglas Barker."

When she had closed the office door behind her Sami told him Carol was a 'high class hooker' who had got on the train in Birmingham 'with just money and knickers in her handbag'. She had given the office number to clients and the nurses had received a few calls.

"They think she's hypomanic, could be drugs," said Sami. "But you were starting to speak about Ina."

Douglas told him that bowel cancer had been confirmed and described his meeting with Dr Burlington.

"What a poisonous little snake in the grass!" said Sami. "What does he think he gets paid all that money for? *He* admitted her from home. *He* saw her first. Then he shoots off around the country to butter up important people, dropping in here occasionally to tell us to talk to Ina about her grief. And now we're to blame for not spotting her cancer! If it wasn't so serious, it would be funny."

"I haven't been laughing much about it," said Douglas.

"I'm sure you haven't, but don't let the bastard grind you down."

"I'd like to go down to see her."

"I'll come with you," said Sami.

****

It was late on a Wednesday evening and Douglas was feeling sorry for himself. He had swapped to clear his holiday dates, and it was his second night on call that week. He reminded himself that during house officer posts he had worked well over eighty hours each week, and in comparison, psychiatry was not arduous. Nonetheless, he was tired. He had aggregated about three hours sleep during the Monday night on call. This had been all the more irritating because most of the interruptions to his sleep were not for 'proper psychiatry', but related to physical problems on the old age wards and to people arriving at the hospital expecting to be seen. An 'open access' policy operated, whereby almost anyone who arrived was deemed appropriate to be seen by the doctor on duty. The policy was not popular among the junior psychiatrists.

"It's a nightmare," said Chris Dunn. "It's mainly folk staggerin' in from the pub after closin' time, when they've run oot o' money or they've fallen oot wi' their woman. So they turn up here pissed as farts and say: "You'll need to stop my drinkin' fir me, doctor." What a farce! And that buffoon on reception, the more trivial somethin' is, the more he seems tae enjoy wakin' ye up through the night. I'm no' sure he knows we've tae carry on workin' in the morning while he swans off tae his bed."

At 10.15 that evening, Douglas saw someone who was uncannily similar to the 'typical boozer' described by Chris. Douglas tried his best to be patient and sympathetic while explaining to the man that it was not appropriate to admit him to hospital, particularly when he was drunk. Douglas was then bleeped to go to the forensic unit where he wrote up night sedation for one of the patients. A nurse was unlocking the ward door to let him out when he heard a familiar voice.

"Hey, Douglas. Big man! How's it goin'?"

Billy Franks' head protruded from one of the dormitory doors in the dimly lit corridor.

"Have you got two minutes, doc?" he said.

"I guess so, Billy, yeah," said Douglas wearily.

The nurse showed them into a dingy interview room where Billy sat on the edge his chair and leaned forward.

"I'll not keep you long, Douglas. You'll be busy, and I'm not busy and that's part of the problem. I'm stuck in here, locked in, hardly seein' the light o' day. And I'm sectioned— a compulsory patient. It's compulsory to be good, to behave, to toe the line. To play the game accordin' to their rules. And that's not really me."

"Hopefully you'll be back with us in the ward soon."

"I'm not sure I will be. The wee smout Dick comes with his consultant, Peterson, to see me once a week. I know I was high and I shouldn't have shouted at the wee shite, but they're not wantin' me back. Even though I'm pretty well now, and the nurses here say that too. It's not just me sayin' that."

"It's not really something I can influence," said Douglas.

"Can you not put in a word? It seems to me that Dick tells Peterson what to do, like the tail waggin' the dog."

"It's not my team, Billy. But maybe I could mention to Dick that I've seen you. That you seemed a bit better."

"Say I'm a *lot* better."

"I'm not sure he'll take notice of what I say anyway, Billy."

"Naw, he is a wee shite, right enough, but you could maybe try? Thanks for listenin'. And is your football team, your fearsome Tangerine Terrors, lookin' good this year?"

"I'm sure we'll do fine. We thumped Dundee last month."

Billy shook Douglas's hand.

"It's been good seein' you," he said.

****

Chris urged Douglas to miss an afternoon of teaching and play golf instead.

"It's mainly academic waffle. Ye can read it in a text book if ye've nothin' better to do. I don't think I've heard one thing since we started that's helped me wi' an actual patient. Nah, about the one good thing at the teaching is chattin' tae Mandy."

Douglas had sensed for a few weeks that Chris was keen on Mandy, and he had been wary about discussing their holiday. He tried to portray the arrangement to Chris as one that was largely based on coincidence; he and Mandy had holidays coming up and they were both keen to go to Greece. Chris saw through this slant, however, and said Douglas was a 'lucky bugger' who should 'look after her properly'. It would have been Chris' usual style to quiz him for details of what he called 'yir latest sexual exploits', but he had not asked about Mandy.

"So what about golf on Friday?" said Chris. "The programme's crap. It's more o' that sociology waffle and then it's somethin' about the 'International Epidemiology of Depression'. So more poor folk get depressed and more rich folk complain about it? If ye were worried, ye'll miss somethin', Mandy'll lend ye her notes. And more importantly, I've won the golf twice and so have you, wi' all the luck o' the day on yir side. By the time ye get back from bloody Greece the clocks'll be changin', and there'll no' be enough light tae get a game in the afternoons. This is it, the best o' five decider before the winter sets in."

Douglas agreed to play. There were no changing facilities at their usual golf course, so Chris's plan was to change in their offices.

"Maybe ye can forget those daft checked golf troosers o' yours, or folk might twig what we're up to. Wear somethin' normal."

Douglas smuggled his golf clothes in to work in a plastic bag, met Chris for an early lunch and was changing in his office, thinking all was going smoothly, when the door opened.

"Douglas Barker, your name's on the door, baby, and what are you up to in here? Where are your trousers, honey?"

It was exotic Carol from Birmingham.

"I've come to the right place for some sex therapy then, have I, doctor?" she said with a giggle.

As she approached him, Douglas retreated towards the window.

"No, you have not. No!' he shouted. "I'm just changing. You should not be in here!"

"Don't be nasty, Douglas Barker," she said teasingly. "This hospital's been such a friendly place so far."

He managed to wrestle one foot into a trouser leg while using an arm to prevent Carol from coming any closer. He was shouting "Stay there!" at her and thinking that the situation could not deteriorate further when Dr Burlington put his head round the half open door. Dr Burlington's head then swivelled from side to side, in a manner that Douglas later likened to a cartoon character.

"Preposterous! Bizarre! Degenerate!" he said.

"I was just changing my trousers," said Douglas weakly.

"Who are you?" said Carol to Dr Burlington.

"Who am I? More to the point, young lady, who are *you*?"

"I'm Carol. Nice to meet you too. You're one of the doctors, aren't you? Isn't Douglas a nice young man? He wasn't doing anything you know. In fact, he was trying to get away from me."

"He was attempting, you say, to escape. He was attempting, you assert, not to consort with you in a sexual manner, and yet clearly he—or you—had removed most of his clothing? I think not. I think otherwise."

"Oh well, think what you like. Does it matter?" said Carol casually. "I'll leave you blokes to chat about it. Bye, Douglas."

With this, she sauntered out of the office.

"I can explain what was—" Douglas started.

"Explanations, I fear, Douglas, are effectively futile. It seems most propitious that I responded to the rumpus in this office *en passant,* since it seems highly probable that my intervention has prevented you from consummating a sexual relationship with a patient."

"No, no," stammered Douglas. "There was nothing like that. I was about to go—"

"Stop there, please. Further obfuscations may but incriminate you progressively. We must talk about this rationally when you are fully dressed and composed. There will be an opportunity, hopefully, to do that within the next working week. No doubt, in the meantime, you will take the opportunity to reflect upon your behaviour."

Douglas sat at his desk for some time after Dr Burlington's departure. He forced himself to rise and go to his car, where he knew Chris would be waiting.

****

At Morag's office, Douglas asked when he might meet with Dr Burlington.

"Is it for a supervision session?" Morag asked.

"I guess you could call it that."

Morag told him that Dr Burlington was away examining for the Royal College and would not be back before Douglas went on holiday.

"You seem more stressed than I might expect of a young doctor about to jet off to Greece," she said.

"Work related difficulties, I suppose you could say."

"Dear, dear, Douglas. Young psychiatrists should not be weighed down by their work. Maybe the situation with Ina has deflated you?"

"Other things too, Morag. But, yes, the Ina situation has been difficult."

"At least your efforts have been appreciated. When you get round to looking in your pigeon hole you'll find a message from her very nice daughter. She thanked you profusely for your help."

"That was kind of her. I'm going down to see Ina today with Sami."

"Only three more days to work!" said Morag. "Relax! Not that I mean you should leave without your dictation being completely up to date!"

Douglas went round to find Sami, wondering why Morag's nagging cheered him up. It was a crisp morning, and the leaves were showing the first traces of autumn as Douglas and Sami crossed the park *en route* for the infirmary. Sami chatted first about cricket and then about patients in the ward. This included the news that Carol had returned to Birmingham.

Ina had been transferred to a surgical ward where they heard that she was being prepared for an operation—"a laparotomy, open her up and see what we can do"—later in the week. In the meantime, they were hoping to "sort out her dehydration". Ina's drug prescription sheet showed that her antidepressant had been stopped.

"I'm not sure that's very clever," Douglas said to Sami. "It was probably helping her depression, at least a little bit."

"Standard practice down here," said Sami. "They don't understand psychiatry so they stop people's treatments. And nobody asked us about it, as usual."

When they went to see Ina, she was in the bed closest to the door in a large ward. She looked grey and helpless, propped up on pillows and with her arm attached to an intravenous drip. She failed to recognise them as they approached, and only after Sami sat on her bed and said hello did she seem to know who they were.

"It's nice to see you," she said croakily. "How are things in the ward?"

"We're just managing to get by without you, Ina," said Sami. "But how are you?"

"Sleepy," said Ina. "Lots of tests. And maybe an operation on Wednesday."

She seemed to have aged since Douglas last saw her.

"Have they said what they think the problem is?" he asked.

"A blockage in the bowel," said Ina, "so maybe they can fix it."

"Do you have much pain?" asked Sami.

"Not too bad. I'm on stronger tablets," said Ina.

A severe looking nurse marched towards them.

"Who are you?" she asked brusquely. "And why are you sitting on the bed?"

"We're from psychiatry," said Douglas, as Sami got to his feet.

"They came down to see me, sister," said Ina.

"Psychiatry!" the sister snorted. "Well, right now we have *things to do*. So if you'll excuse us, doctors?" she said, tilting her head towards the ward door.

Douglas located Ina's case records, wrote that she was still depressed and suggested restarting antidepressants after her operation.

It was a silent and subdued walk back through the park.

****

Mandy was sipping coffee as Douglas ordered another beer. For lunch they had eaten bread and little fish that Mandy assured him were sardines. These were selected by pointing at what looked appetising in the cafe kitchen and, without a shared language, they had become accustomed to this method of ordering their food. They had also become used to the friendly and relaxed atmosphere created by their Greek hosts.

They had spent most of the morning in a secluded sandy bay close to their current seat in the shade. Douglas watched the waves breaking gently on the shingle below the restaurant, and wished he felt more relaxed.

"Too many bones in the fish for my liking," Mandy was saying, "and all a bit too greasy."

Delicious, thought Douglas.

"Are you nearly ready to go back to the beach, Douglas? You'll no doubt need a sleep after that beer."

"What about trying to hire a couple of bikes this afternoon? We could go over to the other side of the island."

"Bikes? In this heat? We would collapse before we got halfway."

"OK, back to the beach it is then. Perfect the suntans."

The holiday had not started smoothly. Their flight was delayed, so instead of being on an island by the first evening, they spent the night in a cheap Athens hotel. It became clear quite quickly that Mandy was not a 'cheap and cheerful' type of girl.

"Not the Ritz, but pretty good value for less than a pound each," said Douglas as he surveyed the room. He did like a bargain.

"It's falling apart, Douglas! Look at the door hanging off the wardrobe. There's no plug in the sink. And the whole place is *dirty*!"

"Oh well, lucky it's just for one night then."

He noticed a large mirror stretching the length of the bed and anticipated having fun beside it. He nudged Mandy and pointed at it.

"That might help things to go with a bang."

"I don't think so, Douglas. I've heard about that sort of thing in this sort of place. It could easily be a one-way mirror, like the one we interview patients behind for the students. And there could be five or six leering, toothless old Greeks sitting watching us from next door."

Mandy changed into pyjamas in the bathroom down the corridor, and insisted they put out all the lights before she got into bed.

Douglas had anticipated a rough and ready holiday, similar to those he enjoyed as a student, but Mandy harboured different expectations. It was the middle of the afternoon when they disembarked from the ferry on the island of Paros. Passengers were greeted ashore by a flock of about twenty locals, mainly older women, who either shouted their advertisements for rooms to let in broken English or held up signs saying such things as 'Cheap Room, Nice Shower'. Mandy walked towards a woman with a well written sign but Douglas tugged her away, reminding her of the plan to sleep on beaches. On the advice of a friend, Douglas strode off in the direction of the nearest sandy beach. Twenty minutes later, he assumed that she would be as pleased as he was when they reached the place his friend had described. A small deserted beach, almost white with shells and sand, sat between rocky outcrops and led down to the bluest of seas.

"And Tim said there's a fine wee restaurant just five more minutes up the road," he told her.

Douglas soon appreciated that Mandy was unhappy about setting up camp on the beach. She was not pleased by the lack of toilet facilities, and was worried about washing and drying her hair. At the nearby restaurant, Mandy was disconcerted, when they chose their food in the kitchen, by various aspects of hygiene to which Douglas was oblivious. He was in good form when they returned to the beach, but Mandy told him.

"I have no intention of 'cavorting in the moonlight' as you so romantically put it. I already have sand in places where nature does not intend it to be."

The night air was chilly, but Douglas slept soundly. He woke to find Mandy standing up and poking him in the ribs with her foot.

"I think it must have been last night's salad dressing. I need a toilet in a hurry. I'm off to the cafe," she said.

She walked quickly up the beach, climbed over scrub and boulders to reach the road, and then broke into a run. As she returned, she grinned delightedly, it seemed to Douglas, when he passed her at speed *en route* for the cafe toilet himself. Thereafter, she was determined not to spend another night on the beach. They walked back towards the ferry, and Mandy accepted the second room they inspected.

Douglas thought they would have an 'island hopping' holiday, but Mandy said she did not wish to move 'now, we've found somewhere habitable'. Douglas agreed that their apartment was very clean with a good shower, but he thought it rather soulless. It faced another building and the walls were a uniform beige. If he had to be in an apartment, Douglas pictured white walls and blue shutters overlooking the sea. Mandy liked the seclusion, and the distance from the sea, saying that along with the cold and her protesting bowels, the noise of the waves on the beach had contributed to her insomnia.

Douglas complied with her wishes, with only a token mutter or two, and consoled himself by getting quite drunk most evenings. Mandy mentioned his 'retsina induced snoring' most mornings as she prepared for 'our usual routine' on the local beach. It was a much less varied and active holiday than he had envisaged, but Douglas did his best to relax, read, swim and get a good suntan.

****

It was his first morning back at work.

"Come in, Douglas. And how was Spain?" asked Dr Burlington.

"It was Greece, actually—Paros," he said as he sat down.

"But you are refreshed? Reinvigorated?"

"I did manage to relax and switch off a bit."

"Switching off, Douglas, can of course constitute a double edged sword, can it not? I trust that you have had time to contemplate and consider. You will recollect our last meeting, in your office, with you in a state of undress and in the company of an attractive female patient."

"Yes, of course I do. It's not a situation that happens often. I was changing my trousers, getting ready to play golf, when she burst in the door."

"Ah, Douglas," said Dr Burlington, shaking his head, "at least you are able, following a fortnight's consideration, to present some sort of explanation, some vestige of an alibi, be it or be it not plausible. It is unfortunate that you did not enunciate this somewhat bizarre account of events at the time of their occurrence."

In August, Douglas had promised himself that he would remain cool and calm in the face of conflict with authority figures, as he had not always done before. But he felt bullied, again, and in danger of breaking this promise.

"If I had had the *chance* to 'enunciate my bizarre account of events' at the time, then I would have done just that. But I didn't get the chance. You talked over me and then you left."

Dr Burlington stood, looked out the window, and addressed Douglas over his shoulder.

"So my listening skills, an important component of my professional armamentarium, in your opinion should be called into question?"

"I often feel that what I say does not register with you," said Douglas.

"No doubt you will anticipate that I do not share your perspective. And your outburst causes me to ruminate about your relationship with your father. Could it be that you have grown up feeling that *he* did not listen to you adequately?"

"What has that got to do with it? I'm talking about *you*, not about my father!"

"You are raising your voice, Douglas, for some reason you are becoming angry. But let us return to your explanation, your excuse, for your behaviour with the young black patient. You maintain that you were preparing to play golf? If one were to accept the veracity of this 'explanation' of events, then one would proceed to the conclusion that you were preparing to abandon your clinical duties in favour of a round of golf."

Dr Burlington sat down and was again addressing his customary spot above Douglas's head.

"It was a study afternoon—lectures. Jim Horsefall was covering me," said Douglas.

"Your tone, Douglas, suggests that you regard the lectures of our academic colleagues to be trivialities, sessions that can readily be sacrificed. At best, your behaviour is far from acceptable. A young psychiatrist must be *unequivocally committed to learning,* as well as to the intricacies of clinical patient care. But I digress, perhaps. You are but three months into what may or may not prove to be a lengthy career in psychiatry. There is time to change. Time for new leaves to be turned over. We shall both have the opportunity to contemplate how you might achieve that. And now, no doubt, your priority is to catch up with what you have missed during your time abroad."

Striding down the corridor, Douglas resolved to cut the finger nails that had bloodied his palms during the discussion with Dr Burlington.

November 1981

Douglas did not often see Harry Cameron, who worked at a different hospital, except on their academic afternoons and sometimes in the pub afterwards. Harry seemed to have fallen on his feet. He was working on a small ward with a consultant who was an active researcher and whose work greatly interested Harry. He had been talking enthusiastically about neurotransmitters and fatty acids until Chris' eyes started to glaze.

"Let's talk about football," he said.

Mandy then described their holiday, or 'adventure' as she called it. She recounted the nights on the beach and in the Athens hotel as if their lives had been in danger. It was a triumph to have survived the heat, the insects and the food. She glanced frequently at Douglas for confirmation during her description. Chris was impressed with her suntan.

"Ye look great, Mandy. Even the beast Barker almost looks healthy."

"There must be lots of vitamins in beer and retsina, then," she said.

"At least it wis you and no' me puttin' up with him fir a while. Perhaps ye told him how tae sort oot Burlington?"

News of Douglas's 'trousers off with the black hooker and Dr Burlington' episode had spread rapidly round the junior psychiatrists to their general amusement. Harry was horrified that Dr Burlington disbelieved Douglas's explanation of events. He mentioned the possibility of moving to another team at the end of January. Harry had been 'elected'—nobody else volunteered—as the first year trainees' representative on a committee that discussed junior psychiatrists' rotations, and he said he would "try to put in a word".

Chris was at the bar as Harry stood up to leave.

"Chris seems to be drinking as ferociously as ever," he said. "He was famous for it as a student. He was spoken to by the university people a couple of times."

"He does drink a lot," said Douglas, "but I wouldn't say it was a problem."

"One definition of a problem drinker is someone who drinks more than his psychiatrist," said Mandy.

"Ha ha. Well lucky I'm just his flatmate, then."

"But maybe keep a wee eye on it?" said Harry as Chris turned from the bar carrying the drinks.

"And I shall also leave you boys to your beer," said Mandy. "I've got stacks of washing and ironing and housework to do after Greece. See you later, Douglas?"

Chris seemed gloomy after her departure.

"Sounds like ye had a great time," he said.

"You've already heard my story. It sounds like a different holiday she was on."

"In her eyes it seems ye can do no wrong. She disnae seem tae notice that ye're an ugly, grumpy bastard."

"Well I suppose you either have charm and charisma or you don't."

"Meaning what? Meaning I don't?"

"Meaning nothing, Chris, meaning nothing. Look, it's a wee bit of a struggle with her just now, if you want to know the truth. She's not very independent. I do like her, but it feels like she wants to be involved in everything I do. Like she wants to be with me all the time."

"Lucky bastard."

"It doesn't feel that way to me," said Douglas.

****

A large hole had developed in Douglas's one pair of black work shoes. He hated shopping, and he was feeling irritable as he hunted for the shoe shop Mandy had recommended. Thinking that he must have been walking in the wrong direction, he turned abruptly and a shopper's heavy bag caught him on the knee.

"Oh, I'm sorry, that must have been sore. And it's you— Dr Barker!"

The shopper was Ina's daughter, Mavis.

"Hullo, no, that was my fault," he said, straightening up and managing not to clutch his knee.

"You're a nice colour. Have you been away?"

"Yes, I'm not long back from Greece."

"Good to get a break. Mum said you went to see her in the infirmary. She was pleased to see you and Sami."

"How did her operation go?"

Mavis told him they had 'opened mum up and saw nothing could be done'. She was now living with Mavis 'for as long as she has left'. Mavis put her hand on Douglas's arm.

"There's no good getting upset about it," she said. "It's a funny thing, but mum seems happier now than she's been for ages. Perhaps it's the antidepressants. Perhaps it's knowing. She says she always thought that there was something wrong inside her and the doctors didn't take her seriously. But you did—and we're grateful for that."

"No need to be," said Douglas gruffly. "Please give her my best wishes."

****

"You have letters to sign on my desk," said Morag before hurrying out of her office.

Next to the letters, Douglas saw Ina's psychiatric case notes with a letter clipped to them. It was from Dr Burlington to Professor Cowdrey, Ina's first consultant at the infirmary.

'Dear Harold,

Thank you kindly for your detailed letter about Mrs Williamina Wylie, recounting first her presentation to your own team and moving thereafter to the wider issue of whether a new dedicated psychiatric consultant post at the infirmary is a development towards which we should be collectively striving. I shall respond in turn to these issues, but might say at the outset that I am less persuaded than you appear to be that the case of this particular elderly lady impinges upon, and illustrates, the desirability of the new post recently under consideration.

As you are aware, Mrs Wylie was referred to me by her general practitioner who made no mention of any physical symptomatology. The patient herself was keen to focus on issues of grief and loss throughout my dealings with her, and I can only assume that she sublimated her physical concerns for reasons of her own, possibly relating to shame and guilt about her conflicting feelings. Be that as it may, she became an in-patient with my team. Dr Samantha Cousins was the junior doctor responsible for her care initially, she having been replaced by Dr Douglas Barker at the beginning of August. While one acts as a guide and a supervisor in one's consultant role, I think you would have to agree that one is to a large extent reliant upon the competence of one's juniors, irrespective of the area of medicine in which one might specialise. As you will no doubt appreciate, I make these observations in response to the suggestion in your own letter that an earlier diagnosis might have been reached and that this may have been to the patient's benefit. I have, naturally, raised this very issue with Dr Barker, who continues to work under my supervision; it would be fair to say that he feels chastened and has undertaken to learn from this experience. That being said, I am uncertain that the overarching competence of junior doctors, whether they practise in psychiatry or in general medicine, compares favourably with that of our own contemporaries. I fear that the prevailing ethos among the medical students of today is one of relaxed frivolity and that, despite the renowned abilities of esteemed academic colleagues such as yourself, there is a rising tide of lessening competence amongst our young medical graduates. As a corollary of this point, I am concerned that errant diagnostic practices may proliferate generally and that, sadly, Mrs Wylie's case may but be illustrative of that same rising tide of incompetence among our junior colleagues.

Moving to the more general issue of the possible psychiatric consultant post, based within your service at the infirmary, I do think, with all possible respect, that you may be generalising rather too widely from a single case. You suggest the need for a consultant 'who embraces the links between physical and psychiatric medicine' and who would be readily available at the infirmary when psychiatric pathology is suspected. As you will recall, I have made the case, both in committee and to you at a personal level, for retaining the status quo. If I can be permitted to utilise my own self as an example, I am confident that I have the skills to ride both psychiatric and physical horses concurrently, and I have always striven to provide my opinions and advice expeditiously whenever these have been requested by colleagues at your hospital. You suggest in your letter that 'just as physicians and surgeons may have psychiatric blind spots, so may psychiatrists when it comes to recognising physical pathology'. While this observation is of course germane, my own experience suggests that such blind spots are relatively rare, certainly at consultant level, and I remain uncertain that one can justifiably extrapolate from the dubious competence of two junior doctors to the need to make a significant change in the *modus operandi* of two services that have cooperated, fully and satisfactorily, in my view, over a protracted period of time.

All that said, I do of course greatly respect your judgement and your opinion, and I look forward to discussing these matters further with you in due course.

With very best wishes,

Sincerely,
Edwin Burlington.'

Douglas read the letter three times. Should he go straight to Burlington and confront him? As he was locking Morag's door, Jim Horsefall was emerging from his own office next door.

"You don't look great, Doug," he said.

"I don't feel great. I've just had a bit of a shock," Douglas said, still hanging on tightly to the handle of Morag's door.

"Coming in for a chat?" asked Jim.

Jim listened patiently to his account of the letter and to aspects of the situation that he did not already know.

"Maybe not much point in going round and grabbing him by the lapels. A lot of it is about merit awards, if you ask me," said Jim.

When Douglas looked perplexed, Jim said that Dr Burlington was keen to be as prominent as possible at the infirmary so that consultants there thought him to be competent and industrious, and thus supported his hopes of getting an improved merit award.

"Pay rises for consultants. An old boys' network where the guys who already have awards vote for themselves to get even more money. The more influential pals you have to support your case the better, and the last thing Edwin B wants is a psychiatrist who isn't him strutting round the wards at the infirmary. So he does his best to rubbish the case for the new post."

He suggested that Douglas should 'try to ignore it and keep your head down'. Douglas was not sure he would be able to follow Jim's advice.

****

That evening in the pub, he described his day to Mandy.

"I thought you wanted to do psychiatry because the consultants are nice people," she said. "You certainly couldn't say that about Dr Burlington."

"Most of them *are* nice. He's an exception," said Douglas.

"Jump ship and come into general practice, if they'll have you. We're not hung up on power and politics."

"I might die from overwork."

"Maybe you would. But anyway, how do I look in this?" she asked.

She stood up and did a twirl in the blue and white checked dress she had bought in Greece.

"Lovely," said Douglas, thinking it resembled a table cloth, "if maybe a little unusual in a Scottish November."

"It's fine as long as I wear my fur coat and warm underwear. There's no point in getting a nice tan and not showing it off."

"'Keep your head down', Jim Horsefall told me."

"Not your style, Dougie."

Only his dementing great aunt, and now sometimes Mandy, called him Dougie. Especially when she pronounced it 'Doogie', he found it exceptionally irritating.

"No, not my style, but maybe it has to be," he said.

"The bracelets go well with it, don't you think? That was quite a flea market in Athens, wasn't it? You talked me into it so you ought to like them. They make a great clinking noise," she said, waving her arm with the silver bracelets to illustrate her point.

His recollection of buying the bracelets was of trying to get her away quickly in the hope of buying some peaches before catching their ferry.

"Very ornamental," he said. "But I guess Jim's right, if only for Morag's sake. If I were to march round to his office and demand that he retracts what he said about my incompetence, then he would know I'd read a confidential letter. And he would know how that had happened."

"So you and Morag would both be in the shit."

"It looks like shit to me, no matter what I do."

"I'm drinking as quickly as you are. You must be talking too much. It's my round and it's quiet, so I'll go up for them."

We're not really connecting, thought Douglas, as she walked to the bar. He didn't feel ready for the commitment and the domesticity that Mandy seemed to want. Should he maybe try to break it off just before she was about to leave psychiatry and move on to her next post in February? She returned from the bar, and leaned towards him conspiratorially.

"Mummy's coming on Saturday. She's heard all about you and she wants to meet you."

"What a pity," said Douglas. "I'm going to the football with Chris."

"What, all day?"

"Yes, I'm afraid so. His team's coming to town and he'll need a minder. He's capable of doing almost anything when the fever of football goes through his veins, particularly when he gets a drink in him. So unless you and your mum want to come to the match, meeting up will have to wait."

"We'd both rather stick pins in our eyes. Oh well, there will be other opportunities."

"Yes, I shall just have to be patient," he said.

****

Douglas was pleased to catch Tam and Sami together in the ward office, although he was less happy to find Dick there as well. He valued the advice of the two nurses, especially when they formed a 'double act'. Sami's forthright views could be tempered by Tam's more measured approach. He wanted to discuss a patient and Dr Burlington.

"I've mentioned before an out-patient I took over from Sammy Cousins. She had only seen him twice, and I've been struggling. He's got a long history of obsessive compulsive disorder."

"OCD," said Dick.

"Yes, thanks, OCD," said Douglas, trying to turn his back on Dick and speak directly to the nurses; they were sitting at the desk, while Dick stood at the filing cabinet reading case notes.

"He's twenty-three now and he's had it since his early teens. He hid it from his parents and friends, and he became a bit reclusive. He did well academically, but things came to a head when he tried to go to university. He has this thing about cats. He was allergic to them when he was a young boy."

"A real allergy, not obsessive compulsive disorder as a child? It does happen sometimes," said Tam.

"Wheezing, asthma, eczema?" Dick chimed in.

"A *genuine allergy,*" said Douglas. "I spoke to his mother. Now he thinks cats carry germs, as well as allergens, and that these are going to make him ill. Whenever he can, he wears a mask. He washes his hands umpteen times a day and if he thinks there might have been a cat anywhere in the vicinity he has to shower as well."

"Does he have contact with cats?" Sami asked.

"The family got rid of their cat when he was a boy, after the allergy was diagnosed, and no, he tries to avoid them at all costs."

"It's a phobia then," said Dick.

Douglas ignored him.

"He scans everyone for cat hairs, in case they might make him ill. To check out if cats might have been sitting on them, he stares at people's groins, anxious as hell. So that can lead to tricky situations."

"You're sure he's not psychotic?" asked Dick.

"I am virtually certain he is not psychotic," said Douglas through gritted teeth.

"What are you doing, anyway?" said Sami irritably to Dick.

"I'm reviewing the notes on my new patient who was admitted in the early hours of this morning. It seems to me..."

"So couldn't you do that in your own office?" Sami demanded. "And let us hear about Douglas's patient?"

"I suppose I could, and then come back to discuss him. Since it appears that Douglas has jumped ahead of me in the queue."

Dick slowly gathered up the notes and left the office.

"Is there a more annoying arsehole on the planet?' said Sami. "Jesus!"

"I love seeing those two together," chuckled Tam. "I've been known to keep Dick chatting in the office if I think Sami's on his way."

"Bastard," said Sami, laughing as well.

"So Alan's quite crippled with all this," Douglas continued. "He doesn't want to go out. The family have a ground floor flat and Alan sits scanning the garden, worried that cats might jump on to the window sills. So he's never relaxed, no matter where he is."

"Not good at all, but where do we come in?" asked Tam.

"He was admitted to the infirmary yesterday after a Paracetamol overdose. They're still concerned down there about his liver damage. The senior registrar phoned me. He seemed like a good bloke, even if he did call Alan a 'nutter', said he thought Alan was depressed and might do it again."

"You think he's depressed?" asked Tam.

"Hard to say. The cat thing's on his mind night and day. So he doesn't sleep much and he's miserable."

"We had a similar young lass last year. She did well with an exposure programme and antidepressants," said Tam.

"I'm assuming you want to admit him to us? Has Dr B OK'd that?" asked Sami.

"I couldn't find him, not that I hunted too hard. But Jim Horsefall thought we should get Alan in here once he gets the all clear with his liver."

The nurses were happy with this plan and Douglas moved on to tell them about Dr Burlington's letter to Professor Cowdrey.

"Speak to Dr Fleck, the physician superintendent," said Sami. "You can't let him away with that!"

"Aye, but what about Morag?" asked Tam. "Doug's over a barrel here. It's not the first time he's fallen out with a new psychiatrist. You remember the young Irish guy, Sami?"

"Shaun. Yes, they couldn't stand each other."

"He left psychiatry. That was a while back, but Dr B has a history. It's maybe easier said than done, but I think Jim's right. Try to keep your head down."

"The bastard shouldn't get away with it, though," said Sami.

"Bastards often do. Haven't you noticed?" said Tam. "It maybe sounds a bit trite, Doug, but if you're a sound guy, then things have a way of working themselves out, no matter how crappy it might seem right now."

"Yeah, well, thanks. I'll try to do nothing. But I can leave it with you to slash his tyres, Sami?" asked Douglas.

****

His team won convincingly, and Chris became boisterous after the football match, singing and holding his scarf above his head despite Douglas's efforts to stop him. Chris did not seem to appreciate the need to celebrate quietly, until a beer can was thrown from across the street and about a dozen opposition supporters started to cross through the traffic towards them. They beat a hasty retreat up a side street and had a drink in a quiet pub. Douglas persuaded Chris to put his scarf in his pocket and go back to the flat to watch the match highlights on television.

"That wis great! My dad would have loved that," said Chris after the highlights.

"Remind me when he died," said Douglas as he passed Chris another can of beer.

"Jist nearly three years ago. Dropped doon wi' a heart attack, stone dead."

"He was young for that to happen."

"He wis young, yeah, fifty-eight. Though he did die happy. It wis jist a few hours after we'd beaten Rangers. Maybe that's why I think about him when we have a good win."

"What was he like?" asked Douglas.

"He wis a wee fella. I suppose when ye look at me ye'll say that's no' surprisin', but he wis particularly small. Mum loved tae stand back tae back wi' him tae show she wis a couple o' inches bigger. No but, he wis a topper o' a guy. Self-educated. Worked all his life in the shipyards and he'd come home and read. Classics, poetry even. Some o' his pals used tae take the piss, sayin' "recite us some o' that Shakespeare, Prof" and that sort o' thing. Sometimes I've seen him wi' his mates after a few beers, and he wid do it—a bit o' Shakespeare or Keats or somethin'. They wid laugh at him, but they admired him, ye know, and ye never heard a bad word about him. I'm tellin' ye this and I'm thinkin' I should've phoned Mum earlier—she'll be in her bed by now—but she still misses him something hellish. Especially on a Saturday. They must have gone tae the pub every Saturday night since I wis about twelve."

"That's a lot different from my parents," said Douglas. "Nights out together were rarer than hens' teeth."

"And yir dad's still like that?"

"He's not quite so bad. He's not a natural socialiser, but his new woman sometimes gets him out to see her friends."

"She sounds a bit o' a terrier. What's her name? Brenda?"

"Belinda. She's quite posh, but nice. She worked at the library and my dad knew her for years. Maybe he always had a bit of a thing for her. I remember my Mum, half teasing, half earnest, saying "I suppose that's you off down to the library again" and I thought it was her way of hinting that he might have done something more useful. Help around the house maybe. It's only recently that I wondered if she knew all along that he was keen on Belinda."

"And yir dad and Belinda got together quite soon after yir Mum died?" asked Chris.

"Yeah. I was away at university by then, so I didn't see it at close quarters, but she had moved in within six months."

"That's speedy."

"Your Mum's not got anyone else?"

"No, and I don't think she's lookin'. She's got loads o' company. She gets on great wi' dad's sister. There's her own two sisters and, like I've said, her brother lives three doors doon. He takes a lot o' lookin' after wi' his head injury. So she wouldnae have the time fir other men. And they would-nae put up wi' her talkin' about my dad from mornin' till night."

"My father hardly mentions our Mum. Her illness must have been tough for him, but he doesn't talk about it. Didn't then, doesn't now."

"How long wis she ill?"

"A couple of years. They thought at first they had caught her cancer in time. Then they treated her thyroid and she perked up for a while. But she couldn't work for about a year before she died. She had a lot of pain."

"Not good. And tough fir you."

"I wasn't at my best," said Douglas, and then took a long swig of beer. "I've not told you about Spider, have I?"

"Spider?"

"She was my girlfriend when we were students. We dis-sected a body together in anatomy. She wasn't my partner, but with four of us to a body, we sat directly across from each other for a year, down at the legs end. You'll remember how intimate that can get. You spend a lot of time together, and we just really hit it off."

"How could her name be Spider?"

"She used to collect them when she was wee, she got the nickname and it stuck," Douglas continued. "So we got very close, and knew when the anatomy finished that we didn't want to be apart, so we started going out. The next year we moved in together. That was a great two years. She was just sort of the one for me, you know. Then she was driving to do a placement up north in general practice when her car went off the road, and that was that."

"What—she died?"

"She did. At the scene. Instantly. Nothing to be done. And nobody has matched up since. This was in the middle of my mother's cancer, and things were all a bit of a daze. I was kind of wrapped up in myself. It was tough, but I feel bad that I wasn't around more for my Mum back then."

"Christ, that's a sad sad story, Doug. What a shitty time fir ye."

"Mum was very brave, stoical. Must have known she was dying, but kept that to herself. Never mentioned it. She knew all about Spider—they got on great—and maybe didn't want to be a burden to me then. She would grip my hand extra tight and look at me funny, like she was trying to memorise everything about me."

"She never talked about it? Her cancer?"

"Only right at the end. Once it was completely obvious. But, hey, you're trying to celebrate a famous victory and here's me going on about death and dying."

"I'm happy tae hear about it. Ye hardly wear yir heart on yir sleeve. In fact, ye're a bastard fir no' tellin' me this before."

"Aye well, some things are hard to talk about. We've finished the beer. Is that home brewed wine of yours ready for drinking?"

On the day of Alan Hardy's transfer from the infirmary, Tam saw him first.

"Alan's a nice young man," he said, "but he doesn't have his troubles to seek. He asked me in the first five minutes if I had a cat."

"Do you?" asked Douglas.

"No, just a couple of dogs. He seemed very relieved to hear that. I think he's quite happy to be here. He doesn't think there should be too many cats about in a hospital, and he was pleased we're not on the ground floor so they'll hardly be climbing in the windows."

They went on to discuss plans for Alan's treatment. Douglas had not got far 'pursuing the mother line', as advised by Dr Burlington, although he wondered if she was a bit protective of him. Tam thought this more likely to be a result than a cause of his illness. They talked about antidepressants, but agreed that Alan's psychological management was less straightforward.

"When we had the girl in last year," said Tam, "we had a good psychologist. She helped us to design an exposure programme. The girl had a thing about germs, too. But the psychologist got pregnant and left, and the new one's a bit weird. Porter Hepburn. Have you met him?"

"No, I haven't."

"And why would you? He stays away from the wards. Says he specialises in complex out-patients, and that he is not the 'hand maiden of psychiatric services'. But I met him in the hospital shop today, and I mentioned Alan. He looked at his diary for about half an hour and said he could come up 'briefly at 3 p.m.' as if he was doing us a big favour."

That gave Douglas half an hour before the psychologist was due to arrive. He and Alan talked while Douglas conducted a physical examination; since the allegations of medical incompetence he had taken to going over patients' physical conditions in detail.

"It looked from the liver function tests that you've been lucky. Almost certainly no permanent damage," he said.

"Yes, I have been lucky. It was stupid. But I'd just had enough that night. Mum and Dad were out, and I'd had a few whiskies," said Alan, sitting up at the end of the examination.

They discussed other aspects of Alan's overdose, which he described as 'the first impulsive thing I've done in years'. He said he would not do it again due to the effects on his parents, his father having been furious and his mother distraught.

"What'll happen in here?" he asked.

"Regular blood tests for your liver. We'll probably put up the dose of your clomipramine antidepressant. And we've got a psychologist coming this afternoon to talk about other approaches," said Douglas.

"What kind of approaches?" asked Alan anxiously.

"To be honest, I'm not sure yet. We'll see what he says. Don't worry."

It was just after three o'clock when Douglas returned to the ward office. Tam was standing with a small bearded man who was holding a briefcase.

"This is Dr Douglas Barker," said Tam. "Our psychologist, Porter Hepburn."

"*Dr* Porter Hepburn," said the psychologist, nodding briskly at Douglas, "and I am hardly *your* psychologist. I provide an occasional service to two wards."

"Yes, quite, sorry," said Tam. "I've started to explain about Alan to Dr Hepburn, Douglas."

"It sounds straightforward to me," said Hepburn. "Obsessional ruminations and rituals with elements of a cat phobia. Yes?"

Dr Hepburn hung on to his brief case while his other hand rested on the desk, beating out each syllable as he spoke.

"Em, yes," said Douglas.

"So we hoped to get a psychological programme going," said Tam.

"Yes, of course you would," said Hepburn, opening his briefcase and extracting a book. "Everything you need to know should be in here. Photocopy the relevant pages and return it to the Psychology Department. As I said, the approach is pretty straightforward."

He held the book, 'Fears, Phobias and Obsessions—A Treatment Manual', between Douglas and Tam.

"Who wants it?"

"And you'll discuss it with Alan?" asked Douglas as he took the book.

"See him?" said Hepburn. "No need for that unless you get completely stuck. It's in the book. Phone my secretary if you're struggling."

He departed, leaving Douglas and Tam looking at each other. Tam broke the silence.

"Before you came in he said that discussing Alan was 'marginally better than being told to do an intelligence test or a personality inventory', so that was him on a good day.

Psychologists have changed. They go on about 'developing our professional identity', or at least some of them do. I think they feel bad because they're not medical. And how could I have forgotten about his PhD—*Dr* Hepburn, indeed. Probably half his patients think he's a medical doctor."

"So we're on our own with Alan's psychology programme. But at least we have a big book," said Douglas, holding it aloft.

December 1981

"And so, Douglas, have you formulated any portentous resolutions for instigation in 1982?" asked Dr Burlington.

Having once hoped to have supervision sessions happen more often, Douglas was now doing his best to avoid them, but was not always successful.

"No, I haven't, not yet. Have you?"

"I suppose one arrives at a point in one's life when one feels that change is not of the essence," said Dr Burlington, making brief eye contact with Douglas. "At your age, by way of comparison, change in appropriate directions can mould and endure. *Appropriate* changes *are* of the essence."

Douglas had extracted a note from his pocket while Dr Burlington was speaking.

"I wrote down a couple of things I wanted to raise with you," he said. "Do you remember the young man, Alan Hardy, from the ward round? The man with obsessive compulsive disorder and a cat phobia?"

"Naturally I do. My recollections of the boy's case are lucid. Perhaps he could have been admitted to hospital at an earlier juncture, before acting out his aggressive self-harming behaviour, no doubt directed towards the parents who found him."

"The overdose was out of character."

"Character, Douglas, is a complex phenomenon. But you will appreciate this progressively, I hope, if you continue with a career in psychiatry. Perhaps more accurately, one should say that character comprises a collection of complex phenomena, these phenomena not always resting easily alongside each other, as is no doubt the case with this boy."

"He took the Paracetamol impulsively and now he regrets it."

"At a certain level, your statement may be an accurate one," said Dr Burlington, moving his head slowly in an anti-clockwise circle.

"Do you have a sore neck?" asked Douglas.

"Neck? My neck? Why do you ask me that? Please focus upon our discussion," said Dr Burlington, beginning to rotate his head in a clockwise direction. "Where was I? Impulsivity, yes, character, and *regret*. He may express regret, of course, for what have been *his actions, his own behaviour*. But I would put it to you that this behaviour, these actions which he *purports* to regret, were interpersonally mediated. That is to say, they reflected his aggressive urges towards those parents who returned to find him. Those parents came home to a young man, suffering and unwell, to find him emitting an unequivocal message reading: "What have you done to me?" He punishes his parents, he shocks and embarrasses them, acting out his punitive revenge for all the difficulties he perceives himself to have endured, at their hands, in the course of his upbringing, and which he believes to have boxed him into this *cul-de-sac* of neuroses, phobias and obsessions."

Douglas sighed loudly.

"That sounds like nonsense to me."

Dr Burlington put his finger tips together and glanced at Douglas before resuming his neck movements.

"You lack experience, Douglas, you lack perspicacity, and at times you do not exhibit respect. If you talk with this boy in the appropriate manner, if you engage patiently with his psychopathology, then you may ultimately comprehend the points I have made to you. Do not be blinkered. Consider the possibilities. Rise above simplistic reductionist assumptions."

From looking out the window Douglas returned his gaze to Dr Burlington.

"Apart from Alan's treatment, there was something else I wanted to raise, although it's not entirely separate," he said.

"Proceed, Douglas, proceed. I am listening."

"Alan was in the infirmary for a week after his overdose. The gastroenterologists were good with his liver, but they understood next to nothing about the psychiatric side of things. They talked about him as a 'nutter' and they just wanted to transfer him to us as soon as possible."

"And your point, Douglas, is what?"

"They didn't want me, a junior psychiatrist, going down there to advise them."

"I would have gone. Indeed, I should like them to have made that very request."

"But you were busy and you're often not here. It seems to me, especially after overdoses, that it would be great to have someone experienced down there to see people. We had a lady sent up last week who took pills when she was drunk and we couldn't find anything wrong with her. She'd had a row with her husband. So she stayed in the ward for 24 hours, it took her away from her family, it caused ructions in her life, and there was no reason for it. That kind of thing could surely be avoided."

"I am afraid, Douglas, that I find your attitude to be preposterously querulous. You are a very junior psychiatrist with experience over a period of four months—*one third of one year*—and yet you endeavour to instruct me about the appropriate configuration of our service."

"I'm not *instructing* anyone," said Douglas. "All I'm saying is that it would seem like a good idea to have a psychiatrist on site at the infirmary. I've seen it work well in Newcastle."

"I shall take note of your view, your *dissenting* view, Douglas. I shall note your fresh faced sentiments. But, as you remarked, I am a busy person and you, also, I trust, will have work to do elsewhere."

****

Having looked at the psychology book, Douglas and Tam invited Anne, the ward's occupational therapist, to join them for a further discussion. Without a psychologist's input, they wanted her to teach Alan some relaxation and anxiety management skills. Tam was not certain, but suspected Anne had a cat that could be used in the course of Alan's treatment. Douglas welcomed Anne's involvement since he liked her poise and intelligent appraisals of patients, as well as finding her very attractive. She was tall, lithe and athletic.

The three of them met in Douglas's office and quickly agreed that Alan did need anxiety management training.

"And you've got a cat, haven't you, Anne?" asked Tam.

"Molly. She's big and black."

"Alan doesn't know that, I suppose," said Douglas.

"I don't see how he would."

"He scrutinises people the whole time, looking for cat hairs.

"But maybe you're used to men staring at you," said Douglas.

"I'll try to take that as a pathetic compliment," she said.

"It could be bad or good that Anne has a cat, because Molly could be part of the exposure programme," said Tam.

"It sounds like you have a plan," said Anne.

"Yes. We would try response prevention for his obsessions and compulsions—try to help him to stop the hand washing, the mask wearing and so on—and for the cat phobia we've started to design an exposure hierarchy," Tam told her. "So he might start with something only slightly scary like sitting twenty feet away from a cat owner, and then step by step confront his fears until hopefully he's finally sitting with a cat on his knee."

"The big problem at the moment," said Douglas, "is that he shits himself at the mere mention of cats. He sweats and he shakes if he's near anything or anyone he thinks might have had recent contact with cats. He really is in a bad way."

"That's a problem, then, if you want me to do relaxation and anxiety management with him," said Anne.

"Do we need to tell him you've got a cat?" asked Douglas.

"I think we do. He'll find out soon enough. That might shake his faith in me, maybe in all of us."

"That is a problem, right enough," said Douglas.

"I think we'll need a non-contagious, non-cat owner," suggested Tam, "like Douglas or me, to act as a sort of go-between under your supervision."

"That sounds bizarre," said Anne, "but it might be the only way? If you guys speak to him about it, I'll do nothing in the meantime, except try to come in to work with not too much of Molly's fluff on me."

"Tam and I can debate which of us becomes your trainee therapist," said Douglas.

****

Since he had followed Harry Cameron's suggestion and kept a closer eye on Chris' alcohol consumption, Douglas had become concerned. He also enjoyed a drink and this may have skewed his earlier impressions, since it was obvious that Chris was drinking heavily. Douglas observed that no day went by without Chris having a drink, he drank very quickly and he had taken to bringing whisky back to the flat regularly.

It was a Tuesday evening and Douglas was reading a psychiatry journal.

"Ye're gettin' tae be quite the academic swot," said Chris, who had been pacing around.

"There's nothing on TV and this is interesting."

"What is it?"

"It's a paper called 'Causes and Treatments for Obsessive Compulsive Disorder'. You remember I mentioned Alan in the ward? Some of this stuff is really relevant. I especially like this bit on the causes of OCD: 'Over many years, psychoanalytic theories have been espoused to explain the causation of OCD. These have included the suppression and redirection of aggressive and/or sexual impulses, and the notion that sufferers with OCD might be arrested in the anal stage of development with unresolved conflicts relating to potty training. There is no evidence, as far as the writers of this paper are aware, to support such theories, and unless and until such evidence emerges, we would suggest that such theories are ignored, especially since they have no demonstrable utility among the treatment options available.' I think that's great. I should make a copy of the paper for my esteemed consultant."

"Maybe no' yir best idea, pourin' more fuel on the battle flames. Anyway, are ye comin' out fir a pint?"

"There's cans of lager in the fridge."

"They're finished. It's gettin' on fir nine o'clock so we've got an hour's drinkin' time if we go now. I can just go mysel' if ye're intent on swotting".

"It's about *patients* and it's *interesting*," said Douglas, "and there was something else interesting in the second lecture this afternoon."

"Aye," said Chris, "I saw ye had yir eyes on that alcohol lecturer. No' a bad bit o' stuff fir a more mature woman."

"For a change it was what she was saying that I found interesting. The bit about the questionnaire for detecting drinking problems," said Douglas, as he picked up his lecture notes from the floor beside his chair.

"Sounded like most o' the Scottish population must be alcoholics from her angle."

"Maybe," said Douglas as he looked through his notes, "but I thought about me and then I thought about you when she put up that wee four item check list. Here it is—the CAGE questionnaire. Remember the C question? "Have you ever felt that you should *Cut down* your drinking?"

"Have we no' all thought that, especially when we see the latest bank overdraft?" asked Chris.

"So you've scored one point," said Douglas. "And then the A question: 'Have people *Annoyed* you by criticising your drinking?'"

"Does it count if the guy that annoys ye is a self-righteous bastard who drinks too much himsel'?"

"It doesn't say that it doesn't. I'll give you half a point there. Any time you guys from the west get criticised about anything it seems to annoy you. Anyway, on to number three, the G question: 'Have you ever felt *Guilty* about your drinking?' And if you haven't, then you should have. Within the last month you've thrown up over your bed and I had to stop you taking your trousers off at that nurses' party."

"As I recall it, ye stopped me from doin' that tae impress the lassie in the short skirt ye were keen on. Douglas, I feel guilty fir *breathin'*, let alone fir sins o' the flesh or drinkin' a bit much. My whole family's like that—guilty about everything!"

"You're not an ideal subject for this test—I'll give you another half point there. But it looks like a whole point for the E question: 'Have you ever felt that you needed a drink first thing in the morning (an *Eye-opener*) to steady your nerves or get rid of a hangover?' Like last Sunday morning when you wired in to that ghastly sweet martini to stop you retching."

"OK, OK, guilty as charged on number four. So what?"

"You scored three out of four, and it could have been higher. She said this afternoon that if you scored two or more then you were ninety percent likely to have a significant alcohol problem."

"Aye, like I said, me and half the population. The big problem I've got wi' alcohol right now is a daft oaf lecturin' me," said Chris, as he looked at his watch and put on his coat, "wi' no apparent concern that the pubs'll be shuttin' very soon."

"But thank you, doctor, for your concern," he added as he left the flat.

"I did try," said Douglas to himself.

****

Following his attendance at a meeting called the 'Placement Committee', Harry Cameron came to Douglas's office.

"I'm a bit shell shocked," he said.

Sweat ran down Harry's red face.

"They swear you to secrecy. It's like the masons," he continued, "so I can't tell you too much. It was nearly all consultants, pretty much all of them showed up, and just a few of us lucky juniors. The things they say! To each other and about the trainees—who they want in their teams and who they don't want. It's like horse trading for who goes where in February."

"I thought there wouldn't be much movement until August?"

"That's right. It was mainly about the senior trainees—a lot of them move in February. You should have heard the lumps getting torn out of some of them! Then one of the consultants threatened to walk out if a particular doctor was sent to his team."

"And it's all a secret?"

"Yes. I can't tell you what Burlington said about you. But he's not your friend, Doug, is he?"

"He's not my closest pal."

"One of the old consultants seems to really hate Burlington, said it was hardly the first time he'd fallen out with a

100

trainee and maybe he should examine himself occasionally. So, at least you're not alone, if you get me. The chairman's Dr Brook. He's a sensible guy—though he was nearly tearing his hair out by the end—and he said he thought it would be good if you got a move. He said he could meet up with you tomorrow to discuss the possibilities."

Douglas liked Dr Brook. Unlike most of the consultants, he was rather scruffy. He wore a battered old sports jacket, and trainees thought he must surely sleep in a polo necked sweater since he was never seen in anything different.

"You're who I thought you were—tricky to pair up the names and faces of all the new doctors," said Dr Brook. "As you'll know, I coordinate the junior staff placements for my sins."

"Harry Cameron told me you chaired the meeting."

"I looked twenty years younger yesterday morning," he said, opening a manilla file on his desk. "This is about you. Not much in here yet, of course. How has it been—your first few months in psychiatry?"

"It's a bit difficult to summarise," said Douglas. "But very enjoyable, fascinating, not without its stresses."

"The right career choice for you?"

"Definitely. There's nothing I would rather do."

"OK. But not all plain sailing? Things between you and Edwin Burlington have been a little strained at times?"

"That's fair comment."

"We heard from him yesterday, of course. And Dr Cameron diplomatically suggested that the difficulties might not be entirely, ah, unilaterally mediated?"

"I've not found it easy to work for him."

"When moving you to another team in February was suggested yesterday, Dr Burlington did not disagree. Indeed, he said that it might be a chance for you to 'turn over a new leaf' or something very like that."

"This 'new leaf' he talks about..."

Dr Brook raised his hand to stop Douglas speaking.

"I do know there may be two sides, but this is about *solutions*, not about disputes or blame. The good news is that you can be offered a move. The bad news is that there is only one slot available. It's with Dr Bill Wiseman in the psychotherapy ward. How would you feel about that?"

"I'm not sure I'm a born psychotherapist," said Douglas.

"It's a bit of a Hobson's choice for you then? If you want a few days to consider the options, then that's fine with me."

"No time needed," said Douglas. "I'll be happy to move. Thank you very much."

"Right. Six weeks to mug up on your Freud before February," said Dr Brook.

****

Anne had to leave the room when she and Douglas went to see Alan about his therapy. His terror was clear as soon as she mentioned her cat, and Douglas continued the explanation on his own. Alan listened apprehensively, then said with a tight smile.

"So you hope to help my obsessions by stopping me from doing them and to get over my fear of cats by having them sit on me?"

Douglas agreed with Alan's bald summary, but emphasised that things would be done gradually, as Alan's anxieties diminished.

Anne had been considering the options while he talked to Alan, and decided that she agreed with Tam; the only way forward would be to teach Douglas how to do relaxation and anxiety management. He could then treat Alan with these techniques and discuss progress with her.

This plan resulted in Douglas's lying on the floor of his own office while Anne sat at his desk. She seemed to understand why he preferred the door to be locked.

"Relaxation is crucial in anxiety management," she said. "Just like you can't sit down and stand up at the same time, you can't be relaxed and anxious at the same time."

She told him she would go through successive muscle groups, getting him to tense these and then relax. She started with the muscles in his face and neck, moved through his shoulders and arms and then down to his fingers. She next focused on his toes and feet before moving up his legs. Douglas's concentration wandered at times as he listened to Anne's melodious voice. After finishing with some deep breathing, she asked him how he felt.

"Great," he said.

"Tomorrow we'll do some imagery. We'll get you to picture a relaxing scene—a beach, maybe. The theory is that you associate the scene with feeling relaxed, picture the scene and then relax rapidly without needing to lie on the floor for twenty minutes. It's a bit like hypnosis. Are you going to lie there all day?"

"I wouldn't mind," said Douglas. "I think I'm going to enjoy Alan's treatment."

****

The Friday before Christmas presented Douglas with a dilemma. The ward staff and the junior psychiatrists had arranged their Christmas nights out for that same evening.

They were at least going to the same hotel close to the hospital. The format of the 'take a party to a party' evening was explained to him; you went for a meal with your own 'party' (the doctors or the ward staff), and then dancing ensued at a more collective 'party'. Douglas felt pressure from both groups to join them. In the ward, Sami urged him to join their table.

"Who else will I talk to about cricket? And don't worry, Burlington never goes. He wouldn't want to mix socially with the likes of us. And if you don't come, Dick could be the only doctor with us, for heaven's sake!"

Dick had paid money to Sami for the ward night out before hearing that it clashed with the psychiatrists' evening. It seemed that Sami preferred annoying Dick to returning his deposit and having him elsewhere.

Mandy and Chris had pressed Douglas to join the junior doctors.

"Surely you want to sit with us," said Mandy. "It's the only psychiatric Christmas night out I'll ever go to with you."

"Ye'll have a better laugh wi' us," said Chris, "and ye'll need tae watch that Mandy disnae see a nicer fella and dump ye. And I thought ye were on a mission tae make me a teeto-taller?"

The pressure from them was hard to resist, and he had signed up to join the doctors. The evening before the party, worries about his relationship with Mandy intensified when he overheard her talking on the telephone with her mother about engagement rings.

On party night, sitting between Mandy and Chris, he was generally having a good time. Harry Cameron was lively company, teasing colleagues about what he alleged had been said about them at the Placement Committee.

On several occasions, Mandy spoke into his ear while he was listening to someone else.

"I peeked in your wardrobe on Wednesday, Dougie," she hissed, "thinking I might spot a nicely wrapped package."

This was followed up a few minutes later.

"Maybe you're going Christmas shopping tomorrow? Best not to have too bad a hangover—to give it your full attention."

She was again wearing the bracelets from Greece, and at one point she held these in front of Douglas's face.

"Perhaps it will be a pendant to match these. Maybe you bought something in Greece when I wasn't looking? Maybe another item of jewellery tomorrow?"

Douglas had given very little thought to what he might buy anyone for Christmas and he was finding her quite irritating. After the meal was finished and the music started up, he circulated round the other doctors' tables and then went over to see how things were going with the ward staff. He was amused to observe Dick shouting above the music into Sami's ear. Occupational therapist Anne sat on Dick's other side and Douglas slipped into the vacant seat beside her.

"You look relaxed," she said. "Or is it drunk?"

"A bit of both, maybe. Perhaps we should introduce some alcohol into Alan's treatment programme."

Douglas had to lean close to Anne to be heard above the music.

"Your hair looks different."

"Well spotted. Not money wasted at the hairdresser then."

"No, you've scrubbed up well."

"Did you just call me a scrubber?" she shouted.

"No, no," he shouted back. "I'm saying that YOU HAVE SCRUBBED UP WELL. DO YOU FANCY A QUIETER DRINK IN THE OTHER BAR?"

"THAT WOULD BE NICE."

Douglas bought drinks in the small bar across the corridor. They were settled in a quiet corner when an inebriated Harry Cameron wandered in and started across the room towards them.

"Hi," he said, as he did a drunken double take. "Oh, pardon me, I'm just looking for a toilet. I get the picture."

He made an inelegant exit, bumping into the barman who was collecting empty glasses.

"What picture do you think he gets, Douglas?"

"Who knows. But if he looked at you it would be a very pretty picture."

"Ha, ha, your patter is truly unimpressive!" she said, but did not move her thigh from where it rested against his.

"Seriously," said Douglas, "it's been good working with you on Alan's case. I've learned a lot. Your patients are lucky people."

"That's good, if it's been educational."

"And it has also been relaxing, very relaxing, of course."

"Yes, I've noticed your relaxation and your enjoyment, sometimes."

Douglas took a long drink of his beer.

"I do sometimes find it hard to focus, especially when we get up to the muscles of the thighs and the pelvis."

"In my professional capacity," she said, looking into his eyes, "I had noticed that it was sometimes a struggle for you when we reached that particular anatomical area. Not all of you always appears to be entirely relaxed."

"What can I say? Is it my fault if the therapist has a very sexy voice?"

Anne put her hand on his.

"What do you think? Further therapy? At my place?" she asked.

****

Douglas tried to appear grumpy about working on Christmas day. In fact, he had volunteered to work until 5 p.m., but he portrayed it, to colleagues and to family, as an unlucky break.

Having spent the previous Christmas day at home with his family, he was quite happy to be avoiding this one. He would drive up on Boxing Day, and he anticipated that two days there would be quite long enough. He still sometimes found it difficult to be with his father and step-mother. He enjoyed seeing his younger brother, but his sister and her family were a strain. Her twin boys, now five years old, fought and squabbled, and this had been constant last Christmas. Neither his sister nor her husband seemed to notice; indeed, they looked around as if to invite others to share the pleasure spread by their wonderful children. So Douglas was happy to be working, but liked chatting to other junior psychiatrists with overdone heroism.

"Just leave Christmas day to me. You go away and enjoy yourself. Try not to think about me, working, here at the hospital."

Most of them assured him that they would indeed enjoy themselves and would not think about him at all, but he anticipated that some might feel favours were owed should he wish to swap nights on call in the future.

Many of the in-patients had gone home to their families for a day or two, and the hospital was quiet as Douglas made his way up to the ward on Christmas morning. Sami had told Douglas that he would have to dress up as Father Christmas and give out presents to the patients. Douglas thought this was a joke, and was taken aback by a giggling Sami, holding up a red cloak and white beard. He prevailed upon Douglas to try them on.

"Perfect fit. Now you need to practice your 'Ho, ho, hos', Douglas."

"Ho, ho, ho," Douglas intoned morosely, much to Sami's amusement.

"Loud and joyful 'Ho, ho, hos' are required! There was a hospital circular about it!"

"I'll do my best. Where are the presents?"

Sami produced a large black plastic bag from under the desk.

"What's that? How can Santa be convincing with that as a swag bag?" asked Douglas.

"Cutbacks. The best I could find. Perfume for the ladies in the blue parcels, socks in the silver paper for the men. They're waiting for you in the sitting room. Come on, Douglas—ho, ho, ho, now's the season to be jolly."

"OK, ho, ho, ho," said Douglas, hoisting the plastic sack on to his shoulder. "It is a far, far better thing I do."

About a dozen patients were gathered in the ward sitting room. Douglas quickly began to enjoy his role, trying to boom out "Merry Christmas, ho, ho, ho" cheerfully as he handed out the gifts. Most of the patients seemed pleased and amused, although one old lady looked at him with alarm and it did not help when he pulled aside his beard saying:

"Don't worry. It's me—Dr Barker."

Douglas's vision was restricted by his hood, and he did not recognise Billy Franks until he was halfway through his 'Ho, ho, ho'.

"I've seen lots of better Santas. Don't give up the day job, son," said Billy gloomily.

After removing the outfit, Douglas returned to the sitting room.

"I didn't know you were back in. I hardly recognised you, Billy."

"And I wasn't wearin' a daft disguise."

"You've lost weight."

"Aye, I have. You maybe never heard. I got sent home direct from forensic and I was OK for a wee while. But now, as you see..." said Billy, as he gazed across the room.

"You've been depressed again?"

"That's what they say. This is no' my favourite time of year. It's three years ago this week that my woman buggered off."

"Not good. Being on your own at Christmas."

"I'm no' on my own, Douglas. I'm in here."

"Better than being at home?"

"Probably. At least there's some company here, and it keeps me off the drink."

"You're just recently back in?"

"Yesterday. I came in last Christmas too. Same situation. And there'll be four or five more like me that was eatin' turkey here last year too."

"I'd better leave you to it," said Douglas.

"Merry Christmas," Billy shouted after him.

****

Douglas arrived at his father's house in time for lunch on Boxing Day. He continued with the mildly martyred tone he had adopted with colleagues, telling his family that although he was not busy, someone had to be there, and it was just unlucky that it had been him.

"But here I am now," he said, "and I'll just have to make the best of it."

The dining room table had been lengthened by means of a card table. The twins sat there and told Douglas it had been decided to save the seat between them for him.

"How kind," he said, noting that his brother was trying to look innocent.

Belinda was busy in the kitchen while the rest of the family sat at the table.

"I'm nearest the door," said Douglas. "I'll go and help Belinda."

Belinda was an excellent cook and would not require too much assistance. She was happily stirring a pot on the stove.

"I've come to help, should that be necessary," he said.

"Douglas, thank you so much," she said, turning from her cooking with her stirring hand high in the air and embracing him with her other arm.

"I hardly had the chance to greet you when you arrived. It is so good to see you!"

As usual, she was a bit gushy.

"Great to be here," said Douglas, as he picked up her spectacles from the floor.

It had been her habit as a librarian to keep her glasses hooked into her hair and, despite numerous breakages, the habit persisted.

"No obvious damage," he said, putting her glasses on the table. "I hear everything went well yesterday."

"It is such a challenge, feeding the multitudes on Christmas day. And now the new challenge, of course, is to make the turkey interesting for the next few days."

"It smells interesting."

"Curry, Douglas. You probably eat lots of that in the flat with your young doctor friend?"

"Chris does make a lot of curries. He's a better cook than I am."

"You should come home more often, and I could teach you to cook. I would love to do that!"

"It's hard to find the time, Belinda. Easier just to get myself a woman who can cook. Like dad did."

"Ha, ha, very kind. Here's the rice—be a darling and take it through."

Douglas was enjoying the meal until Harvey (the 'big' twin) knocked a glass of red wine over his trousers. Everyone except Douglas and his father seemed to find this amusing.

"Just a little more *control* might be appropriate, Helen," his father said.

"Give the boys a break, Dad," said Helen, "they're just excited to see Douglas."

"As they were excited without him yesterday," said her father.

It was decided that they would go for a family walk after lunch and then watch a film on TV. Belinda stayed behind to

111

clear up, and Douglas fell in at the back of the walkers beside his father. They dropped behind the others.

"When did you get the stick, Dad?"

"October. Medical advice."

"Your hip's worse?"

"They say it's my hip. Pain down both legs these days. The left one is rather more severe."

Douglas remembered his father always walking with a limp, ascribing this to military service without divulging further details.

"You seem a little breathless, too."

"Ever the doctor, Douglas. I shall be sixty-five on my birthday."

"Maybe you should have had us when you were younger," said Douglas light heartedly.

"The war took years from the lives of my generation, if it did not actually take our lives," said his father.

It was difficult to introduce levity into conversations with his father.

"But retirement looms?"

"*Looms* seems an accurate description. As I have said to you before, I am keen to work for as long as God and the medics permit."

Douglas struggled to understand how his father derived so much apparent pleasure from his work as a tax inspector.

At this point Harvey ran back to them.

"We're going to play horsies, Uncle Douglas, and you're my horse."

"Great idea," said Douglas, seeing Fergus, the smaller twin, already up on Tom's back.

Banter ensued between Douglas and his brother, with Douglas claiming it to be unfair that he had the heavier jockey and Tom responding that the weight on his back would be a balance to Douglas's growing beer belly. Tom and Fergus won the race easily, and while Douglas continued to protest about jockey weights and unsuitable footwear, he breathlessly wondered whether getting fit might become his New Year resolution.

Douglas seemed to be the only adult who did not enjoy seeing 'It's a Wonderful Life' again. He almost welcomed the twins' regular incursions to demand sweets or to ambush the adults with their new guns. Belinda reminded him that she and his father were going to a party at a neighbour's house, and they started to get ready. The twins, described as 'knackered' by their parents, went to bed quietly.

The two brothers made the evening meal together and Douglas was impressed by Tom's skills in the kitchen. He was now a final year medical student, and having gone to the local university, he had lived at home until recently. He said that Belinda had spent a lot of time "helping me to become a modern man around the house." Tom was the only one of the siblings who felt close to Belinda, and this topic came up at the meal.

"She's done wonders for Dad," he said, "and I don't know where he might have been without her."

"She's just not my type," said Helen. "She never has been, has she Alex?"

Her husband Alex was an industrious, softly spoken solicitor. He prided himself on seeing both sides of every issue, and his opinions were rarely definitive.

"I've not often heard you speak well of her, dear," he said, "but you haven't seen a great deal of her recently, and people do change."

"Not at her age, people don't change," his wife asserted.

113

"She's different from Mum," said Tom, "and to my mind you and Douglas have always struggled with that."

"She is *so* different!" said Helen. "Mum was quiet and consistent. And she was *artistic,* she was *gifted.*"

"Like you, dear," said Alex.

Helen had studied English at university and at that time described herself as a 'future author'. 'My first novel' was started during her student years, and after graduation she took a job in publishing. When the family asked how her book was progressing, her responses became increasingly irritable and dismissive. She said she had decided that her true vocation might be more artistic than literary, and that she was thinking of applying for art school at the time of her marriage. The twins arrived within a year. Having recently read the book 'Games People Play', Douglas thought his sister had been playing 'If it wasn't for my wooden leg' for several years. The impediments she identified that prevented her from becoming a famous author or sculptor—her mother's death, her busy job, her marriage, her twins—were all beyond her control, and without them she insisted she would have realised her considerable potential. Douglas held the view that her main problem was laziness. He had ceased his martyrdom about working on Christmas day since it reminded him of his sister's usual demeanour.

"And Mum couldn't *be* artistic, because she was bringing us up while Dad worked the whole time," she continued. "Then Belinda came along when all the hard work was done."

"I don't suppose we can blame her for that," said Douglas.

"No, perhaps you shouldn't blame her too much," said Alex.

Tom had been filling wine glasses and stacking plates, and he looked annoyed.

"Nobody should be blaming her at all. You don't know what you're talking about," he said. "I was here when Mum died and you guys were off at university. I was here when Dad crumbled. Belinda was a hero, she was a fucking *rock* if you want to know the truth. And to my mind she's stayed that way for the last seven years."

He walked through to the kitchen with a pile of plates and the others sat in silence for some time.

"Tom sounds like he feels responsible, a bit burdened. I should try to come back here more often," said Douglas.

"Perhaps you should," said Helen, "even if there's nothing to feel responsible about. You live much closer than we do. And you don't have two kids and a house to run."

January 1982

Douglas woke in the early afternoon with only a mild hangover. Hogmanay had been disappointing. He and Chris had a few drinks in a local pub and headed for a party at the flat of one of the other junior psychiatrists. Douglas had written down the address but left it in the flat. Chris dissuaded him from going back for it, insisting that he knew exactly where to go. After an hour of walking in the drizzle, they had to agree that they were lost and were not going to find the party. There were mutual recriminations. Chris consulted his watch at one point during their search.

"It's ten past midnight. Happy New Year, ye big useless bastard."

They had turned for home when they spotted a party in a ground floor flat. They were made welcome enough, but they knew nobody. They had drunk or shared the remainder of their whisky when a heated dispute broke out between two women. They left and eventually found their way back. By then it was raining heavily.

While he was dozing before getting up, Douglas thought he heard their letter box rattle. When he went to the door, there was a blue envelope with his name on it. It looked like Mandy's writing. He made a cup of tea and sat at the kitchen table.

It was dated '11 a.m., 1/1/82'

"Dear Douglas (not that you feel that dear to me now),

I had been hoping to see you at the party last night. Perhaps you persuaded Chris to go elsewhere to avoid me, or perhaps you went somewhere with your bimbo occupational therapist. I thought we could have talked last night but you not showing up was a final straw. Please give me back the key to my flat. Things are over between us.

I thought we had something special going, especially when the holiday was such fun. I thought we could have made a go of it together. I knew you were hardly a romantic man but two of the people at the party last night—probably not fair to say who—told me you are a 'serial womaniser'.

I did think you were a bit funny at the Christmas night out. When you vanished Chris said he thought you must have drunk too much and wandered off home. It is good to have a loyal friend. I heard about the occupational therapist at the party last night. It seems like everyone at the hospital knew about it except me—that when I thought I was your girlfriend you went off with some skinny trollop and made me look like an idiot.

How could you!!!??? I think that is the worst thing that has happened to me. How do you think it made me feel? Especially in front of all those people last night. Do you actually care?! I am beginning to think you never did.

I don't want the book token you gave me for Christmas and you will find it enclosed. Perhaps you could buy yourself a book about manners or etiquette or loyalty or something that might help you to become a better person. And I don't want a reply to this letter. I am happy that I only have another month in psychiatry and please avoid me at work.

Mandy."

Douglas sighed, with a mixture of regret and relief, and was re-reading the letter when Chris appeared in his new tartan dressing gown.

"I suppose I might get used to your mother's taste in presents, but that thing is hard on the bleary eyes this morning," said Douglas.

"Fuck off," said Chris as he poured himself a cup of tea, "and it's the afternoon by the way."

"I've just received a Happy New Year message from Mandy," said Douglas, handing Chris the letter.

Chris read it and said:

"As ye say, a happy message tae start off yir 1982."

"A bit strong, eh? We didn't know we were going to get lost last night." said Douglas.

"Christ, Doug, it's New Year's Day, an' I'm no' wantin' tae fall out wi' ye."

"No doubt some of it's justified. But 'serial womaniser'—that's a bit unfair."

" '*Oh wid some power the giftie gie us*

Tae see oorselves as others see us,' as somebody once wrote," said Chris.

"I do recognise the words of the national poet."

"Aye, but ye're no' so hot on insight, are ye? When it comes tae recognisin' yersel'? I've said tae ye often enough that Mandy's a great lass—better than ye deserve. But ye cannae keep yir equipment in yir troosers, can ye?"

"Mandy is a great lass, but she was never right for me. Too girly girly. Too possessive."

"Aye, but who is right fir ye, Douglas? This latest bimbo?"

"She's not a bimbo. She's tasty."

"Tasty, aye. Ye're on tae yir latest lollipop."

"It's not like that. It's actually not like that at all. I've thought Anne was gorgeous from when I first saw her. She's self-contained and she's funny. She likes to be teased, and I just sort of feel at ease with things when I'm with her. I can't put it better than that. Truth to tell, she reminds me a wee bit of Spider."

"OK, so maybe she's no' just another meaningless conquest. Possibly. We'll see. You tell me tae think about my drinkin', and maybe that's right. But perhaps you need tae think about how ye treat women."

"Thank you for your New Year sermon, Reverend Dunn. No, seriously, I do hear what you're saying, Chris."

"Aye, do ye really?"

"If I find the right woman—and it could be Anne—I will treat her well. You watch."

****

Douglas was delighted to hear Tam's report on Alan's progress. Alan had only rarely been wearing a mask and the frequency of his hand washing was reducing.

"His mum brought him back after his pass at home and said she saw a big change. He was grinning away, very pleased with himself. Lots of progress, I might say, in my area in particular, though he did say imagining your sandy beach has been good."

"He told me that picturing himself paddling through the waves was perfect because it's the last place you would find a cat," said Douglas.

"Is the cat owner back to work yet?" asked Tam.

"Anne? I think she's here today."

119

"He's still terrified of contact with cat owners, let alone cats."

"Hopefully we can get Anne into a room with him sometime this week, while he's on a roll."

They agreed that between them they could start taking all the referrals to the psychology department.

"I was sorry to hear that you'll be leaving us, Doug," said Tam, "and it's the psychotherapy ward you're bound for with old Bill Wiseman? You'll like him, but it won't be relaxation therapy there, you know. It'll be interpreting dreams and telling patients that their problems are all down to sex."

"I've heard reports," said Douglas, "and I've started to read Freud."

His aunt had given him an eight book set of the complete works of Freud for Christmas.

"And I've been practising keeping a straight face," he added.

****

The psychiatric trainees took part in a rota to administer electroconvulsive therapy (ECT). Douglas was scheduled for this during January, so he could legitimately miss Dr Burlington's Tuesday ward rounds. This was well timed since Douglas was doing all he could generally to avoid Dr Burlington.

His part in the process was undemanding. A knowledgeable, bossy nurse had been organising the ECT clinics for many years, and she told the new psychiatrists where on the patient's head to place the electrodes and when to press the button to administer the current. Medical students usually left the sessions disappointed. Their preconceptions of ECT tended to derive from the film 'One Flew Over the Cuckoo's Nest' in which un-anaesthetised patients were lifted bodily from their beds by the current and then convulsed violently. So the twitching that ECT induced when patients had received anaesthetics and muscle relaxants often bored the students. It was one of Douglas's roles to try to keep them interested by discussing theories behind ECT, and by getting them to talk with some of the patients before their treatments. Otherwise, he was not sure why he was required. But if it meant that he spent less time in Dr Burlington's company, then he was not objecting.

Douglas did feel, however, that he should keep a close eye on Dr Burlington's thoughts about patients. He did this by scrutinising the case records frequently. Dr Burlington's letters and written notes in the case records were similar to his speech. Douglas began to be amused by some of the more flowery language and took to reading out examples in the ward office, especially when Sami was there.

"Here's a good one—'this lady has been *persistently quixotic* in the care of her handicapped son'—not bad, eh, Sami?"

"Great. What does it mean?"

"Unselfish, I think. And he found her to be '*phlegmatically quiescent*' at interview."

"What a clown! I guess that meant she agreed with him?"

"I think there might be a pattern!" Douglas exclaimed. "Do you see the p and the q? I think he might have some sort of alphabetical system so that one big word triggers another."

"I'm not sure I follow you. Just to make him sound clever?"

"Exactly!" said Douglas, scanning the lady's case notes. "And look at what he wrote yesterday—'Mrs Evans has formed a *critically disharmonious* relationship with a fellow patient'. It must be his system of mnemonics, or whatever you call it, using the alphabet like that."

"I think "stupid twat" is about as good as I can do, Douglas."

"It's fine to know the workings of the enemy brain. We've cracked his Enigma Code!"

"If it helps you get to sleep," chuckled Sami.

****

Alan Hardy agreed to move to the next stage of his cat phobia hierarchy by having a meeting with Anne. The seating in Douglas's office was carefully arranged with a chair for Anne next to the door. Alan went through his relaxation exercises and was picturing a beach scene before Douglas telephoned Anne. She first stood in the doorway, coming closer only when Alan's anxiety felt tolerable. The process was lengthy, but it went well. By the end of an hour, Anne had touched Alan's hands, she was assisting with the anxiety management and Alan was reasonably calm. He agreed to the next stage of seeing Anne's cat in a cage.

"What's she like?" asked Alan apprehensively.

"Molly's big and black and fluffy."

"Oh dear," he said, "it could hardly be worse."

"No, no," said Anne, "it could hardly be better. If you become OK with her, then you'll be OK with any cat on the planet."

"Maybe. If you say so. And when do you think I could get out of here, Dr Barker? When can I go home?"

"Maybe quite soon. But we would need to check with Dr Burlington. Perhaps you could ask him yourself at the ward round? I'm afraid I won't be there."

"I'll be there," said Anne. "Alan and I can both ask him."

After Alan left the office, Anne and Douglas were still sitting in close proximity.

"It's great to see him. He's like a new man," said Douglas.

"Yes, life could open up for him."

"We had fun at the Christmas night out."

"And after it."

"It's a pity, with the holidays and things. We haven't caught up with each other since."

Anne leaned back in her chair.

"Now maybe isn't the best time to talk."

"Why not? Are you needing your lunch?"

"Don't be daft. Look, I thought you knew, then it dawned on me that maybe you didn't, and it seems like you don't. With what you just said."

"Knew what?"

"About Harry. I live at his flat when he's home."

"When he's home?"

"From the navy. He's a lieutenant now. I've been with him a long time."

"That's a pity."

"I thought everyone in the ward knew. I thought they would have told you."

"Nobody said a word."

"Maybe they forget, or something. I suppose he can be away for a long time. But he's due back on leave tomorrow."

"Right, OK."

"So at least you know now," said Anne, "but that doesn't mean it wasn't fun, Douglas. And I'm sure we can still work together."

"Yes, it was fun," said Douglas, as Anne closed his office door behind her.

****

Chris was unsympathetic about Anne.

"The biter is bitten fir a change," he said.

Hoping to discuss the Anne situation, Douglas had waited until the weekend before telling Chris, and then wished he had done so earlier. It was 4 o'clock on Saturday afternoon so Chris was distracted by watching the updating football scores on TV and by the fact that he was quite drunk. Douglas had joined a five-a-side football team, and when he returned there were already several empty beer cans beside Chris' chair. He then moved his attention to a bottle of whisky.

"Celebrating something?" Douglas asked him.

"There's fuck all tae celebrate. We're losin' one nil. Do you fancy a drink?"

"Not me, no thanks."

"Aye, I forgot. Ye're gettin' yersel' fit fir a trial wi' Dundee United."

"The indoor football's good. Maybe you should join up."

"That's better," said Chris, as he successfully tuned in to the football commentary on his radio. "We should've had a penalty in the first half. Aye, and maybe you should join up wi' the fuckin' navy. The fancy uniform might make ye even more irresistible tae women."

124

"That's not terrifically funny. Seriously, you would like the football. When did you last play?"

"Last night. I scored the winnin' goal in the cup final."

"In real life, when did..."

"Fuck!" shouted Chris, and threw his radio across the room. "That wis another fuckin' penalty!"

Douglas retrieved the radio. It was in bits.

"At least we've still got a telly," he said, handing the pieces of the radio back to Chris. "At least for now we do, if it stays in one piece."

Chris was pressing his forehead hard with his fingers.

"Sorry, Doug, man. I'm sorry. That wis out o' order. That wisnae good."

"Can I put the TV off, Chris?"

"Aye. I'll do it," he said, leaning over to switch off the wall plug.

"I'm sorry about yir bird," he said.

"So am I. She's a lovely girl."

"And I'm a pisshead," said Chris, handing Douglas the bottle of whisky. "Away and hide this somewhere."

"I can't think of somewhere you wouldn't find it."

"Right enough. Naw, I've no' been celebratin'. I've been thinkin'."

"About anything special?"

"Mandy."

"Has she been round? Another letter?"

"Na, nothin' like that. She wants tae avoid you, fir one thing. Understandably. So I had lunch wi' her, away from the hospital. A couple o' times."

"Right. And did you get her to pay? I never could."

"Fuck off. She's lovely. I really like her."

125

"Even though my psychiatric training's not far advanced, I'd kind of spotted that. So go for it. I'm out of the picture."

"Ye are and ye aren't. She still talks about ye. And what wid I want wi' your cast-offs? You widnae feel good about it. Nor wid I and nor wid she."

"I'd be fine, and I know she likes you. Christ, if you're keen on her, go for it!"

"And have your enormous fuckin' shadow loomin' over my shoulder?"

"My shadow will soon be a slender one. Give it a few weeks then. Let a bit of water go under the bridge. Get your act together a bit."

"Here starteth another abstinence lecture?"

"Not today. I'm no male model, so I can hardly speak, but your clothes are crap, if you don't mind me saying. And get a decent haircut. That kind of thing."

"Lucky you didnae hide the whisky," said Chris, reaching for the bottle.

****

"What do you think of these, Sami?" asked Douglas, writing in a set of case records. "I put 'she gave a history of being *buoyantly creative*, her talk was *mysteriously nonsensical* and her mood was *cordially diffident*'. Pretty good, eh?"

"Perhaps you need to keep practising. Or then again, maybe you should stop—stop taking the piss? He reads the notes, you know. That's how you and him communicate these days."

"That's the whole idea. Let him see I've cracked his code."

"On your head be it if he works out what you're up to. I should have told you that Morag came round with yesterday's paper. Tam phoned in about it as well."

Sami handed the newspaper to Douglas. Morag had circled Ina's name in the Deaths column. It said that she had passed away peacefully and thanked the doctors and nurses involved in her care. It also gave details of the funeral arrangements.

"Should we go to the funeral?" asked Douglas.

"I don't know, to be honest," said Sami. "I discussed it with Morag."

"It would be good to go, surely?"

"Let's say you and I and Tam went along. If there's not a big crowd we could stand out. Then you could get people saying 'who's the strange threesome?', and that could be tricky for Mavis. She might need to say that Ina was in here before she was in the infirmary. A lot of folk will just think she died from bowel cancer and might not know she was depressed."

"And is that important?"

"It might be. People are ignorant, Douglas. The family might not like Ina to be remembered as a loony."

"People are really that stupid, you think?"

"Yeah, I do. I'll speak to Tam, but Morag thought maybe we should phone Mavis. Express our condolences and stay away from the funeral."

"That seems strange to me, but we can see what Tam thinks," said Douglas.

****

Billy Franks was again causing concern on the ward. All patients had their own 'named nurse' who spoke with them regularly, and Pauline had been assigned to Billy. His mood had risen, he started to make lewd remarks to Pauline and she said he had been "invading my personal space"; so the role of named nurse was taken over by Sami.

"So you think I might be a rapist in the making, do you?" said Billy.

His relationship with most of the staff became fractious and unpredictable. Given the previous difficulties, consultant Dr Peterson, rather than Dick, had been acting as Billy's usual psychiatrist. But now that Dr Peterson had gone on holiday there was something of a hiatus, with Dick avoiding Billy and trying to make decisions on his care through reports from the nurses. Douglas heard about the situation from Billy and from the nurses.

"Dick the wee shit tells Sami to tell me—he tells him to *sell* me—the latest change to my pills or what I'm allowed to do or what I'm no' allowed to do, and he hasn't the decency to meet up with me himself. Thinks he's too high and mighty for that," said Billy.

"I'm the man in the middle here," said Sami. "I'm like some kind of Henry Kissinger peacemaker. It's crazy. And it's not like Dick consults me about his decisions. He just *tells* me—yesterday he left me a *note* on the desk—instructions he wants me to pass on to Billy."

The problems escalated with Billy leaving the ward and coming back drunk. Billy was not generally keen to take medication, and when he had been drinking he was even less amenable. The nurses worried that sedatives might interact with alcohol, and were reluctant to press him to take his medication. So Billy's mood continued to rise.

128

In Dr Peterson's absence, Jim Horsefall was consulted. He concluded that he, Dick and Sami should draw up a plan and then all three of them should meet with Billy to discuss it. Douglas came into the ward office as they were about to see Billy.

"Plan or no plan," said Dick, "we'll need to get him back to the forensic unit. He toed the line there last time."

"That's just a temporary solution," said Sami. "We need to try to keep him here. We usually have a good relationship with him."

"He'll never take his pills," asserted Dick. "He needs a locked ward."

"I don't know him too well," said Jim. "How much does he understand about his illness?"

"Next to nothing," said Dick.

Douglas could not stop himself from muttering a querulous "Eh?", but added quickly:

"Sorry, nothing to do with me."

"Yeah, you shut up, Douglas, even if you might be right," said Sami. "He understands quite a bit about being manic depressive. That doesn't mean he's keen to accept treatment, especially when his mood's up. He often enjoys being high."

"That's not uncommon," said Jim. "We need to try to explain his pills and convince him to take them regularly."

"I don't think he will until we get him behind a locked door, and stop him drinking the pubs dry," said Dick.

"Well let's go and see how we get on," said Jim, leading the others out of the office.

About ten minutes later, loud shouts were emanating from Dick's office. Douglas and a male nursing student arrived simultaneously, just as the door was pulled open by

Sami who was restraining Billy with a headlock and shouting for assistance. Jim Horsefall, minus his glasses, was attempting to hold Billy's legs. Billy was shouting a stream of abuse that included 'fuckin' fascist bastards'. Douglas grabbed the leg Jim was not holding while the student assisted at Sami's end. They managed to get Billy down on to the floor. It was only then that Douglas saw Dick, who had been watching from the far corner of his office. His hands were clasped over his nose and mouth. Blood was trickling between his fingers and he was shaking visibly. Billy had become quiet and limp.

"We will need to move you to the forensic unit, Billy," said Sami.

"Pauline was phoning them for help when I left the office," said Douglas.

"Can we relax a bit, Billy?" Sami asked. "Or are you going to hit us again?"

"He had it comin'," said Billy, his voice muffled from having his head pressed into the carpet. "I'll no' hit the rest of you."

Dick was by this time holding a blood-soaked handkerchief to his face.

"I think my nose is broken. I'll go and find a doctor," he said.

He left with Billy shouting after him:

"You do that! Try to find a better one than yourself!"

Two large male nurses from the forensic unit appeared in the doorway.

"The other nurses are here, Billy. Can we let you go and they can take you round to forensic?" asked Sami.

"OK, OK" said Billy.

Billy sat in the middle of the floor, still surrounded by Douglas, Sami, Jim Horsefall and the student nurse. Billy shook his head ruefully.

"I'm sorry, Sami," he said. "I shouldn't have hit him. But when he started his lecturin', something just snapped."

Billy looked at Douglas.

"I knew resistance was hopeless when the heavy mob arrived. How are you?"

"I'm fine," said Douglas.

"I'll come round to forensic with you, Billy. We can bring your stuff over later," said Sami.

The forensic nurses each took one of his arms, and Billy's head hung forlornly as they escorted him along the corridor.

****

It was Douglas's last week in the post, and Dr Burlington wanted to see him for a 'debriefing session'. Douglas looked out the suit that he usually reserved for job interviews, hoping this might help him to feel less battered by the criticism he anticipated.

"You are dressed smartly and sombrely today, Douglas. You are perhaps fitting me in *en route* to a funeral?"

"No. No funeral today. Ina's funeral was on Monday."

"Ina, yes, Ina. But we are here to discuss you, Douglas, and it is pleasing to see you in more formal attire. The first time we met, as I recollect, you were unshaven and you appeared to have dressed hurriedly. So you have taken on board an element of critique with regard to your professional dress and appearance."

"Well it isn't..."

131

Douglas had resolved to remain passive and he stopped speaking when Dr Burlington raised his eyebrows.

"Douglas. Simply accept my compliment upon your attire today, and share my pleasure that you have *acted on a message*. For we are here to discuss more general matters. Sometimes, I compile notes for the edification of my trainees at these final sessions but, for you, I have not done so; your six months in my team have provided sufficiently numerous lucidly recollected incidents and impressions for notes to be an unnecessary *aide-memoire*. You too will recollect important and pivotal incidents. I am confident of that."

"Yes, though we might see them from different angles."

"No doubt we might. Perspectives, be they clear or distorted, differ between people, and comprise one fascinating aspect of the human condition. Partly for that reason, it may be inappropriate to dwell on *specifics*, and to speak more of *generalities.* That is not to say, of course, that we should diminish the importance of specific events as learning points. You will have, I anticipate, appreciated the importance, from noteworthy incidents (which we need neither rehearse nor discuss), of careful attention to patients' medical symptoms, of the need to exercise appropriate humility in offering advice to senior colleagues about the configuration of medical services and, to be a trifle basic, the desirability of retaining one's trousers while consulting with a patient."

In response to Douglas's splutters, Dr Burlington raised his hand.

"As I said," he continued, "these have comprised specific learning opportunities, and I shall now move on to more general points.

"I had access to a copy of your application for training and to the references furnished by senior colleagues in Newcastle at the time of the commencement of your employment here. The references, in particular, engendered high hopes for your performance. I recall that one consultant pronounced you, in his opinion, to be 'eminently suited to a career in psychiatry'. And while one might occasionally view a statement such as this from a physician as potentially disparaging, in the wider context of his expressed views I was encouraged by the qualities in you that he recognised and described. So, set against my positive expectations, Douglas, I have been dismayed; and I hope you will not take offence if I categorise your overall performance as having been lamentably moderate. Yes, at times your work has veered towards languid mediocrity. You can give the impression of almost horizontal informality. That said, one would not wish to express an unmitigated view, across the board, that your performance and your demeanour have been altogether without positive attributes. Following yesterday's ward round, from which you were absent, your name arose in conversation with my charge nurse, and Thomas praised you highly. He spoke of you with zealous approval, in fact, highlighting what he clearly considered to be your admirably beneficial relationships with several patients."

"It's nice of Tam to say that," said Douglas. "I did think I had done a little better than languid mediocrity during the last six months."

"It is possible that I over-generalised in that particular choice of words, and I am always a man who wishes to accentuate the positives, rather than to dwell inappropriately on negatives. For example, I have noted over recent weeks that your note keeping has improved immeasurably. Indeed, even as a scholar of language myself, it has seemed at times that your descriptions of patients have become *too* assiduously detailed, almost excessively flowery."

"I decided that I should become more organisationally punctilious in my note keeping," said Douglas.

"Yes, Douglas, yes," said Dr Burlington as he rubbed his chin. "And of course, your greatest asset is your youth. Time is on your side! So let us look forward."

"Yes, why not, let's look forward."

"You depart next week for a new post, armed, I hope, with strengths deriving from your rapid learning curve with me, and I know that you are bound for the in-patient psychotherapy unit with Dr Wiseman. Your new consultant has had a long and distinguished career. I was, myself, briefly but formatively, a senior registrar in his team, immediately prior to acquiring my present post. Yes, I note your surprise, since you will not consider me young, and my experience in psychotherapy did not occur recently. I make the point in order to emphasise that Dr Wiseman nears the end of an extremely distinguished career. He is a man worthy of the utmost respect. He has a senior merit award, and this is entirely deserved. You will learn much from him, especially if you exercise respect, and become more rigorous in your approach, more overtly pertinacious in your pursuit of knowledge and clinical excellence."

"I thought you might mention my new post," said Douglas, "and I wanted to tell you that I hope to be energetically futuristic and demonstrably enthusiastic."

He was pleased to see Dr Burlington looking at him with a perplexed expression.

"Good, Douglas, good," he said, standing up and extending his hand. "We have, I think, said enough. I would like to wish you good luck in your career."

****

The last day of Douglas's post proved more difficult than he had anticipated. He was almost moved to his first tears before ten o'clock during the ward patients' group meeting. Most of the patients were under the care of other teams, and he did not know them well, but they seemed sorry that he was about to leave.

"It's been good to see you at these meetings. Most of the doctors don't bother to come," said one lady.

"You were nice when you examined my leg. We'll miss your cheery face," said another.

"And you got us some fine new chairs," said an old man.

"It was Tam who ordered the chairs," said Douglas. "But I am sorry to be leaving."

At the end of the meeting, one of Douglas's own patients, a young man who rarely spoke spontaneously, approached him.

"I'll miss you. I got used to you. You're no' the worst," before turning and ambling away.

"Praise indeed, from him," said Tam as they went into the ward office. "That looked like a tricky meeting for you."

"Don't you start being nice to me. Or I might get upset."

"Nothing wrong with that. The staff will miss you too. You've been good fun. You're a steady pair of hands. And you spend time with people."

Douglas was looking out of the window.

"I thought that was part of the job," he said.

"Not everyone around here seems to take that view."

Dick made his usual noisy entrance to the office.

"Right on cue," said Tam.

Dick's nose remained swollen, and bruising had spread across his face.

"Cues? What about them?" he asked. "I've hunted everywhere for Mary Hill's notes."

Since his injury, Dick had experienced trouble pronouncing 'n', and when he tried to say 'notes' it had sounded more like 'dotes'. Sami had told Dick earlier in the week that he should write things down, rather than speak, especially when discussing medication, since if 'nose' were confused with 'dose' this could lead to prescribing errors.

"I'd better get away, Tam," said Douglas. "I've things to do before lectures this afternoon."

"They're on treatment of deurosis today," said Dick as he hunted in a cupboard.

"He means *neurosis,*" Douglas translated.

"You and I are experts on that," said Tam. "Alan went home yesterday.

"I know," said Douglas.

"He said he'd come back and see us. I hope you will too."

"I will. I'll come and scrounge a coffee when I'm on call. Tell Sami I'll see him in the cricket season, if not before."

In Morag's office, there was a package waiting for him.

"Alan Hardy and his mum left it for you yesterday afternoon," Morag told him.

It contained a comically fat ginger cat ornament. A card read:

'Dear Dr Douglas Barker,

Here is something to remember me by. I hope I am not being too optimistic—not my style I hear you say—but I think I am nearly cured. Without you and Tam and Anne, it would have continued to be a CATastrophe and I cannot begin to CATalogue all the help you have given me. Maybe not good ones but jokes are part of the new me too.

All the very best and thank you again,

Alan.'

"I have a wee thing for you too," Morag said, handing him a book.

"Cooking Made Simple," he read.

"I thought I had seen one called "Cooking Made *Very* Simple". That's the one I went looking for. I'm worried this one might be too advanced for you," said Morag.

"Very funny. It will have pride of place in my library of cookery books."

"Perhaps it will be your *only* cookery book?"

"Possibly, Morag. It's really very kind of you."

The door had been slightly ajar, and Jim Horsefall put his head round it.

"I thought I heard Doug's voice," he said. "Your last day. It's a pity things went the way they did with Dr B. But I'm sure you'll bounce back."

"Thanks, Jim," said Douglas. "And thanks for your help and advice. And for covering all my study afternoons."

"Last time today. And what will it be this afternoon?" Jim asked. "Lectures or golf?"

"Ha, ha," shouted Douglas at Jim's retreating head.

"You're going when you're improving. You are *much* more organised," said Morag.

"Morag, I'm hopeless with presents," said Douglas. "And you've been such a help. It's doctors who are supposed to give presents to secretaries."

"Don't be daft. That's not a present. It's a reminder to look after yourself. Now run along. I've got work to do."

Douglas managed not to cry until he reached his office.

February 1982

The new consultant wanted to meet him at 'nine thirtyish' on his first day. It seemed that Dr Wiseman had two offices and Douglas was to report to 'my smoking room in the ward'.

The room was certainly smokey. Dr Wiseman had set down his pipe in a large ashtray while he welcomed Douglas, and he quickly resumed puffing. Dr Wiseman did not look as a psychotherapist should, in that he was cheerful and portly, and seemed to be open and friendly. Douglas had expected someone more serious and austere.

"Not too smokey for you, I hope. At least we can see each other through it, eh? I can see you at any rate."

"No, it's fine. I'm used to it. I live with a smoker."

"Married a smoker, eh?"

"Oh, no. He's my flatmate. I'm not married."

"They don't let me smoke in the university department. I'm an academic, you know. It's the university that pays me. Brought in a smoking ban last year. If I was inclined to be paranoid, I might think it was a ploy to get rid of me. The stuff I do is mainly about people—case studies—and I'm certainly more interested in *people.* The rest of them up there are more interested in molecules and brain scans. Are you interested in people, Douglas?"

"Yes, Dr Wiseman, I'm very interested in people."

"Bill. You must call me Bill. Or you'll make me feel old."

"I'll try."

"You're not married, eh? I'm married. I'm very married."

Dr Wiseman paused to wave his hand at the many paintings on the walls of his office.

"Do you buy art, Douglas?" he asked.

"No, I don't."

"Perhaps not at your age. But you *like* art?"

"I quite like art."

"I quite like it too. But my wife *adores* art. What do you think of my collection here?"

"Well, I'm not—"

"Best to tell you. My wife painted all of them. Before you tell me they're dreadful, eh?"

"They're striking, very original."

"Tactfully put. My wife does not do muted colours, does she?"

Dr Wiseman pointed his pipe at the largest painting that was in blues and bright red.

"That one's my favourite," he said. "I sometimes use it with patients. What do you see?"

Douglas proceeded warily.

"Maybe, em, a sort of mountain village, in between two hills, with sea in the background?"

"Yes, people often say that. A sort of enormous cleavage, eh?" said Dr Wiseman with a big smile. "But enough of your psychopathology. No doubt you could tell me that you've already spotted my oral fixation," he continued, waving his pipe in the air. "We're here to talk about your new job, aren't we? What do you hope to get from being here?"

"A better understanding of psychotherapy—that would be the main thing."

"A good answer. So I am thinking that you may not wish to be—to become—an all singing, all dancing specialist psychotherapist yourself?"

"I don't have that intention at the moment."

"I know why you're here. Dr Brook came to see me. I haven't gone to the Placement Committee meetings for the last six years. Too acrimonious. It's unsavoury to see consultants shouting and boasting. Comes down to sibling rivalry and penis envy, *big* penis envy that is."

Dr Wiseman continued to give Douglas some of his views on the vagaries of the Placement Committee and on how junior staff were allocated to different teams.

"And have you met Joanie Smith yet?" he asked.

"I know who she is. We've never really spoken," said Douglas.

"Third year trainee. Coming up to the second part of her psychiatry membership exam. Joanie. Funny name, eh? I think she was christened with it, because you wouldn't choose it, would you? Unless you were trying to *diminish* yourself, sneak in under the radar, avoid confronting people with your adult sexual self, maybe. You could ask her about that—I never have. Anyway, Joanie it is. She asked—she almost begged—to stay on for another six months. She *does* want to become a psychotherapist. Signed up for personal analysis and so on. She'll be your colleague. So we'll have one specialist trainee and another passing through with his eye on other things—that could work pretty well."

After telling Douglas to 'get reading, start with some Freud', Dr Wiseman moved on to discuss the duties in his new post.

"Obviously psychotherapy, almost entirely. We have a few out-patient with general psychiatric needs. But like everyone else they'll benefit from psychotherapy. Everyone does, don't they?"

"I'm not sure about that."

"Quite right. Some don't. And people don't benefit from *bad* psychotherapy. So you'll want to know what you'll actually do?"

There were twelve in-patients and some Day Patients, almost all of whom had eating disorders, neurotic illnesses or personality disorders. Douglas would attend the 'Large Group' for all patients each morning—Dr Wiseman came to that only once a week—and in due course Douglas would join one of the 'Small Groups' in which more in-depth psychotherapy was conducted. He would have his own patients with whom he would do individual therapy once or twice each week. Douglas would be taking over these patients from 'your predecessor, young Dr Fielding, a pathologically uncomplicated chap'.

"But enough chat," said Dr Wiseman, knocking out the contents of his pipe, "let's go walkabout. Show you the geography."

"You'll notice," said Dr Wiseman, as they walked up the corridor, "that the ward is a sort of L shape and I'm down at the bottom of the L where all the offices are. That's yours," he pointed out, "three along from me. Still got Fielding's name on it. And round the corner here are all the beds—three dormitories with three beds in each and three single rooms. And this is the nurses' station right here bang in the middle."

Dr Wiseman stopped at two chairs and a desk that protruded beside the open door of a large office.

142

"I like the nurses to sit out here. To be available. Rather than," he said, pointing at the office, "hiding in there. The patients are in their Small Groups just now, that's why no one's out here. Look, good, Norman's in the office. You can meet him."

A small wiry man was sitting in the office writing, and he turned as he heard his name. He wrote a further few words and stood up.

"I'm Douglas Barker, new psychiatrist."

Norman looked at Douglas appraisingly.

"Hullo. Norman Snoddy. I'm the charge nurse here. And you will be with us for how long?"

Norman's studied, serious demeanour was more what Douglas had expected in a psychotherapy unit.

"Six months, probably," he said.

"It is not very long. To learn to work differently. I feel that a year is better," said Norman.

"Six months is a long enough sentence for most of the young doctors, eh?" said Dr Wiseman. "And who's this lurking as well? Our new nurse. Remind me of your name?"

A petite dark-haired woman had emerged from behind the office door.

"Pauline. I worked with Douglas upstairs."

"I knew you were moving, but I didn't know you were coming here," said Douglas.

Pauline flushed. Douglas had held out his hand, thinking he was about to meet someone new, and Pauline was holding it.

"I wanted a change. I've done general psychiatry for three years. I always fancied psychotherapy," she said.

"Good, good," said Dr Wiseman. "I'll leave you to it. Be in my office if required."

Norman continued to observe Douglas.

"Shall we sit in the office," said Norman, indicating a particular chair to Douglas. "One can become territorial. This is my usual seat. We have a few minutes before the Small Groups finish, and perhaps I can orientate you a little. Pauline, since you are new as well, you can join us. She is starting her second week here. We like people to have picked up the basics, get into tune with the *ambience* of the unit before engaging fully with the programme. Our philosophy differs, I think, from what prevails in the rest of the hospital."

"In what way?" asked Douglas brightly, trying to lighten the earnest atmosphere.

"We like to *take time*. We like to *reflect*. We expect our patients to do a lot of reflection, and so we believe that it behoves us to do likewise. It behoves us to examine our feelings, our thoughts and our behaviour. Or else how shall we begin to understand our countertransferences, and the ways in which these might harm or assist? You follow what I am getting at, Pauline?"

"Countertransference? I think so. How we feel about our patients?"

"No, it is rather more complicated than that," said Norman, his speech slowing further.

"I shall give you an example," he resumed, after a lengthy pause. "Last week, I saw a patient. She has chronic anorexia nervosa and I have known her for a long time. I have certainly *seen* her for a long time. Whether I *know* her all that well is more debatable. Anyway, I had been on holiday and this had caused an interruption to her therapy, since I normally see her weekly as an out-patient. Her father left the family, I should tell you, when she was twelve. On the very day she had her first period, in fact. Ever since, she has

144

dreaded abandonment, especially from the male figures in her life. And she was furious with me on my return from holiday. She spoke very little at the session and she had lost weight in my absence. She implied that this loss of weight was to be equated more generally with her most recent loss, *her loss of me,* and that the weight loss was, in fact, my responsibility and not her own. At the end of the session, as one does, I wrote her next appointment in my diary. Later, as I was writing her notes, I checked this again, and what had I done? I had *missed a week*! I had given her an appointment for *two weeks hence*."

He looked slowly from Douglas to Pauline and back again.

"Do you see what I had done?" he asked.

"Missed a week? Turned over two pages in your diary at once?" suggested Douglas.

Norman looked puzzled.

"Well, yes, that is probably the case," he said, "but *mediated* at an *unconscious level,* and mediated by what? Her anger towards me was not *rational*, was it?"

"We all need to take holidays," said Douglas.

"It was *ir*rational. She was responding to me, subconsciously, dredging up the anger deposited long ago when her father left her. This is, of course, *transference*, when a patient responds to you *as if you were someone else*. In this case, she saw me as an abandoning father figure and she became furious with me. And what did I do?"

"You retaliated," said Pauline.

"Exactly. I became angry. Because she was angry, and I felt she had no right to be. Not with me who has stuck by her for several years. I have done the very opposite of abandoning her. So I felt unjustly accused and, feeling niggled, no doubt, I attempted to *punish* her by missing a week of therapy."

"So what did you do?" asked Douglas.

"I telephoned her. It seems that I had written the correct date, for the following week, on her appointment card."

"So you didn't actually punish her," said Douglas.

"No, but it was clear that I wished to—if only at an unconscious level."

"Gosh!" said Douglas. "No such thing as a mistake, then?"

"Well put," said Norman. "Mistakes—bungled actions as Freud called them—are unconsciously mediated, and they are *not* mistakes. They fulfil unconscious wishes. So that is one small example of the need to *reflect,* if we are to *understand*, and we cannot conduct useful therapy without understanding."

"I think this is all going to very interesting," said Douglas. "Are you enjoying it so far, Pauline?"

"Yes. It's very different from working upstairs."

"The Small Groups are over, as you will hear," said Norman, alluding to the noise of voices in the corridor. "I hope we shall work together harmoniously."

"I'm sure we'll do that," said Douglas.

****

"They let ye out early today," said Chris.

"One's new consultant, Dr Wiseman, says that one can scarcely spend time more productively than reading the works of Sigmund Freud," said Douglas, holding up The Interpretation of Dreams.

146

"And what does he tell ye tae read after that? The fairy tales o' the Brothers Grimm? Hansel and Gretel, now that's a cracker. Ye'll enjoy that one."

"You can mock all you like. You may wish to practise psychiatry without insight, but I don't."

"Insight? Insight intae what?"

"Well, this evening I have been extending my insight into dreams. Take you, for example. You mentioned in the pub the recurrent dream you have about flying in an aeroplane and then you start getting anxious and you fall out?"

"It's a helicopter. Ye'll no' find it in the book because they didnae have helicopters when Freud wis makin' up his nonsense."

"Helicopters, aeroplanes, spaceships? It doesn't matter. You could even be flying under your own steam, like Superman. But all of the flying dreams are about *erections*, about sexual *potency*. Like flying, the *penis defies gravity*."

"And the bad witch shut Hansel and Gretel in the big oven."

"It says it here," Douglas continued, "and the *falling* is about fear of *losing* the erection, a fear of *impotence*, or even *castration*."

"Last time I got that dream one o' my legs wis stickin' right out o' the bed. It wis a warnin'. Wake up or ye'll fall out on tae the floor."

"Nonsense. It was a symptom of psychopathology. A repressed fear of impotence and castration. You need to know this stuff. You might be selected to go to psychotherapy next."

"I wid resign before I wid go there! I'd go away and do brain surgery or somethin'."

147

"It's not that bad. It's just like learning a new language—Spanish, or Russian."

"More like Martian."

Douglas did agree that sometimes his new post seemed "a wee bit odd", and told Chris about that morning's Large Group.

"It's usually quite a double act on a Wednesday, apparently. Dr Wiseman was there, along with Norman, the charge nurse. Norman's what you might expect."

"Weird?"

"Very serious. Inscrutable. He sits on his hands with his head on one side. Dr Wiseman was pretty normal when I met up with him on Monday but he seemed to metamorphose in the group into someone who sees the world through huge Freudian glasses. Norman's a bit the same, but he's like that all the time."

"So what were they sayin'?"

"Well, some of the patients with eating problems got talking about vomiting. And Dr Wiseman said to two of them: "So what do you think you have been trying to get rid of?" Silence—so Norman comes in with something like: "Were there particular emotions that you have been finding unacceptable?" "Or perhaps they were unacceptable memories, or impulses?" says Dr Wiseman. The girls sat looking puzzled. Then after the group, Dr Wiseman and Norman chatted away about suppressed sexual feelings, about how the girls might have been victims of incest, and how they were probably vomiting up repressed memories to try to get rid of them."

"It sounds like a madhouse," said Chris.

"I think 'psychiatric hospital' is the more appropriate term," said Douglas.

"Ha ha. I find it worryin'. How can that be helpin' the lassies?"

"I wouldn't knock it till I've seen a bit more of it. They seem to have a good success rate."

"Aye. Maybe folk pretend to be better so they can get out."

Chris had been unpacking some shopping as he spoke.

"I wis goin' tae make chicken stew," he said, "but ye might interpret that as well, will ye?"

"I haven't got to chicken stew in the book yet, but I'm sure there will be a hidden reason for your behaviour."

"Aye, right, and are ye wantin' some all the same?"

"That would be good. But don't forget to take off that smart new jacket before you start cooking. Is this you taking my advice to smarten up?"

"What? Take fashion advice from you? Ye remember it was my birthday last week?"

"Could I forget? I had to be nice to you for a whole day."

"Well I needed tae use my birthday money fir somethin'."

"So you bought a jacket when there are lots of perfectly good pubs where you could have spent the money?"

"Fuck off," said Chris as he took off his jacket.

****

The first patient Douglas saw for individual therapy, Diane, was one of the women who had been talking about vomiting in the Large Group. Diane had been in the ward for more than seven months. She was now twenty years old and had first developed anorexia nervosa when she was fourteen.

This became more severe and her weight had been dangerously low before she was admitted to hospital. Since coming into the ward her weight had fluctuated, and there were recent concerns that she was again losing weight.

Diane was certainly very thin. She was dressed incongruously in a flared skirt and ankle socks, but she was strikingly pretty. Her brown eyes and her bone structure reminded Barker of many of the young women he had seen in Greece. She sat looking sad and remote.

"I hope you don't mind going over things again with me. I know you've done it before," said Douglas.

"Twice before," said Diane. "You're my third doctor here."

Diane first became concerned about her weight early in secondary school after she overheard another girl refer to her as 'dumpy'. She had been a good runner at primary school, and she took this up again successfully, representing her school at the Scottish cross-country championships. She also started dieting and counting calories. She was seen a few times by a psychiatrist when she was fifteen due to her parents' concerns about her low weight and her insistence upon eating vegetarian meals alone in her bedroom. She told him that her weight had risen then, almost to a normal level. Although she remained worried about what she ate and drank, and she never stopped counting calories, she and her family had been happy that her problems were pretty much a thing of the past.

"Until about two years ago," she added.

"Was that around the time your brother died?" Douglas asked.

"Yes, you know about that, obviously. He died in an accident in January 1980. The day after his twenty-first birthday."

"That must have been awful."

"It was," said Diane flatly. "Not just for me. Obviously for my parents too. And my wee sister. She was only twelve at the time."

"And your eating became more of a problem again?"

"Not right away. The family was in chaos. We all went crazy in different ways. Dad worked even harder until he cracked up. Mum joined a drama group and started drinking too much. And my sister couldn't go to school for a while. I was the sanest of all of us just after it happened."

"And your family now?"

"Dad's not too bad. My sister's back at school. Mum's still drinking too much and she's miserable. She's on antidepressants."

Douglas ran through Diane's current symptoms with her. She did everything possible to avoid high calorie foods, leading to battles with the nursing staff at meal times. She exercised whenever she could in the hope of losing weight. Recently she had started, several times each week, to vomit if she felt she had eaten too much, and she also occasionally took laxatives. Although she weighed less than seven stones, she believed that she was overweight.

"I look in the mirror every morning. And I know I need to be thinner than this."

Try as he did, Douglas could not shift Diane from this belief.

"And the groups," he asked, "have they been helpful?"

"The Big Group makes me anxious. I quite like the Small Group, especially on the days when Norman's there. Some of it is helpful. But some of it's over my head."

After Diane closed the door quietly behind her, Douglas felt both intrigued and impotent. She was fascinating, but he was unsure what he could do to help her.

He knew that his other patient, Lucy, was an attractive dark-haired girl. She had given him a beaming smile at the Large Group when he introduced himself two days earlier. He thought she whispered something about him to the patient next to her, after which they looked at him and giggled. He was puzzled to read in her notes that she was admitted after self-harm and with suspected depression; she did not look unhappy. It seemed that she had experienced repeated relationship difficulties with men and her early life had been unsettled. She had been admitted only two weeks previously.

Lucy bounced into his office a few minutes ahead of the appointed time. She was wearing knee length boots and very tight jeans. As she sat down, she moved her chair closer to his.

"This is my lucky day—getting you as my doctor."

"I'm not sure about that," said Douglas. "I'm new here."

"I know. Of course I know. I've been expecting you. I saw you in the corridor last week, but you didn't see me. I knew it was you."

"You knew it was me?"

"Pauline told me you were coming."

"OK," said Douglas. "Well, I've been reading your notes."

"Written by Dr Brian Fielding, I presume?"

"Yes, most of them."

"I thought young psychiatrists would be sexy," said Lucy, gazing at him coquettishly, "but Brian wasn't. He didn't even speak to me all that much. But he did examine me when I came in. He examined me *physically.* Will you be examining me, Douglas?"

"No, no, probably not," said Douglas. "Not unless..., no, in fact almost certainly not."

"Not unless...? Not unless you want to?" asked Lucy, rubbing the insides of her thighs.

"Not unless you become unwell, I was going to say."

"I *might* become unwell. It could easily happen. In fact, I feel a little breathless and light headed right now. And a bit queasy. Perhaps I shall swoon," she said, putting the back of her hand to her forehead. "Should I loosen my clothing?"

"No, you shouldn't! Look, I need to go over some things with you," said Douglas. "Can we start with the overdose of tablets you took before you came in here?"

Lucy described six overdoses in the past year, usually precipitated by feeling let down by a man. At the time of her most recent episode, it seemed that she had strongly wished to die, and a neighbour found her by chance. As she told her story, there were a few flashes of anger, but she generally continued to be frivolous and flirtatious. She offered to show him the scars from cutting herself on the thigh, and at one point she claimed that her chair was uncomfortable.

"Where *is* your couch? I was sure we would have had a couch."

Douglas struggled to terminate the session. He closed Lucy's case records and he looked at his watch a few times, but these hints did not deflect her from, by this time, chatting about her tastes in music.

"We have to stop now," Douglas finally said, "it's well past an hour."

"Time does fly when you're happy, doesn't it?" said Lucy. "And will we meet like this every day?"

"Oh no!" said Douglas. "Probably just once a week. I'll have to speak to Dr Wiseman about how often I see you individually."

"You persuade him to let you see me lots and lots," said Lucy. "I'm sure you want to."

Douglas was holding the door open. Lucy stood very close to him as she left.

"Have a lovely weekend, Douglas. Perhaps next time we can talk a bit more about you?"

"That's not the idea at all," said Douglas, "and we really do have to stop now."

He shut the door behind her and sat down with a long sigh.

****

Douglas opened his office door to urgent knocking. It was Joanie Smith with her cropped blond hair, the other junior psychiatrist working in the psychotherapy ward. She looked up and down the corridor.

"Can I come in? Have you got two minutes?"

Joanie was not unattractive, but reminded him of a small bird when a cat was in the vicinity. She seemed constantly fidgety, vigilant and ill at ease. He wondered how relaxed patients felt with her. She perched on the edge of a chair.

"Two things," she said.

"Fire away," said Douglas.

"Your patient Lucy first. I'm in her Small Group and she was saying something weird. I don't know her too well.

154

Problems with her parents and lots of issues with men, right?"

"I suppose that sums it up," said Douglas, "but I've only seen her once myself."

"Gosh, yes, of course. She spoke like you'd known each other for years. She talked about you on Tuesday, called you 'Douglas', and said how lovely it was that a doctor was 'taking such an interest in me'. The group went on to talk about women whose men *don't* take an interest in them and it was a good session. But then she went on about you again today—weird stuff."

"What stuff?"

"*Really* weird stuff," said Joanie, leaning even further forward. "She said her life had 'just started' and had 'come together' with yours and that her 'problems were over' now that you and she had 'found each other'."

"What?"

"And there was more. She said, 'and I know he loves me.' So one of the other patients asked her 'did he say that?' and she said, 'he didn't need to, it was obvious'."

"Bloody hell!" said Douglas. "When I saw her last Friday she flirted ridiculously and I couldn't get her out of the door. But that's something else!"

"Have you heard of de Clérambault's syndrome—erotomania?"

"Only vaguely," Douglas confessed.

Joanie reminded him that patients with erotomania believe that someone of 'superior social status, including doctors' is in love with them. They falsely interpret perceived 'messages' to convince themselves of this.

"Does she have any other delusions?" asked Joanie.

"No, I don't think so. I can check that out when I see her tomorrow."

"Good luck. You don't often see erotomania. Usually they have schizophrenia when they're deluded like that."

"Thanks for the tip—the warning."

"The second thing is Dr Wiseman. Bill."

"You struggle to call him Bill too?" asked Douglas. Joanie frowned.

"Not at all," she said. "Bill and I are very close."

"Right, OK", said Douglas.

"I want to be a psychotherapist myself, you know," said Joanie confidingly.

"Yes. Dr Wiseman—Bill—told me."

"He did? He mentioned me to you?"

"Yes. On my first day. He told me you would be the other doctor on the ward."

"And what did he say?"

"Nothing much really. Just that you would be in your second six months here and you wanted to be a psychotherapist."

"I've been worried about him," said Joanie, looking worried. "He hasn't been quite himself recently. I'm not sure what it is. He's had the cold shoulder from the other academics. I think he feels *disrespected*. He's a lovely man. He really is. I find it difficult when he's unhappy."

"He seemed jolly enough when I last saw him. Hardly like a psychotherapist at all."

"Happiness and practising psychotherapy are not mutually exclusive, surely?"

"No, no, that's not what I meant. He just seemed, em, fine."

"Well, I suppose that's good. But I was hoping you might keep an eye on him. Two sets of eyes better than one and all that? I do get anxious about him."

"I can try," said Douglas.

"And we can discuss it? You'll report back?"

****

Before his next session with Lucy, Douglas spoke with Dr Wiseman about her. Dr Wiseman had not interviewed Lucy, but he knew who she was.

"I spotted her in the Big Group last week. Saw the way she looked at you. I diagnosed her on the spot—hysterical personality disorder. You shouldn't do that, eh? Make a diagnosis on the basis of a smile and a whisper and a titter? Bad practice. But after that I read her notes and they confirmed it. So I'll probably continue my bad habits, eh? But don't you start. They can be hard going, these girls."

Douglas described his first session with Lucy and passed on what Joanie had told him.

"So you've got a sexualised transference," said Dr Wiseman. "They can be mighty tricky. Best of luck with that one."

This was not the focused guidance Douglas had been hoping for.

He read up about hysterical personality. 'Histrionic personality' seemed to be the more official term. It was much commoner in women than in men, and these women were often sexually provocative, with a history of failed romantic relationships. They wanted to be the centre of attention, they were emotionally shallow and theatrical, their moods fluctuated a lot and they were prone to feelings of intense rejection. Their self-esteem, the book said, was fragile and depended

157

on the nature and degree of attention they were receiving. Douglas also read a paper that suggested hysterical personality was a term invented by men to denigrate women, a description of the extremes of female behaviour which were required to survive in a male dominated world. He thought his sister might get on well with the author of the paper. The literature on treatment looked vague. He read that he needed to help the person 'uncover and understand their motivations and their fears' and to 'begin to relate to others in a more positive and appropriate manner'. One paper advised strongly that the therapist should not be drawn into an intense relationship with the patient, and should remain 'professional, aloof and objective'.

He also read the little he could find on erotomania. It was not helpful to see that 'transference love' was often a 'derivation of the castration complex', and the consensus seemed to be that these patients were psychotic. As Joanie had said, it seemed often to be a symptom of schizophrenia.

He hardly recognised Lucy when she arrived for her psychotherapy session. She had dyed her hair fluorescent yellow. Douglas thought it best not to mention the change of hair colour and started by asking her how her week in the ward had been. She said that it had been 'interesting, a mixture of tears and laughter'. She told him that her highlight had been seeing him in the Large Group, and 'the lovely red tie' he had worn that morning. She was again gazing at him intently and rubbing the insides of her thighs. In line with his reading, Douglas told her he was keen to hear about her relationships with the other patients, hoping this might lead into her more general motivations and fears in relationships. Initially, this seemed to go well. She discussed a girl in her dormitory who she said was already 'a very close friend indeed'. She then mentioned a male patient with whom she had fallen out, saying he was 'an obvious bastard like my very first boyfriend'. Douglas thought they were getting somewhere, until Lucy said:

"But my *important* relationship with the people here is obviously *with you!* And you haven't mentioned my hair. Do you like it? Did you notice?"

"I could hardly not notice," said Douglas with a smile.

Lucy broke into song.

"When you smile, I can tell

We know each other very well."

"Herb Alpert," said Douglas.

Lucy was staring at him rapturously.

"You remember it, Douglas. You remember *our song!"* she said.

"What?"

"I was sure you would remember."

"Remember what? It's a—it's just a record!"

"Just a record. Hmmmm. Perhaps that's what you have to say," said Lucy, tapping the side of her nose, *"as my doctor?"*

Douglas took a deep breath. He reminded himself to remain aloof and professional, and to check for other symptoms of psychosis.

"There are some questions I'd like to ask you," he said.

"You know you can ask me anything you want, Douglas—anything," said Lucy, still gazing at him and now caressing the undersides of her breasts.

"Have you ever heard noises or voices when there's nothing around to explain them?"

"No, I haven't."

"Have you ever seen visions, or seen things other people couldn't see?"

"Only when I've dropped acid, Douglas. But you're a vision, a lovely vision."

"Have you ever felt that you were under the control of an external power or force?"

"Only you, perhaps. No. I haven't. These are funny questions."

"Have you ever felt that you had special powers and that you could do things other people couldn't do?"

"No! Why are you asking me these questions? It's like you're suggesting I'm some kind of crazy person!"

"I need to check out these things," said Douglas, writing in her case notes.

"What is this?" Lucy demanded. "You've gone from discussing *our song*—from *intimacy*—to treating me like a *mad person* in the space of two minutes. What's wrong with you?"

"There is no such thing as 'our song'. That is a figment of your imagination."

"A figment of my imagination! How dare you?" shouted Lucy.

"Calm down," Douglas told her.

"Calm down? Fucking calm down?"

Lucy was standing and glaring at him.

"You go from being warm and loving to *this,* and then you tell me to *calm down*? You say there's no such thing as our song. Next you'll be denying that you love me."

Douglas did not hide his astonishment.

"You think I love you?" he said. "What on earth would give you that daft idea?"

Lucy came a step closer.

"So it's a daft idea, is it?" she shouted.

Douglas nodded. Lucy paused, staring at him, and then continued in a low and level voice.

"I'll make you sorry for saying that, Douglas Barker. I'll make you *fucking* sorry. I thought you were different, but you're not, are you? Like I say, you will be *very fucking sorry.*"

She marched out of his office and slammed the door. Douglas tried to piece together what had happened and to write something coherent in her notes, but he was perplexed and shaking. He walked through to the ward and saw Pauline at the nurses' desk in the corridor.

"Can I have a word?" he said, and they went into the office.

"What did you do to Lucy?" Pauline asked him. "She came through here like a tornado, shouting that you were a lying bastard, and said she was going out for a long walk."

Douglas described the session to her.

"I knew she was volatile and strange," said Pauline, "but now it sounds like she's psychotic."

"I don't know what to make of it," said Douglas. "She came over with a glazed look, as though she thought I was someone else."

"No doubt Norman would call that transference," said Pauline with a giggle, "but to me it's more likely to be plain madness. Hey, Douglas, don't worry about it. I'm here this evening. I'll speak to her when she comes back. You go off and enjoy your weekend."

****

161

Douglas took Chris with him to play football. He was skilful, as well as being surprisingly fast and fit. He would be an asset to their five-a-side team, and he thoroughly enjoyed himself.

For the rest of the weekend, and even while he had several beers with Chris, Douglas felt uneasy and subdued, replaying the bizarre session with Lucy.

He went in early on the Monday morning.

"I heard about Lucy from Pauline, and she is off today," said Norman. "So I can recount only second-hand news. And what I know about your session with her on Friday is of course third hand news. Perhaps you could tell me about that yourself."

Douglas described events again and Norman pressed him for details.

"You knew already that she had feelings for you?" Norman inquired.

"Well, yes, I thought it was clear that she fancied me," said Douglas.

"She *fancied* you, Douglas? I am unsure what you mean by that. She fancied you for what? As a lover? As a father figure? As a saviour? As a composite of her own projected feelings?"

"I'm afraid I didn't think about it all that deeply."

"That is becoming apparent," said Norman. "And she believed that you and she *shared a song*. That you were singing from the same hymn book. That you understood her, you were alongside her, at a deep and personal level."

"You could put it like that," said Douglas.

"And at that point, when she had put all of her eggs into your basket—and I am aware of the double meaning of

162

'eggs' that you might extract from my analogy—you with-
drew, and you quizzed her dispassionately, a clinical doctor
grilling a potentially crazy patient?"

"I thought I should find out if she had schizophrenia."

"So many of the young doctors who come here," said
Norman, shaking his head ruefully, "are hidebound. Their
imaginations are *castrated*—by diagnosis, by models of *illnesses* that they need to put neatly into boxes. This girl was
connecting with you, and you felt a compulsion to *diagnose*
this connection."

"It didn't feel like 'connection'. She seemed crazy—irrational."

"She was saying that she loved you, Douglas. Do you
deem love to be a rational emotion?"

"No, I don't suppose it is."

"Of course it is not! And with someone like Lucy, it is
even less likely to be rational. For who is it that she loves? It
can scarcely be *you*, with whom she has spent so little time.
So clearly, her feelings relate to other experiences and relationships, do they not?"

"I suppose that makes sense," Douglas agreed.

"And your job, through this transference, was to tease
these things apart. To help her to discover the complexities
of her emotions and relationships. My presumption would be
that love, hate and the fear of abandonment sit in a tangled
emotional mass due to the difficulties of her early life."

"That's probably right."

"Group work differs from individual therapy," Norman
continued. "In one-to-one therapy you need to *let the transference develop.* You must *tolerate* the projection on to you
of feelings and emotions from the patient's past. And that
will often include tolerating, and understanding, feelings of

love. It is not always comfortable to feel so urgently loved, but this is often a vital starting point for therapy."

"Even when the urgent love seems to be crazy?"

"Even when everything seems to be crazy," Norman confirmed.

"So what happened with Lucy at the weekend, Norman?"

Norman told him that Lucy had gone for a few drinks, returned to the ward 'still furious', packed up her things and left. They had heard nothing from her since.

"Do you think we should try to contact her?" Douglas asked.

"I would think not," said Norman. "Even while acting, apparently, under the drives and influences of feelings deriving from her infancy, she has ostensibly behaved like an adult. To pursue her would place us in the role of protective parents. We would be acting out the transference ourselves. Indeed, were we to contact her, we might even be steamrollering through the countertransference. No, I think we need to leave things be. I suspect that she will decide to come back into therapy."

"So just wait and see?" said Douglas.

"Yes. Waiting and seeing is an underestimated skill," said Norman.

****

"Any further word from the daft lassie that shouted at ye?" Chris asked.

"Not a peep," said Douglas. "And that's about ten days since she left."

"Ye'll be sorry about that. Just when therapy wis goin' so well."

"I'm not crying myself to sleep, because seeing her wasn't easy, to say the very least. But I would like to know what's happened with her. Anyway, it's not like you to have your nose in a book."

"It's 'Symptoms in the Mind'—mental state examinations and all that. Bob advised it."

"Bob?"

"Bob Robertson—my normal and helpful consultant. And since ye're always readin' yerself these days, I've got nobody tae chat with."

Douglas had been immersed in a book, underlining sections that he considered important.

"This one's good," he said. "Introductory Lectures on Psychotherapy—I should have read it first."

"Aye, maybe there was a clue in the title."

"Ha, ha. Yet again, Freud has helped me to appreciate that my flatmate is teeming with psychopathology."

"Let me guess. I drink too much because I'm orally fixated, and that's because I wis breast fed, or maybe because I wisnae breast fed fir long enough?"

"You might well be right, but that's not the focus of tonight's analysis. I'm reading about the id and the ego and the super ego."

"We did a' that at primary school."

"Then you'll recall that your id is like your primitive instincts—a 'cauldron of seething excitations' as it says here. And like all Glaswegians your cauldron is particularly seething."

"I'm no' a Glaswegian."

165

"Near enough. You behave like one. And the ego tries to represent the id to the world appropriately. It's a sort of mediator between the id and the superego, which is basically your conscience."

"Like I've said before, my conscience is massive. I eat guilt fir breakfast."

"Most of the time, perhaps. But you've got a super ego that is almost entirely soluble in alcohol. And drink makes your ego malfunction as well, so that your seething id is laid bare for all to see."

"Thanks fir that very helpful analysis, doctor. How much do I owe ye?"

"First sessions are free."

"I think that wis about my nineteenth, but I'll no' quibble. Anyway, last time we went out tae the pub, you came home more drunk than I did."

"True."

"I wid also say that my id often seethes a bit less than yours does, especially when it comes tae women."

"Ah, 'women' and 'seething' in the same sentence. How is Mandy?"

"Very funny. She's grand. And last time I saw her she never mentioned ye once, so perhaps she's stopped seethin'."

"Good. So things between you are ticking along nicely?"

"I've seen her a couple o' times. But there's no' really any *things* between us that could *tick along*."

"Really?"

"Aye, really. Now shut up—ye're interruptin' my readin'."

****

Douglas continued what felt like a quiet apprenticeship in psychotherapy. He attended the meetings and ward rounds, and he went into the Large Group two or three times each week. Norman told him he could join his Small Group in March, adding that new members of staff tended to be 'observers more than participants'.

Douglas read a lot during his working hours, and saw his out-patients more frequently than was necessary. His only in-patient was Diane, and she was making little headway. In her individual sessions they got stuck on the issue of her weight and her body image. Their most recent meeting had been typical.

"You were weighed again yesterday?" Douglas asked.

The patients with eating problems were weighed twice each week and they usually dreaded these mornings.

"It was the same," said Diane, "six stones twelve pounds."

"So that's still two stones under your target weight."

"My target weight is stupid."

"No it isn't. It's the healthy weight for a woman of your height and build."

"How could it possibly be healthy? I'm fat as it is."

"You're not fat. The scales don't lie. You're seriously underweight."

"So everybody says here."

"That's because it's true. You are very thin."

"No, I'm not! I look at myself in the mirror. I live with myself! You don't."

When they got bogged down in this sort of debate, Douglas wondered how he could do psychotherapy with what seemed like a fixed delusion. Dr Wiseman and Norman gave him similar advice.

"Softly, softly catchee monkey," Dr Wiseman said. "Try to guide her gently into other areas."

"Eating is *not* her core problem," Norman said. "It is of *symbolic significance*. Focusing upon it enables her to continue to repress her other emotional turmoils."

Thus far, Douglas had not succeeded in talking about other areas with Diane in any depth. He recognised that this was not all Diane's doing, since he continued to feel that his powers of logic and persuasion should convince this emaciated girl that she was not fat.

Douglas was pleased to hear he would be getting a new in-patient who sounded less complicated than Diane. Dr Wiseman had summarised Michael's situation in his notes.

"This 45 year old man presents with three main problem areas. Firstly, he is very anxious, as a virtually lifelong phenomenon. Of late, his anxiety has been peaking into acute episodes of panic which seem to relate to his other areas of difficulty. He lived in a pathologically close relationship with his mother until she died nine months ago. Since her death, he has endured a prolonged, abnormal bereavement reaction. Over the same period, he has experienced progressive difficulties in his work as a bank clerk, and this has focused upon an acrimonious relationship with the manager of his branch. He has been unable to go to work for a month, and it seems best to take him in to hospital for assessment and treatment."

Michael was sweating and tremulous as he sat down in Douglas's office. He was a podgy man with thinning dark hair. He wore a baggy sweater and bell-bottomed jeans that Douglas thought had gone out of fashion ten years ago. Michael seemed to be open, friendly and self-effacing. Douglas liked him almost immediately.

He said he had 'never been a confident person'. He became a more anxious child when he was five years old, after his father was killed in the second world war.

"At least that's what Mom always told me," he said.

"Mom?" Douglas repeated.

"Yes, I called her 'Mom'. She insisted on it. She was American."

His mother had married Michael's father in the USA in the 1930s and he—an Englishman—had insisted on returning home to fight for his country. Michael was an only child, and so he and his mother were left alone in Britain. They moved north 'to make a new start' after the war. He said his mother had also been anxious and 'a bit reclusive'.

"She liked a quiet life, and she encouraged me to do the same. Neither of us was very adventurous. I had a funny accent—a bit American, a bit English—and at school they poked fun at me. I did OK academically—Mom encouraged me to work hard—but when I thought about university Mom said no, it would be safer to work in a bank. So that's what I did."

Michael had continued to work in the bank for nearly thirty years. He declined promotion, partly because this might have entailed a move away from home, and his manager for the past three years had been 'a young man with new ideas, not all of them sensible'. The manager was not very understanding when Michael's mother died, and he felt coerced into accepting and implementing changes with which he did not agree.

"I've crumbled under the pressure," he said. "Mom would have helped me to deal with him."

Michael had kept his mother's bedroom unchanged 'as a sort of shrine, I guess' and he would go in there frequently 'to chat with her'. He said that he continued to 'see' and 'hear' his mother, 'just as clearly as I can see and hear you now'. He also said that 'sometimes when I'm sitting, Mom can walk up behind me and I feel her hands on my shoulders'. At these times, he worried that he might have 'tipped over into craziness'.

Michael expressed mixed feelings about being in hospital. The programme had been explained to him, and he said he was unused to being in groups of people.

"But maybe I need to get used to that. And the people I've met so far have been very nice."

Michael had been assigned to Norman's Small Group, so Douglas would see him there as well as in their individual therapy sessions

March 1982

Chris was out so Douglas answered their new telephone. It was his sister.

"Hullo, Douglas. How's things?"

This was her usual start to a telephone conversation. It was his cue to say 'fine', before Helen launched into an update on her own life.

"Things have been a bit mixed here over the past few weeks, actually," he said, doing his best to leave no pauses. "I'm settling in to the new psychotherapy job, but it's very different, quite complicated and sometimes a bit weird. I don't really know what I'm doing half the time, to be honest. I'm joining one of the small psychotherapy groups tomorrow, so that will be interesting. The indoor football's going well and Chris has joined the team. He's very good. He said he had a trial when he was a teenager, so I said, 'whatever you did I presume you got off with it' which I thought..."

"You thought was very funny," said Helen. "You're prattling. It must be lovely to have a career. You don't know how envious I am."

"I do sometimes get a hint about that."

"Things with me have been *very mixed.* Good news and bad down here, you might say. The first is a bit of both, I suppose. I'm pregnant again. Quite pleased, of course, but

171

I'm sick as a dog, nearly as bad as I was with the twins. And it does *set one back*, doesn't it, *as a person*."

"That's a funny way to look at it," said Douglas. "Congratulations. You hoping for a girl?"

"I can't say I'm not. A girl might be very *peaceful* after the twins. And we're short of peace down here, even more than usual. I've really phoned to pick your brains—your psychiatric brains."

Douglas did not like the sound of this.

"Yes, the bad news down here is that Alex is signed off work with stress and depression."

"That's a surprise. He seemed fine at Christmas time."

"Yes, he was, wasn't he? But he was a bit worried even then. One of his partners embezzled money and then they investigated Alex. A dottled old lady said he'd done something wrong—it turned out he hadn't—but he got stressed anyway and now his doctor says he's depressed."

"I'm sorry to hear that."

"I'm sorry too. I'm very sorry. Now it's like I've got three children to look after. His doctor put him on antidepressants."

"What are his symptoms?"

"Symptoms? Well he's in his bed a lot, or he just sits about, and he says he's stressed. Even though the work thing has been cleared up."

"Is he sleeping OK?"

"How could he? He's in his bed so much. But, look, is this what they do now? Tell people not to work and feed them antidepressants?"

"If they're depressed, yes, that's what we do."

172

"What ever happened to 'get back on the horse and ride it'? We all have things we could get depressed about. What happened to battling on through adversity?"

"It can take time to get better."

"It's going to take for ever if he's here at home. He should be at work, surely. Could you not phone his doctor about it?"

"What?"

"Phone his doctor. Discuss it. Tell him Alex needs to be back at work."

Chris had come in and was listening to Douglas's side of the conversation.

"No. That wouldn't be appropriate at all," said Douglas. "Look, you need to give it time. Antidepressants take a few weeks to kick in."

"*A few weeks*? Surely if you—"

"Sorry, Helen" said Douglas, gesturing at the front door to Chris, "I think I hear someone at the door. You'll be going to Dad's 65th next month? I can chat to Alex then."

"But that's four weeks away!"

Chris rang the bell as Douglas held the telephone towards the door.

"That's the bell again, Helen. Keep me informed. I'll have to go. It does take time. Bye."

"Yir dear sister will be thinkin' we run a brothel or somethin'. That's the second time I've had tae ring the bell tae get her off the phone," said Chris.

Douglas was shaking his head wearily.

"Her husband's depressed, apparently, and she's pregnant."

"That'll no' be easy fir her."

"No, I'm sure it isn't, but nothing ever is. And she wants him back at work yesterday."

"He's off his work? Maybe he's quite bad."

"It was hard to tell. She's not the most sympathetic of people. And she seems to know as much about depression as she does about quantum physics."

"Like most members o' the public. You and yir brother can educate her at yir dad's party."

"I suddenly get the feeling it won't be much of a party," said Douglas.

****

The Large Group still rather puzzled Douglas. When Dr Wiseman came on a Wednesday he very much led the group. He would often select a patient, especially one who had been silent, and would make a statement followed by a question, such as:

"I understand, Diane, that your weight remains on a low plateau and so do you. It seems you are taking no risks with your eating and no risks with your emotional life. Perhaps there are matters of which you are so frightened that you cannot tolerate the dangers involved in contemplating them?"

If this did not lead to a revealing response or to comments from other patients, Norman would chip in to draw out something else, or to point out that another patient shared similar difficulties. It appeared that Norman and Dr Wiseman had evolved a formula, and in the Wednesday Large Groups there was a high level of participation and interaction.

On other mornings, the Large Group could be quiet and apparently passive. Norman and his deputy charge nurse, Fiona, talked about the various types of silence they observed in the Large Groups. Douglas heard from them about contemplative silences, expectant silences, avoidant silences, passive silences and passive-aggressive silences.

"Are these long silences helpful?" he asked.

"Silence is a mode of communication," Norman said. "Self-evidently, a non-verbal mode of communication, and one of our roles is to disentangle the nature and significance of that particular non-verbal communication, just as we would with any other."

"But wouldn't speaking be more helpful?"

"The patients bring the issues to the Group, Douglas. If silence is the issue they bring, then the group is a silent one."

"Dr Wiseman seems to bring in the patients' issues for them," said Douglas.

"I am one of Bill's greatest admirers. He is a very proactive therapist. He endeavours to do a week's work in a single group. It is possible that his Large Group technique would sit more elegantly within a Small Group setting," Norman said.

Despite his ignorance about group processes, Douglas felt relatively at ease in his Small Group by the end of the first week. Both Diane and Michael were in the group, and they seemed pleased that he had joined them. As Norman had advised, Douglas did not take a leading role, but Norman did. Despite his serious demeanour, with only the occasional spark of humour, the patients clearly regarded Norman with warmth and trust. He was gentle and supportive. Nearly all of the patients in the group seemed to want to participate and to disclose things, often apparently with the aim of helping each other rather than of helping themselves.

"It's been really interesting this week. I think I'm learning a lot from watching you at work," said Douglas.

"Thank you, that is a kind comment. The patients seem soothed by your solid amiability," said Norman.

****

As he sometimes did, Douglas was walking around his office as he read a book, and he startled Joanie when he opened the door halfway through her knocking.

"Enjoying the groups?" she asked.

"I'm surprising myself. They're fascinating."

"There's so much going on, isn't there?"

"Too much for my small brain," said Douglas, "no matter how much I read about group therapy."

"Anything to report? About Bill?"

"Em, no. Not really. I can't think of anything."

"But you've been seeing him regularly."

"Oh yes, I've had supervision from him nearly every week. And we both see him in the Wednesday Big Groups and at the ward rounds."

"And you haven't noticed *anything?*"

"He hasn't seemed unhappy."

"Unsettled, on edge?"

"You know him much better than I do, obviously. Maybe it goes over my head, but he seems quite relaxed and cheery. He even suggested that we go for a game of golf in the spring."

"*Golf?* He invited you to play *golf?* He has never invited me."

"I didn't know you played."

"I don't. That's not the point."

In response to Douglas's quizzical look, tears formed in Joanie's eyes.

"I've been in analysis, you know," she said, "for the past few months. I'm sorry to get upset. I've been discussing my worries about Bill, my feelings for him.

"I'm no analyst myself, you'll remember," said Douglas.

"Yes, but you know Bill. My analyst doesn't. My father had chronic depression, you see."

"I'm being a bit slow, Joanie. Maybe you should sit down."

She sat on the edge of his desk.

"My father was depressed and anxious. That's how I remember him—always alone, always fearing the worst. And then he died up in the hills."

"Are you sure you want to tell me this?" asked Douglas.

"Why shouldn't I? I know you'll keep it to yourself. And you're an ordinary person, not like my analyst. I told him—Boris—that I have *feelings* for Bill. Strong feelings. Ever since I first came here. But when I mention this to Boris, he *interprets* it. He says my love for Bill is actually my love for my father, for the man who was psychologically absent during my childhood, because Bill is so *present* in the here and now. And he says that I worry about Bill because I worried so much about my father, and then I project depression and anxiety on to him that he doesn't have at all."

"And might Boris be right?"

Joanie stood up, and sat back down again quickly.

"Sorry, I shouldn't stand up. This isn't Dallas—the TV programme—people always stand up and walk about when they talk to their psychiatrist in Dallas, don't they? Not that you're my psychiatrist of course, but you are *a* psychiatrist. Boris could be right, but I don't think he is. You know Bill. So you might understand why I could just simply, you know, love him *for himself.*"

"I can. But he must be at least twenty years older than you."

"Twenty-six. It does happen."

"It does."

"And I think he likes me," said Joanie, colouring slightly, "but I don't know if that's as a trainee, or as a budding psychotherapist, or as myself—as a *woman.*"

Joanie stood up again.

"Thank you so much, Douglas," she said.

"I don't think I've been any help," he said.

"You have, you *have*! You've kept an eye on things, and you don't think I'm crazy. And you haven't interpreted anything at all. Thank you again," she said as she left.

Douglas reflected that his job was not straightforward. Interpretation of motives and feelings was a skill he needed to develop, and now he had just been thanked for interpreting nothing at all.

****

Douglas was astonished to see Billy Franks sitting next to Pauline in the Large Group. On spotting Douglas, Billy hurried into the middle of the group room.

"It's great to see you, big man. Pauline told me you were workin' here," he said.

Douglas's instant diagnosis was that Billy's mood was again rather high.

"You're surprised to see me, Douglas, by the look on your face," Billy continued.

"I heard someone was coming here from the forensic unit, but I had no idea it was you."

"Well it is me. Larger than life and twice as beautiful, eh?"

"You seem happy," Douglas observed.

"Happy to be here, especially with the sun shining. I'm here *for assessment*. That's what the head man told me."

Dr Wiseman had mentioned to ward staff earlier in the week that a new patient would be arriving. The patient's team had refused to go on treating him, and he was coming in to assess whether psychotherapy might be of benefit.

"That would be Dr Wiseman, he's the consultant here," said Douglas. "You know this is a psychotherapy ward, Billy?"

"Yeah, that's fine, Douglas. You know me—I can chat to anyone."

"It's not exactly chatting. Take your time maybe, Billy? Go slow and suss things out?" Douglas advised, as he became aware that the others had taken their seats.

Pauline had kept adjacent chairs vacant for them.

"Good morning," said Dr Wiseman, looking round the group.

There were mumbles in response, apart from Billy.

"Morning, sir, and isn't it a lovely one?" he said loudly.

"It is indeed," Dr Wiseman agreed. "And you have cued me in nicely. I met Billy on Monday and he came to us last evening. Over the last few years, Billy, you have had long spells in various wards, never here of course, and I think it would be fair to say that you have been searching without success for *stability* and *consistency* in your life. Perhaps you

179

would wish to give the group your own description of your difficulties?"

"Aye, sure, my pleasure," said Billy. "I've just come from forensic but I'm no' an axe murderer, you know. I thumped a guy in the ward upstairs. He deserved it. Douglas, Dr Barker here, he was there at the time. He'll tell you. That was only the second—no, wait, the third—person I've ever hit in my life. I'm no' violent and I'll no' be violent here."

"Good," said Dr Wiseman. "And what about your problems more generally?"

"How long have you got, hah? It's a bit o' a list. They say I'm a manic depressive, and who knows, they might be right. I'm no' sure to be honest with you. Things were pretty much OK until my woman—the love of my life for ever—buggered off down south, and since then I've no' really been right. Unstable, lonely, unsettled, call it what you like. And I've drunk a bit too much sometimes, no' that I've had the chance to do any drinkin' while I've been cooped up in here for nearly three months now, and I eat too much," he said, patting his stomach, "although I couldn't help noticin' at breakfast this morning that there's a few of you skinny young lassies who might do well to get a bit of that particular problem."

Douglas nudged Billy.

"Douglas's giving me the elbow here," said Billy. "He wants me to shut my gob."

"It has been helpful to hear you open your gob, Billy," said Dr Wiseman.

The group moved on in a familiar fashion, with Dr Wiseman introducing patients and topics while Norman acted as co-therapist. Fears relating to sexual relationships were a prominent theme.

180

It was unseasonably warm, and the windows were open. A wasp flew in, causing alarm for several patients as it buzzed around the room.

"Emma and Patricia," said Dr Wiseman, "I notice that the wasp has had a particularly unsettling effect upon you both."

"The fear of a wasp's sting," said Norman, "is of course so very similar to the fear of sex, and to concerns about the harm that can be done with an erect penis."

Billy had removed one of his shoes and he jumped up as the wasp settled on the window sill. He flattened it with an accurate blow.

"Lassies are frightened of wasps," he said. "They've got a real sore sting. Is that no' amazin' though? It's still March and here's a wasp flyin' in the window. And no' any ordinary wasp. It's huge!"

He picked it up by the wing.

"A wasp so early in the year must be a sign of a good summer to come," said Billy.

"On that note, I think we should conclude this morning's group," said Dr Wiseman.

****

"Come in, Joanie," shouted Douglas, in response to knocking that sounded even more urgent than her usual.

"It's Diane," said Joanie as she perched on a chair. "The nurses asked me to see her. She had abdominal pain and she was a ghastly colour."

"She's been losing weight again," said Douglas.

"I know. She's been very worried about it, hasn't she? Anyway, her abdomen felt funny—hard and pulsatile. Then she confessed. She'd been at home over the weekend?"

"Confessed what?"

"She told me that she brought back a lot of ball bearings—her father uses them for something or other—and she swallowed them before she was weighed this morning."

"Shit!" said Douglas. "How many?"

"About fifteen."

"How big?"

"The size of marbles, she said. Enough to put her weight up by a pound or two, I imagine."

"So what did you do?"

"Not much, really, except phone the on-call surgery team. They said they'd come up here to see her."

Diane was sitting up in bed, looking even more haggard and pale than usual. She seemed embarrassed to see Douglas as he sat down on her bed.

"Dr Smith told me what happened," he said.

"It was stupid, wasn't it," said Diane.

"It was hardly clever," Douglas agreed.

"It was an impulse."

"An impulse? But you brought them in from home at the weekend."

"They were in my father's garden shed."

"So you planned it."

"No—well, sort of. I noticed how heavy they were. So I smuggled them back here. It sounds silly, but I thought I could put them in my knickers and then I'd weigh more. But when I tried it this morning they just kept falling out. Just before I was weighed, I panicked. And I thought it would be a good idea to swallow them all."

"I know you get very worried about the weighing mornings, but what made you do something so dangerous, so *extreme?*"

"I see how concerned everyone gets. Then they nag me and pressurise me, and every meal is even more of a battle to make me eat."

Diane's eyes clenched in pain.

"I get spasms now and then," she said. "Dr Smith wondered if that might be when they come out of my stomach and into my intestines."

"I won't examine you myself," said Douglas. "We'll wait for the doctors from the infirmary. I'm no expert on swallowed ball bearings. It still seems like an extreme thing to do."

"I like to please people. And nothing seems to please people more than when I put on weight. It pleases my parents. It pleases the nurses. It pleases you. And it pleases Norman."

"It's particularly important to please Norman?"

"Yes, it is, for some reason."

"Anyway," said Douglas, "talking is hardly the priority just now. We need to get the ball bearings situation sorted."

"Should I drink water to wash them down?" asked Diane.

"I don't know, to be honest," said Douglas. "Let's wait for the surgeons. I'll go and see what Dr Smith wrote in your notes."

Douglas added a few lines about Diane, and was returning the case records to the nursing office. He was horrified to see the two figures in white coats who were approaching from the far end of the corridor. He did not know the smaller, younger man who trotted in the rear, but he knew the curly haired surgeon who strode along in front.

When Douglas was a student in Newcastle, he and two friends devised an Absolute Bastards Chart (ABC) on which they ranked the senior doctors whom they encountered during their training. The surgeon approaching, Humphrey Dodds-Donaldson, had been number one on the ABC nearly every week, and had seemed to harbour particular animosity towards Douglas. When they first met, Dodds-Donaldson had consulted his list of new students with incredulity.

"Can this be *Mr* Barker? Or is it a girl?" he said, staring at Douglas's long hair. "No—it *does* seem to be *Mr* Barker!"

Dodds-Donaldson insisted that Douglas wore two paper hats when he was in theatre observing surgical operations, while one hat sufficed for women with much longer hair. When Dodds-Donaldson addressed him, Douglas felt that his tone was at its most plummy and condescending, and he always seemed to direct the most difficult questions to Douglas, whose answers were usually received with a disparaging sneer. Douglas had not tried to disguise his dislike for Dodds-Donaldson and, if he ever thought about him since graduation, it had been to hope that they would never meet again.

But Dodds-Donaldson seemed very pleased to see Douglas.

"I should have *known it!*" he trumpeted from ten yards away. "It's young Barker! He became a *psychiatrist*. Of course he did!"

Douglas observed him coldly.

"And it seems that you are still a surgeon," he said.

"Wilson," said Dodds-Donaldson to the junior doctor, "let this chap be a warning to you. If you too are lazy and

184

disrespectful, then this could be you in five years' time—a *psychiatrist*!"

Dr Wilson looked flustered.

"Are you the surgical house officer?" Douglas asked him.

"Yes. Jerry Wilson," he said.

Douglas shook his hand to emphasise that he had no wish to shake Dodds-Donaldson's.

"You spoke on the phone, surely," said Dodds-Donaldson.

"It was my colleague, Dr Smith, who called," said Douglas.

"Probably a good idea to leave things to someone more competent," said Dodds-Donaldson. "Anyway, you need our help. Some sort of standard psychiatric emergency, I gather?"

"As I am sure Dr Wilson told you, the young woman swallowed ball bearings."

"Astonishing! Stranger than truth that a patient could do that *in a so-called hospital*, isn't it Wilson? But come on, let's go and see her. Lead on, Barker."

Douglas walked quickly to her dormitory.

"Hullo again, Diane. These are the surgeons from the infirmary."

Dodds-Donaldson stopped at the foot of the bed.

"Classical anorexia nervosa, Wilson," he said. "Emaciated. And lots of that downy hair on her arms—lanugo, it's called, unless I'm much mistaken."

He walked to Diane's side and lifted her hand.

"See the blue tinge, Wilson? Peripheral cyanosis. So, they let you swallow things in here, do they?" he said to Diane.

Without waiting for a response, Dodds-Donaldson pulled back the bedclothes.

"We need to get rid of those pillows. Lie flat. Any pain?"

"Not at the moment. It comes in spasms," said Diane, wincing as Dodds-Donaldson palpated her abdomen.

"She hasn't perforated anyway," he announced. "We need to get you down to our ward, young lady. Some X-rays will show us what's happening. Nothing by mouth in the meantime," he said, before turning and marching off towards the ward office.

"Notes, Barker, notes," he demanded.

"Her haemoglobin is what?" asked Dodds-Donaldson, flicking through the records.

"I think it was 10.2," said Douglas.

"I've seen that one. That was in January. What is it now? This week? Today?"

"We haven't done it since then, I don't think."

"You don't think. I suppose that pretty much sums it up. Who would want to be ill in this place, Wilson?"

"What would be the reason for doing it?" asked Douglas irritably.

"Monitoring the patient's well-being? That sort of thing ever occur to you up here? Come on, Wilson, proper surgical patients will be queuing up. Let's go. Send her down to us, Barker. And do try to stop your patients from swallowing this, that and the next thing."

Later that day, Douglas telephoned the surgical ward from the nursing office, and Dr Wilson told him Diane was settled. X-rays had confirmed that the ball bearings were moving from her stomach into her bowel.

"Mr Dodds-Donaldson said that if you phoned I was to give you a message. He wrote it down," said Dr Wilson.

"Do I want to hear it?"

"Maybe not," said Dr Wilson, "but this is it: 'Tell Barker that I regret not doing more to stop him from graduating. If he wants to continue to practise medicine, then just possibly it is not too late to go back to basics and to start looking after his patients properly.' Sorry—that was it."

"Well you can tell him from me that he can stuff his message up his pompous public school arse!" Douglas shouted. "Thank you and goodnight!"

As he slammed down the telephone, he looked up to see Norman and Dr Wiseman in the office doorway.

They were pleased that Diane was progressing, and seemed just as interested to hear about the history between Douglas and Mr Dodds-Donaldson. Indeed, Dr Wiseman found it highly amusing.

"The message we heard you give him may not have been the most prudent," said Dr Wiseman. "Letting him think that you have an interest in his bottom may well have been a mistake."

"As he surely does in yours," said Norman.

"My thoughts exactly," said Dr Wiseman. "From the moment he singled you out with your long shining locks of hair."

"And then he tries to obfuscate his homosexual desires with bluster and aggression," said Norman.

"Surgeons are often aggressive," said Dr Wiseman. "At heart, most of them are sadists. What better way to act out one's sadistic impulses than by cutting people open with a scalpel? And then to be paid and thanked for gratifying their sadism, turning their perversion into something deemed to be constructive and helpful? For them, it's the perfect solution. But at heart, they are unhappy and conflicted men,

187

Douglas. Feel pity for your public school nemesis, and that may help you to tolerate his psychopathology, eh?"

By this stage, Douglas was also laughing.

****

"Daylight after work," said Douglas, as he and Chris walked to the pub. "Don't you love it when the clocks change?"

"Spring in the air," said Chris. "No doubt ye'll be comin' back intae heat soon."

"Could be."

"When ye've no' had a new woman fir this long, I get concerned that ye might be unwell."

Chris dodged a car and crossed the road ahead of Douglas.

"Anarchist," he said as he caught up.

"I think ye might still be pinin' fir yir Christmas O.T."

"I can't say you're wrong. Anne was lovely. No doubt she still is. Perhaps I'm going through a lull—a contemplative phase."

"The only thing ye used tae contemplate was who ye were goin' tae shag next."

"Nonsense. Anyway, you're the current shagger in the flat, are you not?"

"No comment. And what's the latest news from yir place of work?"

"So we shall not be discussing Mandy's sexual performance. Hardly a smooth change of topic from the Glaswegian psychiatrist, but I'll tell you anyway. The ward round this morning was great."

"Ye should sell tickets."

"Maybe we should. You remember Diane, the girl with anorexia who swallowed the ball bearings?"

"No' an easy story tae forget."

In the bar, Douglas gave a thumbs up when the barman suggested 'the usual'. He told Chris that Diane was making good progress at the infirmary.

"It was discussed at the ward round today," Douglas continued. "And Dr Wiseman, of course, goes into deeply Freudian mode, and he says: 'Diane's actions have a strong symbolic significance. Penis envy and castration complex seem to lie at the core. Surely she was vicariously acquiring the testicles she never had and that she always longed for?', or something very similar."

"And ye managed no' tae laugh?"

"Then Norman says: 'You could be right, Bill, but I'm wondering if her action is more anti-men, more *vengeful*. Is she biting off and swallowing the testicles? Is *she* the castrator? Is she acting out a subconscious fantasy of revenge?' Then Bill comes back with: 'But her first plan was to put them into her knickers, in the very place where the longed for testicles would have been.' Then they chatted about this, to and fro, as if it was the most ordinary thing to discuss. Like football, or the weather."

"And what dae ye think yerself?"

"Probably just a lot of balls," said Douglas. "I think she wanted to put on weight to get the nurses off her back and to please Norman."

"Maybe ye are still hangin' on tae yir sanity by a thread," said Chris.

"And the other interesting thing is Billy Franks. The guy who broke Dick's nose?"

"A local hero, no less."

"He was assigned to Dr Wiseman after Dick's team refused to have him when he left forensic. So he came into the ward. But after a week of causing chaos in the groups—he was a bit high and he just didn't get the whole psychotherapy thing at all—"

"Him and me might get on," said Chris.

"Yeah, you might. So he's been discharged from the ward, and now he's my out-patient."

"Another thing tae help keep ye sane. A normal patient wi' manic depressive illness. So ye'll get him to take his lithium?"

"That's a major part of the plan."

April 1982

The family party that Douglas's father wanted for his 65th birthday was to be a quiet meal at home. Work colleagues had already held a formal event to mark his retirement.

"They keep calling it a celebration," he had said on the telephone, "but that's the last thing it feels like. I had hoped to continue working, but people in high places deem that to be impossible."

On the morning of the Saturday scheduled for the meal, the atmosphere in the house was subdued, in keeping with his father's mood. His sister was yet to arrive and Tom had been sent out to buy carrots.

"Not like me to forget," said Belinda, "but the last few days have been hectic."

"Your glasses bit the dust again?" asked Douglas after she hugged him, pointing to a cracked lens in her spectacles.

"Perhaps a sign my hair is thinning when the glasses won't stay stuck. I'll get new ones on a string once the dust settles."

"Is the dust settling?"

"His retirement do was on Thursday," said Belinda, lowering her voice, "and he just sat about yesterday. In fact, it's good that you're here to *unsettle* the dust."

Belinda hustled him towards the sitting room.

"Your elder son has arrived, Charles," she announced.

Charles had never been a demonstrative man, even in the months surrounding his wife's death. His feelings were often hard to read, but he had always seemed quietly in control. Douglas's first thought was that his father looked defeated, in a way Douglas had not seen before.

He had been gazing out of the window from his armchair, and he turned to smile grimly at his son. Douglas handed him an envelope.

"I got you a Happy Birthday card, Dad," he said, "since I wasn't sure a Happy Retirement card would be right."

His father opened the envelope.

"A very nice card, Douglas. And a book token. Thank you."

Douglas asked about the work retirement dinner and heard that his father had 'endured kind speeches'.

"People tell me I must *take up new interests*," said his father, staring bleakly into the distance. "They say it brightly, condescendingly, as if I were a child who was bored in the school holidays."

"It's a big event in anyone's life."

"And that sounds condescending too."

"It wasn't meant to be, Dad."

Douglas was pleased to hear his brother return.

"At Christmas you looked fatter and now you look fitter, big brother," he said.

"Football and clean living," said Douglas.

"Maybe I believe the football," said Tom.

"Why don't you youngsters eat Belinda's sandwiches and then go for a walk? Catch up with each other," suggested their father.

"We could do that," said Douglas, "if you won't get fed up."

"I need to get used to inactivity."

The brothers walked through the village into open country, and Tom talked about his impending final examinations. He and Douglas were of fairly equal intelligence, but Tom was more conscientious, and they agreed that his finals should not prove too demanding.

"It's more a question of how many prizes and distinctions you get," said Douglas.

Tom was concerned about their father, saying that he had been 'morose' since hearing he would have to retire. They turned back for home and the bright weather broke. Rain was slanting into their faces.

"A well-timed shower," said Douglas, as he guided his brother into the bar of the local hotel.

As he looked around, Douglas thought he would notice changes, but he detected none. Two locals, standing at the worn bar, greeted him casually as if they had seen him the day before.

"It's like I never left," he said as they started their drinks. "And I don't know if that makes me sad or happy."

"Sameness," said Tom. "Seems to drive some people away and keep other people here."

"What about Dad and Belinda? Maybe Dad likes the sameness too much. Should they make a break for it?"

"I can't see it. Belinda tried to plan a holiday in Spain, but she was overruled. She's almost talked him into a week in Ireland, but negotiations are ongoing."

"He is set in his ways. Maybe not a good idea to move."

"No, but he does need to do something. Anyway, what about you? At Christmas you were telling me there was a woman you were keen on."

"That was Anne," said Douglas. "Past tense, sadly. I did really like her, but it turned out she already had someone."

"Not good. I think that's the keenest I've seen you on anyone since Spider."

The brothers took reflective drinks.

"Do you still think about Spider a lot?" asked Tom.

"No. Only every day," said Douglas.

"Shit."

"Subject change, please, Tom. Let me tell you about the new job."

Douglas chatted at length about the interesting time he had been having on the psychotherapy ward, and they were laughing as they got back to the house.

"Nice to hear you boys having fun," said Belinda. "Your father has gone to the station to meet Helen. It's his first outing in two days."

When the car returned, only Helen and their father got out.

"No Alex? No twins?" Douglas asked.

"His mother came down to look after Alex and his depression," said Helen. "So she's got Fergus and Harvey too. While I come up here for some adult company."

"Do you hear that, Tom? Helen wants you to act like an adult," said Douglas.

Helen wanted to sit with her father and 'read a newspaper uninterrupted for the first time in years' while, at Belinda's request, Tom and Douglas dug the garden.

"Your father grew vegetables a few years ago, as you might remember. Maybe if there's an inviting plot, he might take it up again."

The old vegetable border was overgrown, the earth was heavy from the recent rain, and the brothers spent a wearying hour on their task. Their father came out briefly, muttered about 'one of Belinda's schemes', half-heartedly pruned a rose bush, and went back into the house.

After the digging, Belinda said:

"And now pre-dinner drinks. Helen and your father have started already. Through you go."

On the coffee table in the sitting room there were three bottles of sherry.

"Join us, boys. Look what Dad got from his friends at work," said Helen.

"An old man's drink," said their father.

"That hasn't stopped you from consuming three or four," said Helen.

"Maybe that makes me an old man then."

There were ruddy spots on his cheeks, and his words were slightly slurred. It was several years since Douglas had seen his father take more than a single drink. He joined his sons in two more sherries before Belinda summoned them, and he was unsteady on his feet as he sat down at the dining room table.

As Tom poured the wine, Helen said:

"Maybe no more for Dad. He already seems a bit jolly."

"Shouldn't be jolly," said their father. "Out of character."

"We want you to be jolly," said Helen, "but when you're sober."

"Maybe drinking is my new hobby. You should be pleased I've got one. Maybe I'll never be sober again," he said, holding up his glass for Tom to fill.

"You're only sixty-five once," said Tom.

"And thank Christ for that. Cheers!" said his father, taking a swig of wine.

Belinda's duck was complimented, and the conversation flitted between mention of Helen's pregnancy, Douglas's job and Tom's studies. Their father joined in only occasionally.

"Motor bike. Maybe I'll buy a motor bike."

A few minutes later, he said:

"Bread. Maybe bake my own bread."

Before finishing the meal, he was asleep at the table, his chin on his chest. Belinda roused him and escorted him to bed. Helen, who had complained of nausea during the meal, returned to the sitting room while her brothers cleared the table.

Belinda was tearful when she came downstairs.

"I've never seen him like that," she said.

"It is his birthday," said Tom, taking her arm to escort her through to join Helen.

"We never got the chance to sing 'Happy Birthday To You'. I wanted to sing 'Charlie Is My Darling' to him as well."

"That's a pity," said Douglas, while thinking it a rather bizarre song choice.

"And his cake. We didn't do his cake," said Belinda.

"Too much chat about food," said Helen, "for a nauseated pregnant woman."

For a moment, Douglas thought she had said 'nauseating'. The conversation moved to the topic of her domestic situation.

"By September, I'll have three children to look after. Who knows, maybe four if it's twins again. Alex would *have* to be back to his old self by then. *Surely,* doctors?"

"I'm not a doctor yet," said Tom. "I would defer to the psychiatrist's opinion."

"As I mentioned to you on the phone," said Douglas, "recovery from depression can be slow."

"*Slow?* It's going at a snail's pace! Maybe he plays with the twins a bit more, but he's still grumpy with me—*completely unsupportive.* He doesn't seem to want to hear a word about my pregnancy."

"That's not like him," said Belinda.

"He's changed. He's focused on himself," said Helen.

"That's what happens in depression," said Tom.

"It's often part of the illness," said Douglas. "Unselfish people become more selfish. Self-centred people become even more self-centred—if that's possible."

"He used to appreciate at least some of what I did. That's gone," said Helen.

"Sometimes we get taken for granted a bit in a relationship," said Belinda, "like with your dad just now. But if it's a phase—a passing phase—maybe that's OK?"

"But will it pass? *When* will it pass? That's my *point*!" said Helen.

"I just did my psychiatry block," said Tom. "As I said to Douglas, it was very interesting."

"You told me that too," said Belinda. "Maybe we'll have two psychiatrists in the family."

"Surely not," said Helen.

"Maybe," said Tom. "If I can ignore the jibes of my classmates. And my family. I was just going to say that when I saw out-patients with the consultant, a lot of them had depression, but they were getting better. With the right treatment."

"A *psychiatrist!* You're suggesting Alex should see a psychiatrist?" Helen demanded.

"You make us sound like axe murderers, or child molesters," said Douglas. "It's hard to know if he should be referred without hearing the details. I could have asked him if he'd come up today."

"Phone him then. If you won't phone his doctor," said Helen.

"Tell him to phone me if he wants to."

"Would it be so awful for him to see a psychiatrist?" asked Belinda. "A nice person like Douglas? What harm could it do?"

"People might get to know, for one thing," said Helen. "And what would that do to our family's reputation? Or to his career, for that matter."

"Surely the priority is for him to get better," said Tom.

"He might not have to go to the hospital," said Douglas. "Some psychiatrists see patients in their own doctors' surgeries these days. Or perhaps the consultant would see him at home."

Helen continued to talk about her own situation, while Belinda sought views on 'managing' her husband's retirement. Near the end of the evening, Belinda cried again

"Charles misses you all so much. Not that he would tell you. He sees a lot of you, Tom, of course, but then you might disappear too after you qualify."

"Well, as I've said before, you boys will have to visit more, because I can't," said Helen.

As he went to bed, Douglas's head was spinning. Compared with families, group psychotherapy was not complex at all.

****

"I had tae sign fir this. Recorded delivery," said Chris, as he handed Douglas a large white envelope. "It's from the General Medical Council, no less. Have ye no' paid them yir fees?"

"I think I did," said Douglas.

The letter read:

'Dear Dr Barker,

The Chairman of the Council's Preliminary Proceedings Committee asked me to notify you that the Council has received, from Ms Lucy Campbell, a complaint about your professional conduct. This complaint raises a question as to whether, as a registered medical practitioner, you have committed Serious Professional Misconduct, as defined by legal statute.

In Ms Campbell's complaint, it is alleged that:

1. You abused your professional position, while she was a vulnerable patient under your care, by discussing your sexual feelings towards her;

2. You conducted an inappropriate physical examination upon her in your office;

3. You visited her flat where you and she engaged in full sexual intercourse

The complaint is supported by a sworn statement from Ms Campbell.

The decision reached by the Preliminary Proceedings Committee (PPC) will determine whether the case might be referred on to the Professional Conduct Committee of the Council for the purpose of an inquiry into the charge against you. The next PPC meeting will occur on 26th April. Should you wish to offer a written explanation, then this will be considered in the course of that same meeting. Thereafter, we shall write to you again.

Yours sincerely,

A.P. Shearer (on behalf of the General Medical Council).'

Douglas re-read the letter aloud to Chris.

"So who is this Lucy Campbell? Do ye know her?"

"It's the girl who got upset that I didn't love her. The one who left threatening revenge."

"Right. But she's daft as a brush. Surely the GMC would recognise a daft complaint."

"Apparently not."

"I suppose they have tae investigate. Ye better fire off a letter. Tell them ye didnae do it and the lassie's crazy."

"Maybe you could draft the letter for me, Chris."

"Ye know what I mean. That's the take home message. Just tart it up a bit."

"You're right. That's what I'll do. Life is never dull around here, is it?"

****

Douglas gave the letter from the General Medical Council to Dr Wiseman at the start of his supervision session.

"Bloody irritating, eh? Getting a letter from someone who doesn't tell you what gender they are. I take it that we've heard nothing more from Lucy Campbell since she left here in a cloud of dust?"

"No, nothing. And that's been about two months," said Douglas.

"Hell hath no fury like a woman who perceives herself to have been scorned. She seeks a public castration at the hands of the GMC. I take it that there's nothing even remotely factual in her complaint?"

"No! Not a thing!"

"Sorry, Douglas. Don't take offence. It's advisable to check, even when one feels certain, or one might end up defending the indefensible, eh?"

"She did suggest, in a very flirty way, that I should examine her. But I didn't."

"Good. Have you drafted a response to them?"

"Yes, I've got it here," said Douglas.

"Let's hear it."

"'Dear sir/madam," Douglas read,

"I am responding to your letter of 5th April in which you accuse me of professional misconduct with Ms Lucy Campbell. I would make the following points:

(1) Ms Campbell was my patient for a period of just two weeks, and I interviewed her in my office only twice. I have not seen her since the 12th of February.

(2) At no point did I express sexual feelings towards her.

(3) At no point did I examine her physically.

(4) I have never been in her flat, far less had sexual intercourse with her there.

(5) Her diagnosis was histrionic personality disorder, although we thought that she might also be psychotic. Her complaint suggests that she is.

Yours faithfully,
etc etc

Does that sound OK?"

Dr Wiseman advised that the GMC was investigating rather than accusing, and so Douglas should modify his irritated tone. He commented that the GMC might benefit from a brief explanation of the features of histrionic personality and erotomania. He did not like Douglas's implication that anyone who complained about him must be mad.

"You would hope that the GMC will have the sense to throw it out right away," said Dr Wiseman. "This PPC group is the screening body for all the complaints they get. And if you haven't contacted your medical defence union, do that right away. Discuss the letter with them."

As he looked up from writing notes on his drafted letter, Douglas noticed that the walls of Dr Wiseman's office were almost bare.

"Aha, Douglas, I see that you are spotting my new decor. Or the lack of it, eh?"

"It is quite a change."

"My dear wife, Claire, swept in on Monday. We had disagreed over the weekend. She nursed her wrath for two days—and today's theme seems to be feminine revenge and castration—then she pounced. She removed every one of her pictures. In an attempt to make peace, I've implied that my office is a poorer place without them. To be honest, however, I prefer it like this. The intended castration feels more like a penis enlargement, eh?"

Douglas had no idea what to say.

"Sorry. I've embarrassed you. Tell me how things are going with young Diane," said Dr Wiseman.

******

Douglas was enjoying a quiet Friday night on call. He was lying on the bed in which the overnight psychiatrists slept, reading The Dice Man, when there was a brisk and familiar knock on the door.

Joanie came in.

"Was that a 'come in'?" she asked. "The receptionist said you weren't busy."

Joanie was looking glamorous in a long black dress. She sat down at the end of the bed and Douglas sat up.

"I've been at the theatre with my sister," she said. "Then we had a couple of drinks and I was passing the hospital on my way home."

"I wasn't expecting visitors," said Douglas, putting down his book.

"The Dice Man! A bit 1970s don't you think?"

"Maybe. But I like it."

"So you've not been busy?"

"No, but it might be about now that the drunks start to pour in from the pubs—and the theatre."

"Very funny. I thought you might be lonely."

"A kind thought. Was it a good play?"

"A musical. Not my cup of tea. Can I ask you something?"

"Fire away."

"Would you like to have sex with me?"

"Well—"

"No, no, I mean *theoretically*, not *actually* have sex."

"Em, what do you want? A theoretical answer?"

"I want a *real* answer to a theoretical question. An *honest* answer."

"Yes, obviously, I would, but—"

"Douglas! I knew I could rely on you for a straightforward answer! A straightforward answer from a red blooded male, if your reputation is to be believed."

"It's a funny theoretical question."

"I suppose it is—a bit cheeky, really."

"Are you propositioning me, Joanie?"

"No, sorry, I'm not. I'm *not*! It sounds like a bit of a tease when I hear myself, and I like you, so I'm just saying we could, if you were desperate, but that's not why I came to see you."

"Perhaps it relates to Bill?" Douglas suggested.

Joanie moved up the bed towards him.

"Yes, it does," she said quietly. "I went for a drink with him last weekend. It was lovely. But then, at closing time, *we didn't know what to do*. We both just sort of drifted off home. I need to seduce him, don't I? I need to get him past the consultant/trainee thing and make it a man/woman thing."

"I guess you're the best judge of that."

"Yes, you're right, I am. I knew you would understand. And I needed a man's perspective. You are *always* helpful, Douglas. You have boosted my confidence. I shall go home and plan my strategy."

Joanie stood up and grinned at him.

"Sorry, I really didn't mean to tease. I won't kiss you goodnight. I hope you have a quiet one."

After she left, Douglas found it difficult to focus on his novel.

****

204

At the weekly ward rounds, the staff group spent a few minutes discussing each patient in turn, after which one or two patients were considered in more detail. These patients might be brought in to be interviewed by Dr Wiseman or by Norman. It was Michael's week for a more detailed review, but first the staff discussed Diane.

Pauline outlined Diane's persisting difficulties at mealtimes, and the nurses' attempts to encourage and reassure her during meals and on the mornings she was weighed. Unfortunately, her weight remained consistently low. In the groups, she focused with interest on the problems of other patients, but divulged little about herself. In her individual sessions with Douglas, she had talked about the death of her brother and the impact of this upon her and her family.

"But she seems very flat when she talks about it," said Douglas, "sort of *uninvolved.* As if it happened to someone else. She seems depressed to me. She's got no energy and she awakens before dawn every morning."

"When you starve," said Norman, "you do not sleep well. Prisoners of war were exhausted, but they slept very poorly. And in anorexia nervosa, the nature of the affliction is to *deprive yourself of everything*. Obviously, you deprive yourself of food. You deprive yourself also of sex, of the chance of becoming a sexual person, of the chance of becoming a parent. And similarly, you deprive yourself of the escape that might be afforded by a full night's sleep."

"What if we prescribed an antidepressant, maybe amitriptyline?" suggested Douglas. "Her mood might improve and she might sleep better."

Norman was not often in favour of prescribing medication.

"An antidepressant? An external crutch? You would like to see us *doing something* to Diane, taking on the responsibility for what she must do herself. When crutches are removed without healing the underlying pathology, the person surely collapses to the ground, does she not?"

"She's been here a long time. Might it be worth a try?" asked Douglas.

"We can seek Bill's view," said Norman, "but I suspect that he will share mine. Sometimes we become irritated, Douglas, with a patient's lack of progress. Sometimes we take it personally. The task is to be patient with our patient, and to help her find her own way to recover. Changes made in this way tend to endure."

The meeting moved on to discuss Michael's first seven weeks in the ward. There was shared optimism, and large deputy charge nurse Fiona, Michael's key-worker, talked with particular enthusiasm about his progress.

"To me," she said, "he already seems like a different man. He's still very anxious, of course, a lot of the time, and he said he didn't want to come in here today to be seen by all of us."

"I think that would be acceptable, particularly if he is indeed improving. But perhaps seeing us collectively is a demon he should confront before too long," said Norman.

"He is getting more confident," said Fiona, "but I think his 'mom' used to undermine him."

"I agree," said Douglas. "He almost said in an individual session that his mother deliberately tried to lower his self-esteem to make him more reliant on her."

"To ensure that he would never leave her, presumably," said Norman.

"I went to his house with him last week to get some stuff he needed, and it was interesting," said Fiona. "He hadn't been home since he came in here, and he said that the house looked different. He felt different about being there—a bit less 'weighed down'. He wondered if I could go home with him again sometime and he could make a start on getting rid of his mother's clothes."

"You and he have formed a bond, it would seem," said Norman.

"We do get on well," said Fiona.

"You are, of course, somewhat, ah, *maternal*, and no doubt this could be therapeutically helpful," said Norman.

"I'm not quite sure how to take that comment," said Fiona.

Pauline mentioned that within the mealtime encouragement of the anorexic patients to consume more, Michael was 'eating like a horse' and gaining weight. It was agreed to separate him from the underweight patients in the dining room and to advise him to take more exercise. Pauline added that Michael would not go to the weekly group swimming sessions.

"We discussed that when I last saw him," said Douglas. "He told me it's because he's fat and his 'blubber' would hang over his swimming trunks. He thought people would laugh at him."

Douglas kept a straight face and continued.

"I didn't say this to him, but I think there's more to it. I think it's to do with his mother. Does the swimming pool, for Michael, represent the womb with its warm lapping water, and is his fear of swimming really about his ambivalence towards his mother? Does he fear experiencing the conflict

207

between his love for her and his anger towards her, if he were to *return to the womb* by going swimming?"

Douglas saw that Pauline was looking at him with a concerned expression, but Norman seemed delighted.

"Douglas!" he said. "I had no idea that we thought along such similar lines. You really are beginning to *get it*!"

"It was just a thought," Douglas said modestly.

"A very good thought," said Norman, "and I am sure that mother related issues hold the key to his recovery. The positive maternal transference he has with you, Fiona, should be developed further. I think I sometimes experience, in the Small Group, the more negative aspects of his transference. Perhaps he splits his mother—the good object he loves and the bad object he hates—and responds to me as the bad object. As he does, perhaps, with his manager at work. I am a manager here, of course. Yesterday, I pointed out that people had again arrived late for the start of the group, as you will recall, Douglas. Michael became irritated on behalf of the late comers. And when I interpreted his annoyance, as a transference phenomenon, he became yet more irritated."

"And it couldn't have been that you were irritating, could it?" asked Fiona.

Douglas thought he saw a flicker of a smile before Norman responded.

"I think not, Fiona."

"He does seem to get a lot out of being in the ward," said Douglas. "He's surprised how much he likes being with the people here. He enjoys trying to help 'the girls', as he calls them, and he seems surprised that they like him."

"The ward community can be helpful in many different ways," said Norman, "and his progress is gratifying. In summary, Michael has started to address his psychopathology, and we must keep right on going, since it seems clear that we are assisting him."

****

Douglas recounted to Chris his 'swimming pool as a mother's womb' interpretation, and Chris shook his head at length.

"Did ye ever think," he said, "that folk don't get crazy thoughts because they're ill? Maybe it's the thinkin' crazy thoughts that drives ye mad in the first place. You need tae look out."

"I am merely learning the language of psychoanalysis," said Douglas, as he left the room to answer the telephone.

It was his brother-in-law.

"Helen told me to phone you," said Alex.

"That wasn't quite the message I gave her."

"She's not here to ask about that. She's at her Women's Discussion Group. But that's what she said."

"I said you could phone me if you wanted—your choice."

"Oh, right. Well we're speaking now."

Douglas asked him about symptoms of depression. It seemed that Alex had made only a little progress and Douglas suggested that recovery might be speeded if Alex were to ask his general practitioner about taking a higher dose of antidepressants.

"Quicker would be good," said Alex, "especially since Helen can get a bit impatient."

"I did get that impression. And because she's my sister, I can also say that she might be a bit unsupportive."

"True. I've been thinking recently that the support in our marriage has been something of a one-way street."

"Has Helen seen your doctor?"

"No. Dr Duncan did suggest it. She said her priority was to look after the twins while I went to see him. And then of course there's her pregnancy."

"She sounded horrified when Tom wondered if you might see a psychiatrist."

"I know. I am thinking about it. Again, I'll talk to Dr Duncan. Douglas, it's good of you to speak, but I'll take up no more of your time. I need to get the boys to bed."

"OK, Alex. I hope you get back to your old self soon."

"There's a cup o' tea here fir ye," shouted Chris.

"Thanks. That was Alex," said Douglas, as he joined Chris in the kitchen.

"I know. I was listenin'. If ye had started tellin' him about castration complexes or swimmin' pools, I was ready tae grab the phone."

"He sounds like he's still quite depressed," said Douglas.

"I thought ye reckoned yir sister was half o' his problem?"

"Yeah, she might be. She can certainly lower my mood. But I'm not the right person to be discussing it with him—or with her. Would you see a psychiatrist if you were depressed?"

"Of course I would. As long as I got tae pick the one I saw," said Chris.

****

"You have a new look," Douglas said to Billy Franks at the start of his appointment. Billy was in a light blue suit and he walked around the room in the manner of a model on a catwalk.

"You too could look as good as this, Doug," he said, hanging up his jacket before he sat down. "You will no doubt be takin' my precious blood again, and I wouldn't want you spillin' it on my new gear."

"I'm no fashion expert, Billy, but do you think the suit matches the rest of your outfit?"

Billy was wearing red trainers and a yellow Bob Marley tee shirt.

"Rome wasn't built in a day. I'll need to play cards with someone with nice blue shoes and a fancy shirt."

"You've lost me, Billy."

"Poker. That's how I got the sharp suit. Playin' cards through the night with somebody even dafter and drunker than me. The crazy bastard bet his suit on a pair o' tens. Hard to believe, don't you think? I'll soon be irresistible to the lassies of this fair city."

"I hoped your life might get a bit quieter. It doesn't look like that's been happening."

"It's spring, Doug, for heaven's sake! The rutting season. No doubt you've been rutting yourself. The time for hibernation is over."

Douglas extracted details from a discursive Billy about his mood and his symptoms. His energy was excessive, he was sleeping poorly and he was impulsive with money and alcohol. He was generally very cheerful, but at times irritable and aggressive.

"Your lithium level was low in last week's blood test," said Douglas. "Have you been taking your pills regularly?"

"Religiously. Every Sunday morning!"

Billy laughed uproariously.

"Did you read the stuff I gave you about lithium, Billy?" asked Douglas.

"I've had all that before. Dr Broken Nose Dick gave me a mountain of stuff to read. It saved him from speakin' to me. How is he, by the way?"

"He's OK. But you should read that stuff. It's important you know about lithium and understand why you should take it."

"No need to get narky, Doug."

"I'm not getting narky, Billy. I'm your doctor, and I want you to stay well. And if you were to take lithium regularly for a change then there's a good chance you might stay well. You might not need to keep coming in and out of hospital. Your life might settle down."

"There's more to life than settlin' down. That's for old people. Or for boring people. It's no' for me. I'm havin' a great time."

"You've not been having a great time since I've known you. You were never happier than when you were settled with Maggie. When you were working."

Billy became suddenly sombre.

"That was a while ago," he said.

"Only four or five years. I was thinking that if you had a more structure, something to do during the day with other people, then that might help? Company and a bit of a routine?"

Douglas went on to describe workshops at the hospital that could help patients to rehabilitate. Billy did not initially seem keen on the prospect, but he brightened when he heard that occupational therapist Anne was in charge of the workshops.

"The bonny blonde with nice tits? OK then, nothing to lose. An appointment with a sexy lady."

Douglas said he would write to Anne about Billy and got ready to take his blood.

"To be honest," said Billy, "there might not be much point huntin' for lithium in the Franks bloodstream. I've no' taken it for a week. I get busy. I forget."

"OK, no blood test. But you might read that information?"

"If I really can't sleep, I just might."

May 1982

"Let's do your next supervision session on the golf course."
Dr Wiseman had said.

Douglas felt uneasy, despite the official sanction, as he
drove away from the hospital. He had previously played only
with friends or relatives, and he was unsure that his etiquette
would be up to scratch, especially since he had heard that the
golf club was a snooty one. It was also hard to know what
balance to strike between deference towards his consultant
on one hand, and camaraderie with a golfing companion on
the other. His anxieties eased slightly after Dr Wiseman,
waiting for him outside the clubhouse, guided him into a
parking space. Dr Wiseman was wearing green plus fours
and tartan socks.

"Sorry about the fancy dress," he said. "It's my policy to
look like an idiot on the golf course. Then nobody's surprised when I play like one."

As Douglas extracted his clubs from the car, Dr Wiseman grabbed Douglas's golf shoes and clapped him on the
shoulder.

"While you may show me a modicum of respect at work,
Douglas, this afternoon we are not at work. Anything goes,
eh? As long as you let me win, of course!"

As they warmed up on the first tee, Dr Wiseman told
him:

"We're right behind a ladies' competition today. No doubt they'll be chatting between every shot. So we'll have time to chat too, eh?"

As he teed off, Douglas felt inquisitive eyes upon him from the clubhouse, and was relieved when his drive went fairly straight down the first fairway. Dr Wiseman had a short, swift and uncomplicated golf swing.

"I don't hit it a long way," he said. "So I'll struggle to compete with a strong young chap like yourself unless I putt very well."

He did putt well, Douglas played erratically, and Dr Wiseman was quickly three holes ahead.

"I fixed that dreadful surgeon yesterday," said Dr Wiseman on the seventh fairway.

"Who? Dodds-Donaldson?"

"The very man. I was on his appointment committee. He was after a consultant job, senior lectureship in the university. He seemed to be the front runner. But I asked him a few questions to reveal his ignorance of matters psychiatric, and he got shirty. I told the committee how rude and arrogant he'd been when he came to see young Diane. Even the surgeons thought he was too obnoxious to appoint, and they gave the job to a chap from Manchester."

"Well done! Excellent news," said Douglas.

"What goes around sometimes comes around," said Dr Wiseman.

Douglas began to play better, and by the time they waited on the tee at the short fourteenth hole, the match was all square. Dr Wiseman was bending to and fro from the waist, with his fists pressed into the small of his back.

"I'm starting my excuses early—I've had a bad back these last few weeks," he said.

215

"I've got Paracetamol in my bag," offered Douglas.

"Already taken some. You'll be thinking it's from too much sex."

"Em, no, I hadn't been thinking that at all."

"Well you'd be right. I've been having no sex at all. Mrs Wiseman continues to persecute me in all areas of my life."

Douglas quickly hit his ball.

"You know Joanie pretty well, eh?" said Dr Wiseman as they left the tee.

"Joanie? I don't know her all that well."

"She speaks highly of you. If truth be told, Douglas, she is the cause of my wife's rage. She suspects that I have a bit of a thing for Joanie, and she may not be wrong."

For the remainder of the round, Douglas tried to change the topic of conversation, but Dr Wiseman returned to discussion of Joanie. He wanted to know whether it was 'crazy for an old chap like me to think I might make it with a lovely young thing like her'. Douglas told him he did not think it was crazy, and said he knew Joanie thought well of him.

Douglas's earlier feeling of uneasiness had given way to one of surreality, as his consultant appeared to seek relationship counselling. Distanced from concerns about his golf swing, he covered the last four holes in level par and won the match.

"You came on to a great game," said Dr Wiseman. "Well played. Even if your victory does make it impossible for me to give you a good reference, eh? But many thanks for the game and for your advice."

Douglas drove home thinking how curious it was that both Dr Wiseman and Joanie seemed to feel he had given them advice. If their relationship did not work out, would they think he had given the wrong advice?

****

His letters were done now by a typing pool, and Douglas had asked Morag to handle his correspondence with the General Medical Council. Morag telephoned to say that she had signed for a registered letter.

Following the positive predictions from colleagues, Douglas had been further heartened by reassuring contact with his Medical Defence Union. The experienced doctor there had written to the GMC with a strong rebuttal of the allegations and told him that 'in my experience of similar cases, common sense does prevail'. He was thus feeling relaxed as Morag handed him the letter.

It came from a firm of London based solicitors on behalf of the GMC.

Cowdrey, Frost and Johnston: Solicitors to the General Medical Council

To: Dr Douglas Barker,
Senior House Officer in Psychiatry
Hillend Hospital.

842-6 Holborn Crescent,
London
28th April 1982

Dear Dr Barker,

GENERAL MEDICAL COUNCIL: COMPLAINT

On behalf of the General Medical Council, notice is hereby given that in consequence of a complaint made against you to the Council, an Inquiry is to be held into the following charges:

"That, as a registered medical practitioner, while providing psychiatric care to Ms Lucy Campbell:

(a) You expressed sexual feelings towards Ms Campbell and suggested that you and she might engage together in sexual activities,

(b) You conducted an unnecessary and inappropriately intimate physical examination upon Ms Campbell in your hospital office,

(c) You visited Ms Campbell's flat where you and she engaged in full sexual intercourse,

(d) Through the above actions, you abused your position during the care of a vulnerable patient with a psychiatric disorder and that, in relation to these alleged facts, you have been guilty of Serious Professional Misconduct."

Notice is further given to you that on Monday the 26th day of July 1982, a meeting of the Professional Conduct Committee will commence at the London premises of the Council at 10 a.m. in order to consider these charges against you, and to determine whether to erase your name from the Medical Register or to suspend your registration therein. In the meantime, you may continue to practise.

You may appear in person, or be represented by any counsel or solicitor of your choosing, or by any member of your family. If you choose not to appear in person, the Committee have the power to hear and decide upon the said charge in your absence.

Yours sincerely,
Cowdrey, Frost and Johnston
Solicitors to the General Medical Council'

Douglas' hand shook as he passed the letter to Morag.

"What do you think of that?" he asked, and watched as Morag's face registered progressive puzzlement and concern.

"You poor man!" she said. "This is absurd. I know it's serious, but it's completely absurd."

Douglas slumped in his seat.

"The GMC don't think it's absurd," he said.

"But it's the word of a disturbed patient against yours, Douglas. How can they entertain it?"

"I've no idea, Morag. They did get the first bit right. She was my patient in February. But the rest is pure fantasy."

"I don't think anyone down there has a clue *what* they are doing," said Morag with an angry snort.

Douglas stood up and sighed heavily.

"I guess I should speak with Dr Cumming from the Defence Union again. He sounds ancient on the phone, but very sensible."

He got straight through to Dr Cumming and read him the solicitors' letter.

"I am surprised," said Dr Cumming. "*Very* surprised. First thing to do is to get you a solicitor. I'll brief him and then you can come through to Glasgow and meet up with both of us?"

"OK," said Douglas. "But what do you make of it?"

"My first hunch is that there's more to it than meets the eye. You've had no other complaints against you, I take it?"

"No, none," said Douglas indignantly. "Well, none that I know about."

"That's probably none, then. Once we've got a solicitor involved we can try to make some inquiries—solicitor to solicitor—with their people. We can try to find out where the GMC's coming from. If you can come over in two or three weeks, hopefully things will be clearer by then."

For the first time, Douglas felt seriously worried about the GMC. If they were stupid enough to entertain this crazy complaint, could they be trusted to reach sensible conclusions?

****

"This is gonnae be hellish," said Chris. "The GMC thing disnae happen till the end o' July, so until then ye'll be mopin' about and I'll have tae do that supportive psychotherapy stuff on ye."

"It's you who needs the supportive psychotherapy," said Douglas. "Three nil."

His football team had beaten Chris' team on the preceding Saturday.

"A fluke, a minor setback," said Chris. "We're still gonnae win the league."

"Aberdeen's going to pip you at the post."

"We'll see. Talkin' about Aberdeen, Mandy's mum's comin' doon from the wild north the first weekend in June. I've been meanin' tae mention it."

"You want me to meet up with her? Tell her you're not as dreadful as you seem?"

"No. In fact, Doug, I'm wantin' ye *no'* tae meet up wi' her. Mandy thinks you and her mum meetin' might be tricky and I can see her point. Introducin' her mum tae me, and then tae my flatmate, the ex-boyfriend bastard that took her tae Greece? All a bit complicated."

"OK, I can nip out to the library or the pub."

"Aye, but Mandy's got these two new girls in her flat, right? So we were wonderin' if her mum could stay here. While you were no' here, if ye're gettin' me?"

"That's a funny arrangement if you ask me. You'll need to get hoovering and dusting and changing sheets. But my psychiatric training has helped me to recognise when I'm not wanted. I can go to my dad's for the weekend."

"That's good o' ye, Doug."

"You'll have time to expand your wardrobe even further. But perhaps there won't be long enough for elocution lessons to take effect."

"Mandy's mum speaks real broad, apparently. She's from Fraserburgh. We'll probably no' understand a word we say tae each other."

"The two of you might get on then. But it's serious stuff, is it not, Chris—when you meet the mother?"

"Aye, it does feel a bit serious. But I like her a lot. More than any lassie I've known."

"I would never have guessed," said Douglas.

****

"I could see myself lying peacefully in the bath. I was still a wee girl, and I was talking to my father who was sitting on the edge of the bath" said Hannah, one of the patients in the Small Group. "And then he got up and said, 'it's time to go', and he left and I started to get sucked down towards the end of the bath. I was sucked down into a sort of straitjacket."

"How did it end?" asked Norman.

"I woke up in a panic, tangled in the bedclothes."

Norman nodded slowly, with his eyes closed, and then looked round the group.

"You may not know this, Hannah," he said, "but did you experience a difficult birth?"

"That *is* a funny question," said Hannah.

"Even by Norman's standards," said Michael with a laugh.

"I don't know about my birth," said Hannah, "but I can ask my mum."

"I had a difficult birth," said Michael. "A 48-hour labour, mother kept telling me."

"You called her 'mother', not 'mom'. It's a breakthrough!" said Robbie, a young man who spoke only occasionally.

"Perhaps not surprisingly," said Norman, "my question did not seem like a funny one to me. You awoke in a panic,

Hannah. Through the daytime you often experience panic. And *your* main symptom when you first came to us, Michael, was anxiety."

"I'm sure this must be going somewhere," said Michael.

"The distinguished analyst, Otto Rank, wrote about the origins of anxiety," said Norman.

"It's fight or flight, isn't it?" said Michael.

"Physiologically, that may well be the case," continued Norman, apparently irritated by the interruptions, "but Rank was asking a *psychological* question. He was asking where anxiety comes from *originally*. And he concluded that it arose from the *trauma of the birth experience*. The expulsion from the safe haven of the warm womb—perhaps the bath in your dream, Hannah—is for all of us a traumatic and unsettling event. For Otto Rank, the anxiety invoked during our birth becomes the prototype of all future anxiety."

Michael was looking round the group, grinning widely. Nobody seemed keen to meet his eye.

"What about rebirthing? They do it in America," said Robbie. "Maybe that would help Michael."

"Ha, ha, Robbie, very funny," said Michael.

"Rebirthing is something entirely different," said Pauline.

"I had a weird dream too," said Diane, looking towards Norman. "I was going to mention it to Dr Barker, to Douglas."

"Are you able to tell the group?" asked Douglas.

"It was horrible. But I will tell you about it. My brother died, as you know," said Diane, taking a deep breath. "I often dream that I'm back at his funeral, but this was different. He was in his coffin, behind the minister who saying nice things about him, and then the coffin lid comes up slowly and my brother stands up—alive. I've suddenly got a gun—a rifle—and I shoot my brother, lots of times. He collapses back into his coffin but nobody seems to hear it or see it. Nobody except me. And the funeral just carries on, as if nothing has happened."

She sobbed, and Michael reached over to take her hand.

"And do you remember how you felt during the dream?" asked Norman.

"That was the worst thing," said Diane. "I felt pleased. When I shot him, I was happy."

"A puzzling emotion for you, Diane," said Norman.

He went on to suggest that Diane's and Hannah's dreams could be discussed further in their individual therapy sessions.

Norman, Pauline and Douglas went to the ward office to review the group. Pauline smiled at Douglas.

"I'm not an anxious person," she said. "Does that mean I had an easy birth experience, Norman?"

"You sound sceptical," said Norman.

"I was reading," said Douglas, "that the prototype of anxiety comes a long time before the birth experience. No doubt you've heard of implantation anxiety?"

"No, I've missed that," said Pauline.

"R.D. Laing wrote about it," Douglas continued. "As I understand it, there we are, the fertilised egg in the fallopian tube. We swim to the top of the uterus and then we have the horrifying thought that we might slip right past the endometrium—the lining of the womb, in case you nurses have forgotten—and come straight out the other end. It's the fear that you might never get implanted in the uterus at all, and begin and end your life as a fertilised egg. Now there's a scary thought."

"He must have been taking the piss," said Pauline.

"I don't think that would have been his intention," said Norman, "but the theory does stretch even my imagination."

"You don't have to answer this, Norman," said Douglas, "but do you always believe everything you say in that group?"

Norman pressed his fingertips together.

"I endeavour to be sincere," he said. "Today, I was not outlining my own theory on the cause of anxiety."

"Do you say outlandish things to relax the patients? To give them permission to talk about almost anything they want?" asked Douglas.

"Even if that were true, Douglas, I could hardly admit to such a strategy," said Norman.

"Perhaps if you hadn't talked about Otto Rank, Diane wouldn't have told us about her dream," said Pauline.

"Who knows? It was quite some dream, was it not?" said Norman. "Women, of course, feel disadvantaged, from infancy onwards, by their lack of a penis—forgive me, Pauline—and Diane's wish fulfilment in her dream is clearly to produce an oversized penis and to kill her brother with it."

"I think you do believe that," said Douglas.

"That she wanted to rape and kill her brother, at a subconscious level? I believe *that*, indeed I do. And speaking of women with murderous fantasies, Douglas, I hear that your General Medical Council are taking Lucy seriously."

Norman and Pauline commiserated with him about his situation with the GMC.

"But at least now I know that my anxiety has little to do with that," said Douglas, "and it was probably due to getting stuck during labour. Or maybe because the umbilical cord was cut too quickly."

"Your black humour may be an asset, Douglas. It is unfortunate that we have heard no more of Lucy. It hampers us in reaching a full understanding of her motives," said Norman.

"It seems pretty simple to me," said Pauline. "She fancied him and she couldn't have him, and she's the kind of person who'll do anything to get her own back."

"I hope you know you can count on my support," said Norman.

****

Douglas arrived early at the Medical Defence Union building for his appointment with Dr Cumming. In the waiting room, among the many women's magazines, he finally found a Golf Monthly. It was hard to focus on the article debating Nick Faldo's chances of winning the Open Championship at Troon. There had been something about entering the old, imposing building and something about the severe demeanour of the receptionist that underlined the seriousness of his situation. At best, the inquiry was going to be very stressful. At worst, he would no longer be able to practise as a doctor.

Dr Frank Cumming emerged, exactly on time, through the door that bore his name. He looked very similar to the picture Douglas had formed from their telephone conversations. He was over sixty years old, he stooped slightly, he had a shock of unruly white hair and he wore a battered tweed jacket.

"Dr Barker, Douglas," he said. "You look just as I thought you would from our phone conversations. Perhaps a bit taller than I imagined."

226

As they entered Dr Cumming's office, a dainty man in an elegant suit stood up and extended his hand.

"Vincent Green," he said. "I am your solicitor, at Dr Cumming's request. You can of course fire me at any time."

Douglas was shown to a seat at the end of the long table, as Dr Cumming and Mr Green returned to their places on either side of him. There was a high pile of papers in front of Dr Cumming.

They started by asking him details about his undergraduate and postgraduate careers. It seemed that Dr Cumming already had most of this information and was confirming its accuracy.

"We've been researching you already, Douglas," he said at one point.

They moved on to ask about his current post and his six months with Dr Burlington's team, before questioning him in detail about his contact with Lucy Campbell.

"And you have never visited her flat?" asked Vincent Green at the end of Douglas's account.

"No, of course not!"

Mr Green put his hand on the table in front of Douglas.

"I'm on your side, Douglas," he said. "In London, the GMC barrister will not be on your side. He will behave like an enemy. And he will ask you much nastier questions than that one. Your own barrister will be pleasant and supportive, but the GMC's man will not be."

"So you're not my barrister?" asked Douglas.

"We should have clarified," said Dr Cumming. "Vince is your solicitor, so he does the research, makes the case—"

"Does the donkey work," said Vince Green.

"Specialised donkey work, Vince, as you well know," Dr Cumming continued. "He will be there in London, guiding the barrister, consulting with you. Our defence union would not have deployed him on your behalf unless we knew him to be excellent. Even if he does look a little young and trendy."

"It keeps on getting more complicated than I thought it was," said Douglas.

"Yes, no doubt it does. I've been doing this job for twenty years and I still forget what a bewildering thing it can be, especially for a young doctor. Are you needing a cup of tea?" asked Dr Cumming.

Douglas shook his head.

"One thing we need from you," said Vince, "is a photo-copy of all Lucy Campbell's notes. The most important thing, of course, will be your own notes about her. These will be available to the GMC too."

"I mentioned to you on the phone, Douglas," said Dr Cumming, "that Vince would try to make contact with the solicitors at the GMC. The old boys' network of legal people sometimes gives out more information than might be shared with mere mortals."

"They were their usual frosty selves," said Vince. "I ended up telling them there was no evidence of any wrong-doing on your part. I said I would push to see the minutes of their Preliminary Proceedings Committee and/or to secure a motion dropping the charges against you. At this point they divulged that there was more 'evidence', as they called it, over and above the statement from Lucy Campbell. Inci-dentally, the chap I spoke to said that he interviewed Lucy Campbell and found her to be 'sincere and mature'. I found that a bit of a surprise."

"Perhaps she can come across like that," said Douglas, "even if I never saw it."

"Anyway," said Vince, "they said they had a photograph. They refused to say more, except that it 'supported the charges' made by Lucy Campbell."

"A photograph of what?" asked Douglas.

"They wouldn't tell me a thing. And they said they also have a letter from 'another source', which they got in January."

"January? Before I ever met her?"

"Indeed," Vince confirmed. "They refused to identify the author of the letter. All their solicitor said was that the GMC 'harboured additional concerns about Dr Barker's professional conduct' when they considered the letter alongside Lucy Campbell's complaint."

"So what could it be? Another complaint?" asked Douglas.

"If the GMC had received a formal complaint, then they would probably have investigated it—if they had taken it seriously. They seem to have taken this letter seriously, so you would have heard about it if it had been a complaint."

"I've had no dealings with them at all before this," said Douglas. "It doesn't make any sense to me."

"Maybe a note from a disenchanted patient?" said Dr Cumming. "Did you have any of them?"

"Probably. But I can't think of any."

"Keep thinking," said Vince. "It seems they want to play it close to their chests and produce rabbits out of a hat at the Inquiry."

"Douglas," said Dr Cumming, "you are looking very fearful. I can understand that. But in my experience, if you haven't done it, then you haven't done it, and a personable young man like you will walk away unscathed."

Despite further reassurances, Douglas was anxious and dazed as he walked to the railway station. He calculated the time until the inquiry at a little less than ten weeks—sixty-seven days—and he wondered how slowly those days might pass.

****

Billy Franks was quieter and more constrained.

"I've come straight from the workshop in my overalls," he said.

Billy was attending three days each week and was enjoying learning to frame pictures. He said he liked the company and 'having something to get up for'. He was sleeping and eating much more regularly.

"I see Anne on Mondays," said Billy. "She told me I had to take my lithium or I wouldn't get to go to the workshop. We sort of made a deal."

"Anne's not daft."

"She's not. She's an awful nice lassie. You'll have heard the news about her, though? Her man was killed in the Falklands."

"I had no idea," said Douglas.

"He was on one of the ships that went down. I feel real bad about it. The first day I was there I was soundin' off about the whole Falklands thing. I was sayin' it was ridiculous to be down there at all, and if the Argies were occupyin' the Isle of Skye then how happy would we be about it? That's what I think, and I can't stand Thatcher, so that doesn't help. But I shouldn't have said it, because then Anne tells me that her man's in the navy, and he's down there fightin' for the country and so on."

"You weren't to know," said Douglas.

"No, but I just wish I had held my tongue. Especially now. Now that he's dead. And she's off this week, so I can't say sorry to her. It was the picture framing instructor who told us. He thought we needed to know. Maybe so that blabbermouths like me don't say the wrong thing when she comes back."

"I'm sure you won't, now you know."

"Aye. The whole thing does make you think though," said Billy.

June 1982

Douglas left early for his father's house on the Saturday morning when Mandy and her mother were coming to stay.

"Your father wants to convene a meeting about this Medical Council business. He suggested that we do it after lunch," said Belinda within a few minutes of his arrival.

"That sounds a bit formal," said Douglas.

"He thinks it will save you repeating yourself and we can hear what everyone thinks."

It was soon apparent to Douglas that his father was more positive in his outlook. He seemed to have regained control during the past two months. He and Belinda had spent time travelling in Ireland, and his father described this as 'most enjoyable despite the weather'. He had resumed gardening, and told Douglas he must return in a month to sample his potatoes. He was looking forward to watching cricket on TV over the summer 'not interrupted by work, if perhaps by Belinda'.

Tom's final exams were imminent, and he had moved back home to 'escape the rowdy elements—the students like Douglas used to be'. For someone so close to his finals, Tom seemed relaxed, and it was clear that Belinda was very happy to have him there.

Douglas felt it was likely to spoil a contented atmosphere when they gathered to discuss the GMC situation. Belinda started proceedings.

"You've spoken to Tom and your dad on the phone, and they probably understand it better than I do. But who are these GMC people, Douglas?"

"They're the body in charge of doctors," he told her. "Like the Law Society with lawyers, I suppose. They regulate doctors and medical students, and they decide whether you can practise medicine or not."

"But who are they? Doctors?" Belinda asked.

"Yes, doctors. Though my consultant says they're "failed doctors". He says that any doctor who wants to sit in judgement over other doctors shouldn't be allowed to do it," said Douglas.

"Someone has to do it, surely," said his father. "But go back to the beginning and tell us about this girl who complained."

Douglas started by describing the way the psychotherapy ward operated. He recounted details of the sessions with Lucy and her behaviour thereafter. He had brought the letters from the GMC with him and he passed these round.

"Who's on these committees?" asked Tom. "Would psychiatrists have looked at this?"

"I don't know," said Douglas.

"And what's wrong with the girl? Explain, please, for the lay person," said his father.

"Well, she could be psychotic—mad. She might have delusions that I loved her and that we had a relationship. But it's more likely she's got a hysterical personality disorder."

"And that means what?" asked his father.

Douglas described to his family the characteristics of people with hysterical personalities, concluding with:

"Their whole life is a drama. And if you cross them, if you don't give them what they want when they want it, they can be very unforgiving."

"As you're discovering," said Tom.

"She sounds just like Polly who used to work at the library," said Belinda. "She caused chaos and we had to get rid of her."

"It's quite common," said Douglas, "especially in milder forms. It's like traits on a spectrum, and the people we say have a 'disorder' are along at the severe end of it."

"However you look at it," said his father, "this woman is obviously crazy. But move on—tell us what happens from here."

Douglas described the meeting with Dr Cumming and Vince Green, and his understanding of what might happen at the inquiry. By the time he finished, Belinda was tearful, and put her hand on Douglas's.

"This is all *so unfair*. A nice, well-meaning young man like you, and you have to put up with *this*!"

"Steady on, Belinda," said Charles Barker. "Any more wailing and weeping and these two might be diagnosing you."

"Belinda's emotions are real ones, that's the difference," said Tom.

"Anyway," said Charles, "cream will always rise to the top. We should not be despondent."

After further comments and reassurances, his father ushered Douglas into the garden. From an exposition on his plans for a pond, Charles had moved on to strategies for controlling moss in the lawn when Belinda shouted through the kitchen window.

"Douglas, your sister's on the phone."

Helen knew that they had been discussing his 'brush with the authorities', as she called it, and said she was sure that 'your usual charm and chat will see you through'.

"Dad sounds better on the phone—more positive," she said.

"He is," Douglas agreed. "And he's looking better—leaner and fitter. Who would have thought it at his birthday weekend? I haven't seen him so cheerful in years."

"Unlike Alex and me," said Helen. "I'm knackered, even if the nausea and sickness are better than at this stage with the twins. I think it *must* be a girl."

"I suppose it is generally the males in your life who cause the problems."

"Alex is much the same," she said. "But he is going to work now for a couple of hours in the afternoons. His doctor did refer him to a psychiatrist, but he's still waiting for the appointment. Could you hurry things up? My baby's due in eleven weeks."

"It's out of my hands, Helen. Some services just have long waiting lists."

"No strings you can pull?"

"No, none."

Douglas enjoyed the rest of his weekend there. As he said to Tom, it felt 'more like a family' than at any time since the start of his mother's terminal illness. After checking on the Sunday afternoon with Chris that there was 'no longer a woman in my bed', Douglas headed back to the flat.

****

"You've been evading my subtle hints all week. So spill the beans. How did it go with Mandy and your future mother-in-law? Was it a three in a bed romp all weekend?" said Douglas after work in the pub.

"Ask me a serious question and I just might answer ye," said Chris.

"Please, if you will, Christopher, describe events with your current girlfriend, Amanda, and her mother, who together resided at our humble abode last weekend."

"I'll ignore yir sarcasm. It wis good. A bit difficult, but good. That's only the second girlfriend's mother I've met and it's no' easy, is it?"

"I've only met two mothers as well. There was Spider's mum, of course. She's fine and I'm still in touch with her. But then there was Frances. Her mum was a violent alcoholic, and I've managed to avoid mothers since."

"Well Trish wisnae violent and she wisnae an alcoholic. She wis good fun."

"So it's 'Trish', is it? That sounds cosy."

"It wis quite cosy, actually. Once Mandy relaxed. We had a fine meal out on the Saturday night, and then Mandy cooked lunch on the Sunday. I'll probably go up there wi' Mandy later in the summer. Meet her dad, and that. He's a golfer, plays up north o' Aberdeen."

"Gee, Chris. This all sounds like serious stuff!"

"You and me are different when it comes tae women. Hares and tortoises, or somethin' like that. Though you do seem tae have been a hibernatin' animal since the New Year. But maybe ye'll soon be sniffin' around that Anne lassie again now her man's no longer wi' us?"

"Even by your own high standards," said Douglas, "that is a distasteful comment, with the chap hardly cold in his coffin. I've heard she's devastated. Another pint?"

"Ye'll notice that I've drunk less than half o' mine. Changed days."

"You've been waxing lyrical about Mandy and Trish and playing golf up north. You've been speaking instead of drinking."

"Nah, Doug. Ever since the GMC have been on yir back, yir drinkin' has been creepin' up."

"Poacher turned gamekeeper! You bastard!"

"It maybe takes a drinker tae spot another drinker. That's all I'm sayin'. You said it tae me and noo I'm sayin' it tae you."

"Thank you, Holy Willie. Any other advice?"

"Aye. Get me a packet o' crisps wi' my pint," said Chris.

****

The ward staff noticed changes in Diane. She had started to eat more, albeit in an erratic fashion, with evening binges on bread and chocolate. She went to the pub on a few occasions, having previously avoided the calories in alcohol. She seemed both more anxious and more animated, and she wanted to go out running every day.

"She is coming to the boil," Norman remarked, "but she still needs to *run away* from whatever is boiling up."

In their individual meetings, Douglas had become accustomed to Diane's being quiet and controlled. This time, she was fidgety and animated. Her hair had been cut short, accentuating her eyes, and she was looking at him more directly than usual as they discussed her eating and her weight. She changed the subject abruptly.

"Norman said in the group last week that we can't always love people just because they aren't here. Just because they are dead. He said it to Michael and Patricia, but I've been thinking about it a lot."

"About your brother?" asked Douglas.

Diane put her hands under her thighs and stared at the floor for a long time.

"It's my birthday on Saturday," she said finally. "I'll be twenty-one, like Lewis was when he died. My parents want me to go home for a family party."

"That would be nice, wouldn't it?"

"Nice!? What would be *nice* about it?" demanded Diane.

It was the first time Douglas had seen her angry.

"I'm sorry," she continued, "but it wouldn't be nice at all. For one thing, it would be what they did with my brother. It would be as much about him as about me. They're still grieving, and every family get together seems to boil down to his absence. My sister feels the same."

"You said that was one thing. What were the others?" asked Douglas.

Diane was shredding a tissue and again gazing at the floor.

"I'll tell you something that I think Norman already knows. He hints at it. My eighteenth birthday was a big deal, a bit like they want things to be on Saturday. Afterwards I went out with friends. I was eighteen, officially able to drink, officially able to get drunk."

Diane again sounded angry.

"My friends got me home and put me to bed. I was pleased that my parents had gone out. But Lewis hadn't. He came into my room. I don't have to spell it out. He called it his 'birthday present'. Not just that time, but when he did it again. He called it another instalment of his birthday present."

"That's awful," said Douglas, swallowing hard. "It happened a lot of times?"

"I lost count. Maybe five or six or seven. And he made me do things."

"It was still going on when he died?"

"That's the thing. I got better at avoiding him, but yes, it was still happening. So when he died, when he crashed his new car, it was like I had been *willing it to happen*. He died, and I was pleased. I was actually *pleased*."

Diane started to sob and Douglas rummaged in his drawer.

"Tissues—they're here somewhere," he said, before handing her the box.

"Can I ask," he said, "if your parents had any idea what was going on?"

"None at all. Lewis could do no wrong in their eyes. He never could, then or now."

"So they still don't know?"

"And I'm not going to tell them," she said decisively. "But maybe you could tell Norman? I don't want to discuss it in the groups."

"I can understand that. And I will tell Norman. It's a bit of a bombshell," said Douglas.

"It feels like a bombshell to me too. Like it could make everything explode," said Diane.

They discussed how Diane might handle the proposed birthday celebrations with her parents, and the session ended. Douglas was quickly on the telephone, inviting Norman to come round to his office.

"She's right, of course," said Norman, after hearing about the session, "it is hardly a surprise. But then I have been the therapist in her Small Group for a year. Her ambivalence towards her brother has at times been transparent."

"What about my sessions with her? Any tips?" asked Douglas.

"You make therapy sound like a horse race, or a plumbing manual, but I can appreciate your struggle to do what is best for the girl. She is clearly guilty and ashamed, apart from anything else."

"She was very ashamed to be pleased that her brother was dead."

"Indeed, and her shame will perhaps have different, additional sources. The victims of incest often feel shame and guilt, as if they had brought it upon themselves. As if, wittingly or unwittingly, they had *encouraged* the abuse, fearing that their own emerging sexuality had almost made them a legitimate target. There is much that we do not yet know. Your task, in my view, is to tread gently but firmly in your individual sessions. You need to help her to explore, but not in a voyeuristic fashion. You must not, in any sense, abuse her again through your therapy. Yet you must not retreat from the exploration. If you do, then she may perceive your retreat as not just a lack of interest and involvement, but as evidence that you also blame her. Evidence that you too might feel ashamed and disgusted by her, thus confirming her own feelings. You have a delicate balance to strike."

"It sounds like a tightrope," said Douglas.

"I hope I can provide something of a safety net," said Norman. "For both of you. In a few short weeks, Douglas, you will be moving on to another new post in your training. Unlike what the man says on TV, 'you have started but you cannot finish'. Six months of psychotherapy is sometimes like a ship passing in the night. I may suggest to Bill that I become her individual therapist following your departure."

"I thought for a moment that you called me 'a shit passing in the night', but you didn't, did you? Thanks for coming round. Your tips have been helpful," said Douglas.

Norman sat back in his chair and smiled.

****

Douglas went up to Morag's office to collect the photocopies of Lucy's notes. Morag brushed his thanks aside, and he handed her a letter.

"This came in yesterday from Vince Green. Depressing stuff," he said.

Morag read the letter.

"He says he remains confident of a positive outcome," she said.

"Yes, but he's not that confident, is he? Or why would he ask for 'statements supporting your work and your character in the event that you are found guilty of serious professional misconduct', or something very like that?"

"You almost quoted the man accurately, but he wrote '*in the most unlikely event* that you were to be found guilty'. It's a contingency plan. *If* you are found guilty. Who have you asked?"

"Who have I asked? To provide the character references? Well, nobody."

"Who were you going to ask?"

"I'm Scottish, Morag. I can't start asking people to say nice things about me. And if I am found guilty, then what good will it do to have people telling the GMC that Dr Barker is actually a nice guy? When they believe I go around having sex with my patients?"

"Neither of us knows how these GMC people operate, Douglas. As I say, it's a contingency plan."

"I'll think about it," he conceded.

Morag quizzed him about how he was switching off from his 'GMC ordeal'. He told her he had joined Sami's cricket team and was 'losing to Chris at golf'. She advised him to start using his recipe book and to buy a smart suit for London.

****

In the Small Group Michael suggested that he might be ready to go home. This seemed to surprise the group members who told him he had not been there for very long. They asked him why he thought he was well enough to leave.

"I feel much better, "he said. "I've been here nearly four months. Isn't that long enough to get well?"

The other patients looked at each other. Most of them had been there much longer.

Two days later, there was talk about work, and Michael suggested that he could soon return to the bank.

"What about your manager?" asked Hannah. "You've told us how difficult he is."

"Somehow he doesn't seem as difficult to me now," said Michael.

"You've practised in the Group with authority figures like Norman and Douglas. Maybe that has helped," said Hannah.

"And maybe you've been here too long yourself, Hannah, if you're saying stuff like that," said Robbie.

"Douglas isn't an authority figure," said Michael. "He's too nice. And he's too young."

Norman had pressed his fingertips together beneath his chin. The patients knew this was a prelude to his speaking, and they waited.

"Your comments are revealing on at least two levels, Michael," he said. "You do not regard Douglas as an authority figure. Doctors constitute authority figures for most people. You say he is too young, and yet your manager at work is also young. Indeed, perhaps this is one of the reasons that he has been a particularly challenging authority figure. You did not demur, I noted, when Hannah suggested that I may represent an authority figure to you."

"He's been practising on you," said Diane.

"Have I?" asked Michael, looking perplexed.

"That was certainly my impression," said Norman, "and it seems noteworthy that Diane corroborates this impression, in line with Hannah's earlier suggestion."

"Michael likes to challenge you, to spar with you," said Diane to Norman.

"Indeed," said Norman. "I have felt sometimes like one of those large faces on a fairground stall at whom Michael has been throwing balls. I dodge the balls, if I can, or if I cannot, my task is to spring back up."

"What a strange picture that is," said Michael.

"I am explaining my feelings," said Norman, "by way of an analogy. I feel that I have been the authority figure at

243

whom you have thrown the balls, the one you wish to knock down. Douglas, on the other hand, might represent the warmer, the more caring side of authority for you. The side that can be loved. While at the same time, your anger towards authority figures—your father who left and then died, your mother who needed you too much to let *you* leave—was projected on to me."

"That sounds right," said Douglas.

"Maybe," Michael said doubtfully.

Norman went on to espouse a theory that Michael had been terrified of his own anger towards authority figures, fearing that this anger might be so powerful as to destroy both them and himself.

"When I bounced back from your barrage of balls, as it were," said Norman, "you saw you could be angry, and that was OK—I survived and you survived."

"Well, I hadn't thought about it like that at all," said Michael. "You might be right. And I guess if I were to disagree with you, then it would just back up your argument."

"I hope you didn't mind me not seeing you as an authority figure," said Michael on the day of his discharge.

"Not really," said Douglas. "Perhaps as I get older I'll get a bit more gravitas."

"More gravitas, less friendly?" said Michael. "I think it's been the feeling of having friends in here that has made the biggest difference."

"I suppose people get better for a lot of different reasons," said Douglas.

"For me, it's been the friendships—feeling accepted, feeling part of something."

"Nothing to do with releasing your repressed anger towards authority figures, then?" asked Douglas.

"I don't think so. But maybe I'm in denial. Maybe that means I should have agreed to stay for another few months," said Michael.

July 1982

Douglas tried not to whimper as he limped into town. His right shoe felt as if it were embedded in his Achilles tendon. He had put on his dress shoes, hoping to match them with a new suit for the GMC hearing, and now wished that he had not.

Seeing a bench under a tree, he sat down and removed his shoe and sock. His heel was bleeding. He found a crusted handkerchief in his pocket, and applied it to the wound. While he was doing this, someone sat on the bench beside him.

"Do you need any help with that, doctor?" a woman asked him.

It took Douglas a few seconds to register that it was Anne, the occupational therapist. She had lost weight, and she looked gaunt, but she also seemed amused at his predicament. Douglas was flustered.

"Hi, hullo," he said. "Shoes I don't normally wear. Hellish blister. I've come to buy a suit. But how are you?"

"I've got tissues. You might be less likely to get an infection from them than from that tramp's rag you seem to have found," she said.

Anne extracted a wad of tissues from her bag.

"Put your leg up here," she said, indicating her knee. "It's lucky I was passing."

She applied the tissues to his heel and then secured them with adhesive tape.

"That's a well-stocked handbag," said Douglas, feeling a little more at ease now that he was sitting upright and replacing his shoe. "I haven't seen you."

"No, you haven't."

"I was very sorry to hear about your fiancé."

"We weren't engaged."

"No, but—maybe you don't want to talk about it?"

"I have been talking about it," she said, putting her hand fleetingly on his arm. "Almost too much. I've met two wives locally who are in the same boat, as it were. We plan to go on meeting up. There's a lot to say. It happened six weeks ago, but it feels like a lifetime."

"It probably does."

"Look, Douglas," said Anne abruptly, "you may not be the best person to talk to about this. About Gareth. And I know you have your own worries. News travels."

"The GMC? It is a worry. But nothing compared to your situation."

"I'll survive," said Anne, shutting her handbag decisively.

Her hand was shaking, and Douglas resisted his impulse to reach for it.

"Do you want to go for a drink?" he asked.

"It's ten o'clock in the morning, Douglas."

"I didn't mean now. Sometime."

"I don't know," she said as she stood up. "A coffee might be better. Maybe in a few weeks? We might both be in better shape by then."

Douglas continued to sit on the bench and gazed after her until he lost her among the shoppers.

****

"Thank you for sending copies of the case records promptly," said Vince Green.

Douglas stood up to relieve the now familiar cramping in his bowel whenever GMC related matters were discussed. He wished the cord on his telephone was longer so that he could have walked around his office.

"There are a couple of points to discuss," Vince continued. "I'll be starting to brief the barrister this week, so we need to be clear on a strategy, start thinking about any witnesses we might want to call."

"Yes, witnesses," said Douglas.

"I was very pleased to see your own notes. These were detailed and legible. They'll give the GMC a good impression of your competence. Perhaps needless to say, you should re-read the notes since the GMC barrister will no doubt be picking over them in his cross examination."

The cramping in Douglas's bowel worsened.

"It was also helpful," Vince continued, "to see the entry from Joanie Smith, registrar in psychiatry. Her description of Lucy Campbell tallies closely with your own. She mentions erotomania and delusions. Not to put too fine a point on it, do you think we shall be able to demonstrate that the girl is crazy, psychotic?"

"I'm not sure," said Douglas. "We never found any other delusions, apart from thinking that I loved her. So probably not."

"That's a pity. And if we were to try to make her out to be a crazy and fail, then we might lose sympathy with the panel. Are you still there, Douglas?"

He had been silent for several seconds.

"I was just thinking," he said.

"To move on to the nursing records," said Vince, "these are also detailed. There's a long exposition from Norman Snoddy, Charge Nurse, mainly hypothesising about the absence of a father figure in Lucy Campbell's early life. It's the sort of thing the GMC would probably consider to be psychiatric waffle. I thought I'd mention that in case you were going to offer up any similar theories during your own evidence in London."

"I wasn't planning to."

"Good. There's another detailed entry by a staff nurse on the day Lucy Campbell left hospital. It looks like it's signed by Pauline someone."

"Pauline Brown," Douglas told him.

"It's a helpful entry for us," said Vince. "She wrote about Lucy Campbell's 'erratic and unreasonable behaviour' and her 'irrational claims about Dr Barker's feelings for her'. That's good stuff. What's she like, this Pauline Brown?"

"She's nice. Sensible."

"Could be a good witness then. I'll discuss it all with our barrister, Simpson Stone. You'll like him. He went to a posh school and that seems to impress the GMC. I've only lost one case down there when Mr Stone has been on board."

"Let's hope it doesn't become two," said Douglas.

"I can't see it. Chin up. I'll speak to you again in London if there's nothing else to clarify on the phone before that."

Douglas went round to the ward, hoping to find a nurse to chat to about anything other than the GMC.

****

"You're due to see Diane this afternoon," Norman said.

Douglas had missed that morning's Small Group, and Norman and Pauline had come round to his office.

"We thought we should update you about her before then," said Norman. "Do you want to start, Pauline? You were there last night."

"Where should I begin?" said Pauline, fiddling with an earring. "Last weekend, Diane decided to tell her little sister about Lewis—the dead brother—tell her about the sexual abuse. Her sister has been struggling, apparently, and Diane told the sister about Lewis in case it had happened to her as well. So that her sister could get help if she needed it. The sister's fourteen now, I think."

Douglas nodded.

"So Diane thought she'd be old enough to understand. Luckily, Lewis hadn't done anything to the sister. Is she called Barbara?"

Douglas nodded again.

"Barbara was horrified," Pauline continued. "And although Diane had sworn her to secrecy, she couldn't keep it to herself and she told her mum. Her mum then told her dad, and he came charging in here last night, shouting at Diane."

"*Shouting at Diane*?" Douglas echoed.

"He said he didn't believe a word of it. Diane was a liar, she was sick in the head. That's the edited version. His language was something else. We had to butt in and ask him to leave."

Pauline said that Diane had been "completely in pieces" since. The other patients, having heard her father, brought it all into the Small Group, and gave her much needed support, clearly believing Diane's account of events with her brother.

Douglas expressed his astonishment that she could be disbelieved by her parents.

"In my experience, it is not uncommon," said Norman. "It can be easier to believe that someone lied, or imagined events, rather than to think that a family member may have behaved in such a depraved manner," said Norman.

"And the family idealize Lewis," said Pauline.

"Since his death," said Norman, "he has become the perfect son who can have done no wrong. And nothing must threaten to explode that myth for Diane's father, it seems."

"How is she now?" asked Douglas.

Pauline told him that Diane was asleep, with her friend Hannah sitting beside her bed.

"So she probably won't be fit to see me this afternoon?" said Douglas.

"You sound hopeful that she might not be, Douglas," Norman observed, "but it is important that you do see her. We must not retreat from her. We must not mirror her father's behaviour."

"I don't think I'll know where to start," said Douglas.

"The beginning is the most usual place," said Norman. "In this instance, I would ask her to recount exactly what she told her sister and how she told her."

Douglas exhaled loudly and shook his head.

"If you like, Douglas, I could see her with you," offered Norman.

"Could you really?" asked Douglas.

"I could and I would," said Norman. "I have only paperwork scheduled. Also, as we discussed, I mentioned to Bill the possibility that I might take up her individual therapy following your departure. Bill agreed, and if we were to see her together today it could perhaps be something of a transitional session. Then I could continue to see her thereafter."

Douglas sighed with relief.

****

Diane was deathly pale, and she sat even more rigidly still than usual. She was quite composed but Douglas was happy when Norman took the lead. He questioned her meticulously about the discussion with her sister, clarified her motives for telling Barbara and praised her for taking this altruistic risk.

"But isn't this exactly what can happen when you start to tell people things?" said Diane through her first sobs.

"People can become upset, of course," said Norman. "But if the alternative is to exert an iron control over your own suppressed emotions, over your own secrets, is this a price worth paying?"

"It will never be the same again," said Diane. "I've broken my family apart."

"You are the victim, Diane, not the perpetrator," said Norman. "Would you really wish to have lived the rest of your life harbouring a secret—harbouring a *lie*—and tolerating, each time you saw your family, their idealised picture of your brother?"

"I don't know, Norman. I don't know what's worse. I don't know what could be worse than this."

They moved on to talk about her father's fury. Norman said it was 'very early days', and that it was impossible to know whether her father might become calmer and more disposed to listen to Diane's account of events. With clear trepidation, Diane agreed to Norman's suggestion that a family meeting might be convened a few weeks hence.

After the session, Douglas said to Norman:

"I'm very glad you were here. I learned a lot from listening to you."

"Contrary to what you seem to think, Douglas," said Norman, "I did not do well. I became *involved*, I became *emotional*. I *told* Diane things and I asked her very leading questions, when I should have been exploring. I should have explored what *she* thought and felt, not expressed what *I* thought and felt."

"But you needed to support her," said Douglas.

"I did feel a very strong impulse to protect her."

"I can't see what's wrong with that. Surely she needs support and protection."

"Countertransference, Douglas. My own need to be the good father she does not have at present. My need to show her that not all men are angry or abusive or unsupportive."

"Gosh," said Douglas. "It seemed to go pretty well under the circumstances."

"You are kind, even if you are insightless, Douglas. Her circumstances are indeed difficult. I have seen similar situations before. They can end up being therapeutic, for both the patient and her family. Or they can split a family so far apart that there is no point of return. For Diane, I am optimistic of a good outcome. She has many strengths as well as many problems," said Norman.

****

"So," said Dr Wiseman, "since you'll be enjoying a wee trip to London next week, this is our last formal get together, eh?"

Despite the irritant effects of the pipe smoke on his eyes, Douglas would miss his supervision sessions in Bill Wiseman's office. They talked about where Douglas might be working in his next post.

"Joanie's heard already. She's off to Child Psychiatry." said Dr Wiseman. "She's been beautifying our new flat. She's a natural nest builder. I do want to thank you again for your part in getting us together."

"Well, I—"

"Joanie's very grateful too, of course. My wife isn't, naturally. So keep out of her way, eh?"

"I've never met your wife."

"Anyway enough about me. It's your session, not mine. What do you want to talk about?"

They discussed Diane, and Dr Wiseman advised him, 'for your own education', to hear about developments by keeping in touch with Norman.

"See if you can get him out for a few pints, eh?" suggested Dr Wiseman. "I'm supposed to give you trainees feedback, advice and so on at the end of your time here, so I talked to Norman myself. He's seen you at close quarters in the groups. We agreed about you."

Dr Wiseman waved the stem of his pipe in Douglas's direction and continued.

"You're a sound chap. Steady and sensible. But don't become a psychotherapist, eh? It's not that you don't see things in the patients. You often do. And they like you. But no, you're a bit too extraverted, a bit too *practical*. Psychotherapists are usually deep thinkers. I don't know if you've noticed, but I'm not always a deep thinker myself. Norman is. Norman can *keep himself back*. I struggle with that. As far as I can see, you can hardly do it at all."

He held up one hand towards Douglas and put the pipe back in his mouth with the other.

"That's not a criticism, Douglas," he continued. "Just an observation, eh? Would you want to be a psychotherapist?"

"I've found it very interesting working here," said Douglas tentatively.

"I'll take that as a 'no'. Unless I'm completely wrong, you'll be a pretty decent psychiatrist. Norman agreed with that. And a bit of psychotherapy will always come in handy, no matter what area of psychiatry you end up in, eh?"

"I'm sure you're right."

"Anyway, Douglas, what about your friends at the GMC? Do you want to talk about that?"

"Not really," said Douglas. "Stay calm and respectful was your take home message when we discussed it last week."

Dr Wiseman nodded emphatically.

****

"Thank you, chef, that was another excellent curry," said Douglas.

"Well now ye can get on wi' the washin' up," said Chris. "As soon as this GMC thing's over, I'll stop feelin' sorry fir ye and ye can do some cookin' yersel'."

"You might feel even sorrier for me if I get struck off."

"At least then ye would have plenty of time tae learn tae cook. And bake. And dae a' the housework."

"It's an exciting prospect," said Douglas, as he took the plates over to the sink. "Perhaps if I were cooking then the kitchen might look a bit less like a bombsite. Just look at this mess."

Chris snatched the mop from Douglas's hand and reminded him that he was due to contact his father. His sister Helen answered his father's telephone.

"Gosh," Douglas said. "I didn't expect you to be there."

"Well I am. I've been here for a week," said Helen.

"Alex and the twins with you?"

"The boys are," said Helen, sounding clipped and bitter, "but Alex is not. He has gone to stay with his mother—'for a break', as he described it."

"I suppose that might be good for him. He's not far away when he's at his mother's, so he'll be able to keep in touch with you and the boys."

"How could it *possibly* be good for him?" Helen demanded. "How could it possibly help to be with that battle axe? She's an old crone. I've never heard her have a good word to say about anyone."

"I suppose you do get people like that," said Douglas.

"It was straight after he finally saw the psychiatrist that he went back to mummy," said Helen. "It was hardly a coincidence. The psychiatrist must have told him to do it."

"I don't think he would have. Maybe it was one of the options they discussed."

"*She.* The psychiatrist is a woman. I hoped she might have had more sense."

"So you're up there for a break yourself?"

"A break? Yes, well it's the start of the school holidays. Belinda and Dad are hovering. I'll pass you over."

"Just a quick hello from me, Douglas," said Belinda.

She was pleased to have Helen and the twins there, but when they got on to the subject of the GMC, the telephone went silent. Douglas heard muttering before he heard his father.

"Sorry, son. Belinda getting emotional again. I had to tell her to get a grip, go away and do something. Tearful women aren't much of a help, are they?"

They talked about Tom who had passed his exams and was now on holiday with medical student friends.

"I shall send you a copy of your young brother's graduation photograph," said Charles. "He managed to look very presentable on the day. We are very proud of you both, Douglas. I hope you know that."

It was Douglas's turn to feel emotional.

"Thanks, Dad," he managed to say.

"Any further word from your legal people?"

"Nothing new. I have to go early on Monday to meet with Vince Green and the barrister chap."

"I wish I could do something useful," said his father. "Something to help."

"Vince Green's very optimistic, Dad. He says it'll last two days, three at the most. I'm on holiday after that. Perhaps I could come and see you for a few days?"

"Do that very thing, Douglas. You may manage to talk some sense into that sister of yours if she's still here."

"We all have our limitations, Dad."

"Look after yourself, son. I'd better go and check on Belinda. The very best of good luck."

His father rang off rather abruptly, and Douglas went through to sit with Chris.

"Dad and Belinda seem even more worried about the GMC than I am," he said.

"That sounded like yir sister ye were speakin' to," said Chris.

"Alex has gone to stay with his mum. It was quite good speaking to her. She didn't mention the GMC once."

"OK, I'll no' mention them either. But Mandy said tae tell ye she hopes ye get away wi' it. And would ye no' like me tae pretend tae be the GMC lawyer cross examinin' ye about all the patients ye've been shaggin'? We could do a role play. Would ye no' like the practice?"

"No, I wouldn't," said Douglas. "What's on TV?"

****

Dr Wiseman had told Douglas to 'disappear at lunchtime on Friday', and at the start of the Small Group Norman announced that it was Douglas's last morning.

"It's a pity that you're leaving us now, just before your court case. I hope that goes well for you," said Diane.

Douglas could not conceal his surprise.

"You didn't think we knew about it?" asked Hannah.

"I didn't," said Douglas. "It's, eh, not exactly a court case."

"What is it then?" asked Robbie.

"Perhaps Douglas doesn't want to talk about it," said Hannah.

Douglas felt like one of the patients. He hesitated, and looked round the group.

"I think the group has a dilemma," said Norman. "Douglas has been a therapist here, a doctor, who has been invested with the authority of a parental figure. And parents seldom openly discuss their difficulties."

"It might be better if they did," said Patricia.

"Douglas is hardly a parent figure," said Hannah.

"And we're not children," said Robbie.

"If I might say so," said Norman, "you are responding to my observations in a somewhat concrete manner. I am talking about *boundaries.* There are boundaries which it is sometimes best to observe and respect. There are boundaries that people can step over, accidentally or deliberately, and then regret having done so."

"So we shouldn't ask our parents things and we shouldn't ask Douglas about his court case?" said Patricia.

"We're talking about Douglas as if he wasn't here," said Diane.

The group members looked at Douglas in unison.

"It's an inquiry, a hearing," he said, "at the General Medical Council. I can't really talk about it, actually. It's about a patient."

"We know it's about Lucy," said Diane.

"There's not many secrets around here," said Hannah.

"She was very strange," said Diane.

"Whatever she says you did to her, we're sure you didn't. She talked rubbish when she was here," said Hannah.

"What did she say he did?" asked Judith, a patient who had recently joined the group.

Norman cleared his throat loudly.

"As Douglas has indicated," he said, "this particular topic should not be pursued further. You can see it, if you wish, as a parental secret. As an issue that perhaps draws attention to the need for boundaries with one's parents. An issue about setting boundaries and about the feelings that the boundaries may cause."

To Douglas's relief, the patients moved on to discuss relationships with their parents and he was able to sit quietly.

When the session finished, Hannah hugged him. Diane tearfully shook his hand.

"Thanks, Norman. You deflected them from cross examining me," Douglas said in the ward office.

"That was not my main intention," said Norman, "even if you did resemble a rabbit in the headlights."

"It looked deliberate to me."

"Patients, like all of us, are both intrigued and horrified by the activities of their parents. This is exemplified, of course, by the discovery that parents have sex. This morning the patients were confronted with this situation. They caught an intriguing but horrifying glimpse. Do they, or do they not, wish to step into the parental bedroom and see what is happening?"

"And I thought they were just being nosey," said Douglas.

"We have not made a psychotherapist out of you, Douglas, have we?"

"Maybe I'm a wee bit more of a psychotherapist than I was in January."

"Possibly. I hope you will keep in touch with us," said Norman.

Douglas went round to complete the emptying of his office. He had just picked up a bulging cardboard box when Joanie came in through the open door.

"Douglas!" she shouted. "I nearly missed you! Let me help you with your stuff."

He and Joanie managed to take his remaining possessions to his car in one journey.

"Just look at all this junk," said Joanie as they packed the car. "But it does include lots of psychotherapy books. I'm impressed."

As Douglas shut the car boot, he turned and Joanie grabbed him around the waist. He could not recall being hugged more tightly.

"Thank you for everything, Douglas," she said finally. "You've been marvellous. Tell that to those bastards at the GMC from me."

****

Douglas had been sitting on the end of his hotel bed for some time, long enough to become accustomed to the dingy walls, the smell of old cigarette smoke and the holes burned into the carpet by careless smokers. The room was without decoration of any sort, and he wondered if art works had been removed by previous occupants. It was a downmarket hotel in a scruffy area of London. At least it was within walking distance of the GMC headquarters and, by London standards, it was cheap. The GMC had not offered to pay for his accommodation.

On the day before, he had played cricket. He took three wickets, his team won and he hardly thought about the GMC all afternoon. He then diverted his attention from the inquiry by celebrating with his teammates well into Sunday morning. Until he got to the station, he focused on little else but his hangover. On the train, he sat across from two chatty middle-aged women. Once they discovered he was a doctor, the fat lady in the window seat quizzed him about her hip joints before moving on to her daughter's pregnancy. By the time they reached the Midlands, the slimmer woman was discussing details of her husband's colostomy.

He found the women irritating and distracting in fairly equal measure, and now in his hotel he could find nothing to

261

help him escape from thoughts about the inquiry. It felt like the night before an exam, but not like any exam he could prepare for. He had no notes and no text book. There was no syllabus, and there were no previous papers to help him anticipate the questions he might be asked.

He realised that he had been sitting for some time with his head in his hands. He was not hungry, but decided he would go for a meal. Then he would find a pub and have a few drinks. He did not know how else he might try to distract himself until it was late enough to go to bed.

****

It was a fairly short walk from his hotel to the GMC headquarters, and Douglas arrived early for his meeting with Vince Green and the barrister. A friendly receptionist showed him to a waiting room, saying that she would tell his counsel he was here. Had he not been feeling distanced and light headed, Douglas thought he might have found her quite sexy.

He had been waiting for less than a minute when Vince Green appeared in the doorway.

"I shall take you to our office through the Council's labyrinthine corridors," he said as he led Douglas briskly along the plush red carpet.

"Nice hotel?" he asked.

"Bit of a dump, actually," said Douglas.

"Perhaps I should have recommended somewhere," said Vince.

"It's only for a couple of nights. I just booked two nights."

"I'd be surprised if that's not long enough. They only have two witnesses," said Vince, as they arrived at a door marked 'Inquiry Counsel'.

A very tall man stood behind the desk, dressed in a black gown and wearing a wig. Douglas had expected less formal attire.

"This is Simpson Stone, your barrister," said Vince.

Three chairs were set out near the window of the large room.

"Let us sit over there, Dr Barker," said Simpson Stone, moving towards the window. "I have it on good medical authority that desks impede communication."

He rearranged the chairs by a few inches and indicated one of them to Douglas.

"You appear to be as terrified as most doctors in your position," he observed. "And perhaps you did not sleep soundly."

"No. I didn't," said Douglas.

"Mr Green has briefed me with his customary detail and precision. I have scrutinised the copies of Lucy Campbell's records—but perhaps I am going too fast. I take it that you feel prepared for today's proceedings? You have an idea of the shape events will take?"

"Only a pretty vague idea."

"Initially, you will sit and watch," said Mr Stone, "while they present their witnesses. They will lead and then I shall cross examine. You may or may not be called upon today. When you take the stand, I question you first and then the GMC will cross examine. Their barrister today, Eva Shapiro, is quite sharp. In my view, she can be a little *too* sharp, and may lose some sympathy as a result. You've seen her before, Vincent?"

"Twice," said Vince, "and I agree. Sharp but a little too abrasive."

"The Chairman of the panel today," Mr Stone continued, "is an academic pathologist, Professor Nelson. He has three doctors with him, along with a lay person. The five of them together are the judge and jury, as it were. They may also ask questions of the witnesses. You will soon get the picture once we are up and running. I shall be on one side of you and Mr Green will be on the other, so you can ask us if things require clarification as we proceed."

Douglas was unsure how much of Mr Stone's explanation he had followed. He had been trying, beneath the wig, to guess Mr Stone's age, while feeling slightly reassured by his relaxed manner and plummy vowels.

"It sounds like a law court," said Douglas.

"It is. They call it an inquiry, but in effect it is the same adversarial model that you will find in a court of law," said Mr Stone, reaching inside his gown to retrieve a pair of spectacles and opening the file that rested on his thighs.

"You may find it tiresome, Dr Barker," he said, "but I should like to rehearse a few details about Lucy Campbell."

Douglas once more described his contact with Lucy and his bewilderment about her complaints.

"The GMC has moved against several psychiatrists in recent years," said Mr Stone, "with regard to alleged sexual relationships with patients. I defended one such case. But this one differs in that it seems to comprise, essentially, a matter of Lucy Campbell's word against your own. Usually, there is more than one complainant, and/or there are external corroborating statements. Perhaps they will table written evidence, Vincent?"

"There was mention of written evidence, as I said. But we have no idea of its nature," said Vince.

"And they do have another witness," said Mr Stone. "One presumes he will be important to their case. A Dr Edwin Burlington."

"*Burlington? Dr Burlington!* What has it got to do with *him*?" exclaimed Douglas.

"That may become clear today," said Mr Stone, "but give us some clues, Dr Barker, if you would. Tell us about Dr Burlington."

"He's an arrogant, self-seeking idiot."

"Your assessment of his character may be useful to me when I come to question the man," said Mr Stone, "but what might be more helpful is an account of your relationship with him, along with any hunches you may have as to why the opposition might have called him as a witness."

Douglas attempted to summarise the difficulties he had encountered with Dr Burlington. As he described their differences of opinion about the diagnosis and management of patients, focussing mainly on Ina, and then their disagreement about the appointment of a liaison psychiatrist at the infirmary, Douglas appreciated that he sounded like a querulous junior doctor inappropriately questioning the wisdom of his consultant.

"We just didn't get on," he concluded rather weakly. "I'm not trying to say I knew better than he did. He was just very difficult to work for."

"So there was conflict between the two of you" said Mr Stone. "Vincent and I did rather assume that he was to be called as a character witness of the negative variety."

"Your secretary Morag tipped me off last week," said Vince, "after she heard he was coming here today."

Douglas blinked, trying to re-focus his vision.

"We've got our own character witness tomorrow," Vince continued. "Dr Jim Horsefall."

"Jim Horsefall? What can he have to say?" asked Douglas.

"Morag was quite clear in telling me he would be a good person to ask," said Vince. "And he kindly agreed to attend at short notice. He sounded keen on the telephone to defend your good name."

"We have probably chatted at sufficient length," said Simpson Stone. "We can talk further, if required, once we have taken our seats, but I tend to recommend an early arrival in the chamber for defendants, Dr Barker, in order to acclimatise to the novel surroundings. It usually helps to settle the nerves. So, shall we go?"

****

The chamber for the hearing did indeed comprise 'novel surroundings' for Douglas. The room was huge, and he took his place at a long table, flanked by Simpson Stone and Vince Green. The GMC legal team would sit at the table opposite, and to his left was a raised area for the chairman and his panel. To Douglas's right was a chair and a lectern where witnesses would give evidence. Vince Green pointed above the witness stand.

"That's the balcony for the public and the press."

"The *press*? What would the press be doing here?" asked Douglas.

"Oh, it will be in the papers," Vince told him. "Did you not get your photo taken at the front door when you came in?"

"No! No, I didn't."

"No need to sound so horrified, Douglas. You probably surprised them by coming early. Anyway, you're looking good for a picture. New suit?"

"Yes," said Douglas in a very small voice.

"Here come the opposition," said Vince, as the GMC legal team made their entrance.

Followed by two men carrying brief cases, the team was led by a wigged woman who swept in at high speed, her black gown flowing behind her. To Douglas's surprise, she wore a short skirt that revealed her plump thighs and a pink blouse over her large breasts. She glared at him as she passed.

The panel had meanwhile come in less theatrically from a door behind their own large table. The chairman, Douglas presumed, sat in the middle of the five panel members on a large red chair that resembled a throne. This would be Professor Nelson who, with his large bushy eyebrows, looked rather formidable. Without forewarning, he said sonorously:

"The defendant will please stand."

Douglas did not realise that this order was directed at him until Vince nudged his arm.

"Your full name, please," said the chairman.

"Dr Douglas Hamish Barker."

"Your date of birth?"

Douglas hesitated at this unexpected question.

"Em, twenty-ninth of July 1955," he said.

"You may now sit," said the chairman, "and we can introduce ourselves. I am Professor Nelson, Honorary Consultant Pathologist. I shall be chairing proceedings on behalf of the Council. Please identify yourselves in turn," he said to the panel, extending his left arm.

A man with very long sideburns at the end of the table said:

"Harold Davies, General Practitioner."

Next to him, a man wearing a blue bow tie announced briskly:

"Walcott, Consultant Physician."

"And on my immediate right," said the chairman.

"I'm Roland Grimshaw, Consultant Orthopaedic Surgeon," said a man with a neatly trimmed grey beard, smiling and making eye contact with Douglas.

The last panel member, who wore a red jumper and sat to Douglas's extreme left, also smiled.

"And I am the lay member of the panel, Philip Jones, a retired headmaster from Cardiff," he said.

Professor Nelson cleared his throat and glanced towards the balcony. Douglas saw that a sizeable crowd had gathered there.

"Miss Shapiro," said Professor Nelson, "do you wish to make an opening statement for the Council?"

The GMC's barrister stood up and walked round to the front of her table.

"I do indeed, sir," she said. "The panel has already viewed the statement of the complainant and an item of written evidence."

Her delivery was clipped and precise.

"We shall expand this evidence," she continued, striding over towards Douglas. "And we shall demonstrate that *this doctor*," as she pointed at him, her finger no more than eighteen inches from Douglas's nose, "has abused his trusted position as a junior psychiatrist. We shall demonstrate, beyond any reasonable doubt, that he conducted an inappropriate sexual relationship with his patient, our complainant."

She dropped her accusing finger and walked back to her own table, where she patted a pile of notes.

"We shall further demonstrate, sir," she said, "that this doctor's turpitude and immorality have not been confined to actions affecting today's complainant, and that his more general behaviour, not to mention his dubious competence, fulfil criteria for Serious Professional Misconduct, and that his name should thus be expunged from the Medical Register without delay. Thank you."

She pirouetted dramatically and returned to her seat.

"And Mr Stone," asked the chairman, "do you wish to make a statement on behalf of Dr Barker?"

"Not at this stage, sir," said Simpson Stone as he stood up. "It suffices to tell the panel that all charges are denied and will be vigorously contested."

"Very well," said Professor Nelson. "Miss Shapiro, please proceed to present your case."

"I shall indeed, sir. I call upon Miss Lucy Campbell to give evidence."

As a clerk scurried off to find Lucy, Miss Shapiro stood in front of her desk, staring at Douglas with an expression of distaste. Lucy appeared, demure in a dark skirt and jacket, with the clerk guiding her by the elbow as if her mobility or her eyesight was failing. She looked at the chair and at the lectern.

"Stand if you can," said the clerk softly.

Lucy took her place at the lectern, gripping the sides with white knuckles. Douglas thought she was trying to look as apprehensive and downtrodden as possible.

"Thank you for attending, Miss Campbell," said Professor Nelson. "Miss Shapiro will speak with you first, followed by questions from Mr Stone, and then the panel may have some additional points to raise with you. Is that clear?"

"Yes. Thank you," said Lucy quietly.

"It is difficult in this large room, Lucy, if I may call you that, to make yourself heard," said the chairman, "but if you could do your best to speak up loudly then this will facilitate proceedings."

"I'll try. I don't have a loud voice," she said.

"Before I proceed, sir, to interview Miss Campbell" said Miss Shapiro, "I would wish to move that I do so *in camera*. We shall be discussing Lucy Campbell's ordeal, we shall be hearing about Dr Barker's salacious behaviour, and—"

"Objection," said Simpson Stone, rising to his feet.

"Yes, Miss Shapiro," said Professor Nelson, "no leading statements, please. Continue."

"We shall be discussing Miss Campbell's ordeal, covering sexual events and details of her medical history. It does not seem unreasonable that the public, and employees of the various media, are excluded from listening to, and possibly reporting upon, such matters, and I would thus submit, sir, that her evidence is taken *in camera*."

The panel murmured and nodded to each other.

"We agree that this is an appropriate request," said Professor Norman. "Miss Campbell's evidence will be heard *in camera*. Please clear the public gallery."

Amidst some discontented mutterings, the balcony was cleared of spectators.

"Thank you," said Miss Shapiro, turning to Lucy Campbell. "Will it put you more at ease if I also refer to you as Lucy during your evidence?"

"Yes, that's fine," said Lucy.

Douglas thought she said it with a slight lisp.

"Can you tell us your age and occupation, Lucy."

"I'm twenty-three. I'm a bar worker, but I haven't been well enough to work since last October."

"Indeed. I understand that. You have raised the matter of your illness, and this is where we shall start. I would wish the panel to understand your illness in order to appreciate fully your frailty and vulnerability."

Miss Shapiro took Lucy slowly through her medical history from the point of her first contact with psychiatric services after repeated self-harm and failure to attend school at the age of fifteen, through two subsequent referrals with outpatient appointments, and then to her presentation in August 1981. She had been seen at the infirmary after taking several overdoses of painkillers, and then for some months in the psychiatry out-patient department before her admission in January.

"And when, Lucy, did you first encounter Dr Douglas Barker?" asked Miss Shapiro.

"I met Douglas—Dr Barker—in November, last November."

"And where did this meeting occur?"

"In the psychiatry out-patients, in the waiting room," said Lucy.

Douglas did not try to hide his incredulity.

"But you were not then his patient, Lucy?" Miss Shapiro continued.

"No, I wasn't. He came and sat in the waiting room and talked to me," said Lucy.

"*What*?" exclaimed Douglas.

"Please, Dr Barker," said the chairman, "you will have your say in due course. You must be silent while other witnesses testify."

271

"And what did Dr Barker say to you at that first meeting, Lucy?" asked Miss Shapiro.

"He told me who he was. He said he had just started in psychiatry and asked me why I was there. He said I was beautiful, and that he might be able to help me in other ways."

"And what did you take that statement to mean?"

"Sex," said Lucy. "He meant sex. He winked at me."

Vince Green and Simpson Stone both placed a hand on Douglas's arms.

"We'll get our chance to speak," whispered Mr Stone.

"So, in November," said Miss Shapiro, "Dr Douglas Barker made a clear sexual advance towards you while you were depressed and vulnerable. And then what happened?"

"He saw me there again a few weeks later. He sat down beside me and asked if I wanted 'a cosy get together', and he put his hand on my knee. But then the doctor came to get me for my appointment and it was just before Christmas when I met him in the street. It was late in the evening and I'd had a few drinks. He invited himself up to my flat."

"And then, Lucy?"

"And then we had sex," said Lucy, this time with a definite lisp.

"He persuaded you to have full sexual intercourse with him?"

"Yes," said Lucy demurely.

"Indeed," said Miss Shapiro, pausing to glower at Douglas. "He had sex with you, knowing you to be a psychiatric patient, exploiting your depression and your vulnerability, your frailty on this occasion being compounded by your intoxication with alcohol. Is this correct?"

"Yes," said Lucy, "it is."

She had not looked in Douglas's direction.

"And did you have sex with Douglas Barker on any further occasions, Lucy?" asked Miss Shapiro.

"Only after I was in hospital. After I was his patient."

"It is very difficult for you, Lucy, and I appreciate how upsetting it must be to recount," said Miss Shapiro, "but can you continue? Can you describe what happened?"

"The first time I went to Douglas Barker's office," said Lucy, glancing at him for the first time, "he told me to take off my clothes. He said it was a routine examination. And then he examined me, em, all over. It was intimate, you know. And he told me we could carry on where we left off—that's what he said—at my flat, the next weekend."

Douglas stared at her, willing her to meet his eye.

"So he took me to my flat again," Lucy continued, "and we had sex. After that he told me our relationship couldn't continue because I was his patient."

"So, he had sex with you twice, he subjected you to an unnecessary intimate examination, and then he announced that you and he would not be having a continuing sexual relationship. And how did this make you feel, Lucy?"

"I was very upset," said Lucy timidly, looking up at the panel. "I thought he loved me."

"I believe that we have seen, during Lucy's upsetting testimony," said Miss Shapiro, while pacing to and fro, "some ham acted innocence from Dr Barker—"

"Objection!" shouted Mr Stone.

"Sustained," Professor Nelson confirmed.

"And I would deem it timely," continued Miss Shapiro, "to introduce some confirmatory evidence."

She extended her hand towards one of her team and he passed her two envelopes. Miss Shapiro passed one on to Lucy.

"You have three copies of the same sheet, Lucy, as you will see. Perhaps you would like to read it to the panel," she said.

Lucy looked squarely at the chairman and read:

"My love is like a red, red rose

That's newly sprung in June."

"Thank you," said Miss Shapiro, taking the sheets from her. She walked to the chairman to give him one, smiled smugly at Simpson Stone as she gave one to him, and kept a copy in her hand.

"And tell us, Lucy, when you first saw this," she said.

"Douglas—Dr Barker—wrote it. In his office."

"We have, of course, checked this against Dr Barker's entries in the case records, and it does closely match his characteristic handwriting. But explain, please, Lucy, why he wrote these lines."

"It was to me," said Lucy. "My birthday is in June. He was saying he loved me."

"Where did this come from?" Vince whispered urgently.

"I've got no idea," Douglas whispered back. "I've never seen it before."

"A brief but clear love note," Miss Shapiro was saying. "It could hardly be anything else, as I am sure we would all accept."

She paused to look round the chamber.

"Before our further item of corroborative evidence is tabled," she continued, "I would ask you, Lucy, to divulge some personal information about Dr Barker. I do not wish to lead you here. But might I ask, if he were naked, would Dr Barker be recognisable from behind?"

Lucy seemed to stifle a giggle.

"Yes, he would," she said. "He has Australia on his bottom. It's a birthmark. It's just like the shape of Australia."

"Fortunately," Miss Shapiro announced, "it will not be necessary for Dr Barker to bare his buttocks publicly, I hope, in order to corroborate this statement."

She handed a photograph from the second envelope to Lucy.

"Could you please describe what you see, Lucy."

"It's a picture of a bottom. I can see Australia. It must be Douglas's bottom."

"Thank you, Lucy," said Miss Shapiro.

"The photograph was sent anonymously to the Council," she continued as she walked slowly past Douglas and his legal team, showing them the photograph as she went, before approaching the chairman and handing it to him.

"I would wish to submit as evidence this photograph of male buttocks, presumed to be those of Dr Barker, the defendant," she said.

"God almighty," Douglas whispered to his legal team, "that did look like me."

"And there, sir, I shall conclude my questioning of Lucy Campbell," said Miss Shapiro, before sweeping triumphantly past Douglas's table and returning to her own.

Douglas thought Lucy still looked amused by the photograph, but Professor Norman interpreted her demeanour differently.

"Are you able to continue, Lucy?" he asked. "Can you take questions from the defendant's counsel?"

"I can. I'm OK," she said.

Simpson Stone began by questioning her gently about her psychiatric history. It seemed that he was trying to gain her confidence, and perhaps to demonstrate that he did not wish to upset her gratuitously. Douglas glanced at the panel during this interchange. The chairman, the orthopaedic surgeon and the headmaster were attentive and appeared to be taking notes. The physician looked bored, and was the doctor with the long sideburns actually awake, he wondered.

"You have mentioned on several occasions, Miss Campbell," Mr Stone was saying, "that you were suffering from depression?"

"That's right," she said.

"And you have been prescribed antidepressant medications?"

"No, I haven't."

Simpson Stone looked to the panel and then turned back to Lucy.

"That perplexes me," he said. "You say you have been depressed and yet no doctor has prescribed antidepressants."

"No, they haven't."

"Doctors do get things wrong, of course. But you have seen a lot of doctors—well into double figures, I would think—and they all seem to have disagreed with your diagnosis. They have all seen things differently from how you see things, perhaps?"

"I have been very depressed at times," said Lucy with a catch in her voice.

"Oh, do please sit, Miss Campbell," said Mr Stone gallantly, "if my line of questioning is upsetting you."

"I will sit down," said Lucy quietly, as the clerk came forward to help her into the chair.

"We may return to the matter of your diagnosis, but I do have a small related point in the meantime. I see from your case records that a consultant in adolescent psychiatry, seeing you in 1975, wrote that he considered you to be a 'very creative thinker indeed'. What do you think he might have meant by that?"

"Objection," said Miss Shapiro. "He is asking the witness to interpret a medical statement."

"This is scarcely a medical statement," said Mr Stone.

"Please answer the question, Lucy," said Professor Nelson.

"I don't know what he meant. I would have been just sixteen then," she said.

"Perhaps it is not difficult to interpret," said Mr Stone. "Perhaps he meant that you were prone to tell tall stories, to make things up, just as—"

"Objection," shouted Miss Shapiro again.

"Sustained," said Professor Nelson. "You are answering your own question, Mr Stone."

"I shall move then," said Mr Stone, "to a *specific* story, the story about Dr Barker's alleged advances in the hospital waiting room. On the first occasion, Miss Campbell, from your earlier account, you seemed to suggest that Dr Barker must have spoken to you for quite some time?"

"A few minutes, yes," said Lucy.

"He sat beside you, in a busy hospital waiting room, in full view of staff and patients, you say on two occasions, even putting his hand upon your knee, and making sexual advances for several minutes?" asked Mr Stone with astonishment.

"There are private parts of the waiting room, places to sit for people who don't want to be seen. For people who don't want everyone to know that they're seeing a psychiatrist. For people like me," said Lucy, with slight petulance.

"So you were hiding yourself away from public view in a private area?"

"That's right."

"And yet Dr Barker saw you there, you allege? You claim that he saw you, as you hid from the public gaze, with sufficient clarity to cause him to visit his unwelcome sexual advances upon you, Miss Campbell? Come, come. How could this be?"

"I don't know," said Lucy emphatically. "He *just did*!"

Simpson Stone moved away from Lucy, with his back towards her, facing the panel, and slowly repeated:

"He just did. Hmmmm. Well, well."

He turned back towards Lucy.

"Let us move on. You mentioned, Miss Campbell, that Dr Barker subjected you to an intimate examination in his office."

"Yes, he did."

"And you were what—lying on a couch?"

"No. It's a small office," said Lucy. "He doesn't have a couch. I was on the floor."

"You were on the floor? Dr Barker told you to take off your clothes and to lie on the floor of his office for a physical examination? And you complied with this request?"

"Yes, he said I had to," said Lucy, this time with a pronounced lisp.

"And you complied. As a compliant person might comply," mused Mr Stone. "And yet, here we have that same '*compliant*' person competently bringing this serious complaint to the attention of the General Medical Council? Do I detect some creative thinking?"

"I had to complain," said Lucy adamantly, rising from her chair, "in case he did it to someone else."

"Hmmmm, in case he did it to someone else," said Mr Stone reflectively. "You highlight the point, albeit inadvertently, that it is perhaps surprising you are today's only complainant, if we are to believe that Douglas Barker prowls the hidden nooks and crannies of hospital waiting rooms, hunting for pretty girls to misuse. But, I feel we have listened to enough tall tales for one morning. I have no further questions."

Simpson Stone returned to his seat, after a disdainful glance at Lucy, and Douglas smiled at him grimly.

"That was good," he said.

"I would like to be sure, Lucy," said Professor Nelson, "that you would feel able to respond to points from our panel?"

"Yes, I'll try," she said.

"Any points? Questions, gentlemen?" he asked the panel.

"I have one," said Mr Grimshaw, the orthopaedic surgeon. "I was interested to read a copy of your case records, Lucy. You will not have seen these. Both Dr Barker and a Dr Smith wrote that you might have 'erotomania'. Do you know what that is?"

"No. I have no idea."

"They felt you had the illusion, or perhaps the *de*lusion, that Dr Barker had feelings for you when this was not actually the case. Is this possible, do you think?"

"No," said Lucy decisively. "He said he loved me. He had sex with me. He wrote that I was his red rose."

"So it couldn't have been your imagination, then?" asked Mr Grimshaw.

"No, it couldn't, not at all," said Lucy combatively.

"Thank you. That was my question," said Mr Grimshaw.

"Any other points from the panel?" asked the chairman, meeting with shakes of heads. "In that case, Lucy, thank you. You may now go."

Lucy smiled up at the panel as she departed, again being guided by the clerk.

"And there we shall end the morning session. You have a further witness, Miss Shapiro, and lunch is already slightly late. We shall reconvene at 2.15," pronounced Professor Nelson.

"Hang on a minute," said Vince Green, as Douglas started to get up.

"I need to get out of here. Go for a walk," said Douglas.

"Give Lucy Campbell a good start," Vince advised. "You don't want to bump into her in front of the press."

"The writing in the Burns poem does appear to be your own," said Mr Stone.

"It does, but I've no idea how she got it. And I've no idea who could have photographed my arse," said Douglas, shaking his head. "I feel like I'm going crazy myself."

"I have the impression of a resourceful girl, Dr Barker," said Mr Stone, "but also of someone whose malevolence will not ultimately hang together as a credible whole. At least that is what I am hoping."

"I have to go. If I see her, I'll run," said Douglas, before making his way out of the chamber at speed.

****

Douglas blundered out of the front door of the GMC headquarters, and headed for Regent's Park, stopping to buy

280

a sandwich *en route*. He found a fairly tranquil open space and sat on a bench to eat and to try to relax.

For the second time within half an hour, Douglas worried that he was becoming psychiatrically unwell. He thought he caught sight of movement, first near a large oak tree and then behind a rhododendron bush, but when he looked again more intently, he saw nothing there. He rubbed his forehead vigorously and returned to his sandwich. When he looked up again, he clearly saw a man in a checked shirt, partly obscured by bushes, training a long lens upon him. Another photographer emerged from behind the oak tree. Douglas jumped up, annoyed but relieved that he was not developing a paranoid psychosis, and spent the rest of the lunch break walking briskly.

Back in the GMC chamber, as Dr Burlington took the stand, Douglas tried to conceal his profuse sweating, fearing that he might appear anxious and guilty. He distracted himself by gazing at Dr Burlington's orange and green checked suit. Surely nobody could take this man seriously? Following introductions and questions elaborating Dr Burlington's professional background, Miss Shapiro asked him to explain why he had been called as a witness.

"I shall attempt to do just that, Miss Shapiro, Chairman," he said. "I had occasion, in January of this year, to write a letter in which I aired some cautionary deliberations about Douglas Barker to the General Medical Council, after he had been working in my team since the preceding August, and I—"

"Objection!" said Simpson Stone. "We have not had sight of this letter."

"It is not evidence in this case, sir," said Miss Shapiro to the chairman. "As Dr Burlington had begun to explain, it was a cautionary communication, marking the card, as it were, of a junior medical practitioner who was exhibiting worrying behaviour."

"Indeed, Mr Stone," said Professor Nelson, "while the letter in question is on file here with the Council, it does not relate specifically to this case, and there is no requirement for you to see it."

"Thank you, sir," said Miss Shapiro. "Dr Burlington?"

"I felt compelled," he continued, "to communicate, in epistolary format, my concerns about Dr Barker in three principal areas. Since they seem less germane to the current inquiry, I shall mention the first two areas with relative brevity. In clinical settings, he could be carelessly deficient, and yet he felt able to disparage energetically the considered views of his consultant. This point related to my second area of concern, in that his apparent disrespect for senior colleagues extended into overt criticism of one's carefully considered plans for the future configuration of our services. These were areas of significant concern, and in my view reflected a *worryingly anarchic attitude,* even though I have touched upon them only in outline today."

As he spoke, Miss Shapiro seemed disconcerted by Dr Burlington's characteristically addressing a point several feet above her head. Douglas wondered if she might be more accustomed to men addressing her breasts, and then wondered why he was wondering about this at such a time.

"And please explain, Dr Burlington, your third area of concern, a matter of close relevance to the current inquiry," Miss Shapiro said.

"Indeed I shall. The third area relates to potentially odious proclivities in the sexual aspects of Dr Barker's behaviour, and I shall describe a specific incident, if I may. One wishes to monitor closely the performance of one's juniors, in accordance with published GMC Guidelines, especially when there may be pointers to *causes for concern*, and I chose to visit Dr Barker in his office during a working day. I believe it was during October. The door was partly ajar, and upon opening it, I can report that I was horrified at the prevailing scene. There was Dr Barker, in his hospital office, consorting with an attractive young female patient. He had *removed his trousers*, and he seemed to be attempting to embrace her."

"He had no trousers on, Dr Burlington?" asked Miss Shapiro, looking around the chamber, and Douglas heard laughter from the public gallery.

"Indeed. The man was trouserless. Upon my arrival, he hurriedly replaced them, of course."

"And had you not arrived at his office when you did, doctor?"

"I am pleased that I did. One can only imagine what was about to occur," said Dr Burlington sombrely.

Again looking smug, Miss Shapiro turned to the panel.

"It seems that a pattern may be developing," she said. "I have no further questions for Dr Burlington."

"We need to talk about this," muttered Simpson Stone.

"I can explain," said Douglas.

"Mr Stone," said the chairman, "do you wish to question the witness?"

"I continue to feel, sir, that we should have received advance notice of the line of this testimony. I have no questions, since I have yet to discuss the matter with my client," said Mr Stone.

"And the panel?" asked Professor Nelson. "Any points for Dr Burlington?"

"If I might," said the Welsh headmaster, Philip Jones, "I would like to know what happened next. You say, doctor, that you found Douglas Barker without his trousers and with this young patient in his office. Then what happened?"

"I relayed my concerns, quite forcefully, and she left the office."

"She was fully dressed?"

"She was."

"And what did you and Dr Barker then say to each other?"

"I made it clear to him that his behaviour was horrendously inappropriate."

"And he said?" asked Philip Jones.

"He said very little. He mumbled that he had been changing his trousers. In his office, in the middle of the day. He later informed me that he was doing so as a prelude to leaving the hospital to play golf."

"I see," said Mr Jones. "Almost sufficiently unlikely to sound plausible?"

"Not to me," asserted Dr Burlington.

"And then there might have been two pairs of trousers in evidence, doctor? A pair for Dr Barker to work in, and another pair to play golf in?"

"Maybe. I do not recall."

"You do not recall. And it seems to me like an important detail," said Mr Jones.

Dr Burlington did not respond.

"If I might say this, doctor," continued Mr Jones, "it seems to me that you do not care much for Dr Barker. You do not seem to like him."

"My feelings—" started Dr Burlington.

"Objection," cried Miss Shapiro. "Irrelevant."

284

"I was making an observation," said Mr Jones.

"No need to answer, Dr Burlington," said Professor Nelson. "Are there other points? No? Then thank you for attending, doctor. You may stand down."

While Miss Shapiro was confirming that she had no other witnesses to present, his team were emphasising to Douglas that they needed to discuss the "no trousers incident". Simpson Stone stood and addressed the chairman.

"I wonder if I could request a brief break in proceedings, sir, before Dr Barker takes the stand?"

The physician beside the chairman was nodding approvingly at this suggestion, and Professor Nelson agreed.

"Very well. An opportune time for a cup of tea. We can resume in twenty minutes."

****

Douglas described to Simpson Stone and Vince Green events on the day when he was changing for golf and Carol burst into his office. Vince was amused but Mr Stone was unsmiling, referring to it as 'an added complication'.

This did not ease Douglas's anxieties as he took the stand. Even although the chairman and his panel were some distance away in the large chamber, Douglas found it unnerving to be looking directly at them as he spoke. In order to 'establish your solid credentials', as Simpson Stone had notified him, he was asked about successes in his career to date. His university blue in cricket was mentioned, drawing approval, Douglas thought, from the doctor with the long sideburns. Mr Stone questioned him benignly about his year in general medicine and his experiences during psychiatric training. Mr Stone then moved on to the incident with Carol, saying that he hoped 'we could lay this story to rest'. Douglas explained how the situation had arisen, while hearing titters from the public gallery behind him. The orthopaedic surgeon and the retired headmaster were also amused.

"And who was this patient, Dr Barker?" Simpson Stone asked him.

"She had come up on the train from Birmingham. She only stayed in the ward for a few days. She wasn't my patient," Douglas replied.

"And what was the nature of her illness?"

"They thought she was elated in her mood—hypomanic—or that she might have been taking drugs. She was disinhibited."

"So a disinhibited patient burst into your office uninvited where she found you in a state of partial undress. She was quickly followed by Dr Burlington, and he appears to have misconstrued the situation?"

"Yes, he did," Douglas agreed.

"It seems unfortunate that the GMC have not produced the patient in question to give evidence, does it not?" asked Mr Stone.

"It would have helped," said Douglas.

Miss Shapiro got to her feet.

"As a point of information, Chairman, the lady in question could not be traced. The Birmingham address in her case records did not exist. Indeed, she may also have given a false name to the psychiatrists."

Simpson Stone moved on to question Douglas about Lucy Campbell, establishing the details of his professional contact with her.

"And so that we are entirely clear," said Mr Stone, "you had not met Miss Campbell before she became your patient on the first of February this year."

"That's right. She did seem vaguely familiar, and I assumed I had seen her around the hospital in January."

Douglas proceeded to deny speaking to Lucy in the waiting room. He described her flirtatious behaviour while she was his patient, and he denied conducting a physical examination on her.

"And while she was a patient in the ward," said Simpson Stone, "she asserted that you had a relationship together. She said that you loved each other. And how did you respond to this?"

"I hadn't seen anything like it before," said Douglas. "We wondered if she might be deluded, psychotic, but she had no other delusions that we could find. So we thought she probably had erotomania."

"Please explain," said Mr Stone.

"Erotomania is when a person believes that someone eminent—usually someone like a politician, or a film star, or a singer—is in love with them, and it isn't true."

"And it will be noted that Dr Joanie Smith, as she recorded in Lucy Campbell's notes, also regarded this as the likely diagnosis," said Simpson Stone.

Simpson Stone walked away from Douglas and addressed the panel.

"So, we have a patient with delusions about a doctor, with delusions about a non-existent relationship with that doctor. And this is a patient who was recorded some years previously as having an overactive imagination. For reasons that are unclear, the General Medical Council has taken this patient's delusions seriously and has elected to pursue this innocent doctor. I have no further questions."

Professor Nelson asked Miss Shapiro if she had questions of her own.

"I most certainly do, sir," she said, rising to her feet and giving Simpson Stone a dismissive glance as he passed her.

"And I shall start with some clarification about the nature of erotomania," continued Miss Shapiro, standing beside Douglas and then wheeling abruptly towards him.

"Do patients with erotomania have special skills, special talents, doctor?" she demanded.

"Em, no, they don't," said Douglas.

"No psychic powers then?"

"No."

"What about X-ray vision, doctor, does that happen in erotomania?" asked Miss Shapiro teasingly.

"No, of course not."

"Thank you for that clarification. And yet, without psychic powers and without X-ray vision, Lucy Campbell was mysteriously able to describe a very particular birthmark on your left buttock, doctor? How can this be?"

"Em, I'm afraid, I just don't know," stammered Douglas.

"It is *very curious indeed*, is it not, doctor?" said Miss Shapiro to the panel. "And no doubt it is a matter to which we shall return in due course."

"If I might interrupt," said Professor Nelson, "I sense that your cross examination of Dr Barker will not be brief, Miss Shapiro?"

"No, it will not be brief, sir" she said, "nor will it need to be terrifically lengthy."

"Nonetheless, the clock has reached an hour," said the chairman, "from which we shall not be able to conclude that

288

aspect of proceedings this afternoon. We shall therefore complete Dr Barker's evidence in the morning."

The chairman pointed his pen at Douglas.

"I must tell you, Dr Barker," said Professor Nelson, "that since you are engaged in unfinished testimony under oath, you are deemed to be *in purdah* from now until the recommencement of proceedings tomorrow morning. That is to say, you are not permitted to associate with anyone who is involved in any way, or to otherwise discuss, any aspect of this case with any person during the intervening period. Is this clear to you?"

"I think so," said Douglas.

"Your legal team can clarify the parameters with you," said the chairman. "Today's proceedings are closed."

As the chamber emptied, Vince Green and Mr Stone explained that *purdah* was a legal safeguard against evidence being 'compromised' while a witness was in the middle of testimony, so Douglas must try to speak to nobody about the case and should attempt to remain as socially isolated as possible until the inquiry continued the following morning.

"But I can give you these to read, Douglas," said Vince Green, extracting an envelope from his brief case. "They might cheer you up this evening. It's the testimonials from colleagues and patients. Morag got them for you."

****

On the way back to his hotel, Douglas found a telephone box. Chris did not answer at the flat. He then had a faltering conversation with his father, attempting to reassure him and to explain why he could not discuss proceedings due to the *purdah* situation. His father sounded puzzled and anxious.

Douglas sat on his bed and surveyed provisions for the evening—a ham sandwich, two packets of crisps and three cans of beer. He looked at his watch. It was just after 6.30 and he anticipated a long night ahead. Perhaps, if he were careful not to talk to anyone, he could go for a walk later on. He wondered if it might be a dodgy neighbourhood after dark, but thought there should be some light until ten o'clock.

His only reading material was the package that Vince Green had given him. Along with a copy of a note from Morag to Vince saying that she had approached people 'because I anticipate that Dr Barker will be too shy to ask himself', there were four testimonials. The first was from Chris.

'Dear sirs,

DR DOUGLAS BARKER

Dr Barker and I met just less than a year ago when we started our psychiatry training together in August 1981. I do know him well, however, since we have shared a flat together for the last ten months.

While my opinion is not being asked here, I would like to record the fact that the charges against Dr Barker are completely bizarre and ridiculous. Whether the patient concerned is psychotic or malicious is open to question, but Dr Barker's innocence is not. As his flatmate, I would have to have known if anything like these allegations had been happening. So I can say that him being up in front of the GMC does not make any sense at all.

I have always found Dr Barker to be an honest and straightforward person. He takes his work as a psychiatrist very seriously and he reads a lot of books and papers. He is a very ethically minded doctor, and he talks respectfully about his patients for whom he shows a lot of care and concern. I cannot imagine him mistreating a patient in any way, let alone behaving as the GMC seem to think he might have done. He expects high standards of himself and of others working in medicine and he is very aware of his responsibilities in working with vulnerable patients. These are responsibilities that he would not abuse.

Yours faithfully,
Dr Christopher Dunn.'

Douglas struggled not to be upset by Chris' tone of indignation.

It took Douglas a few moments to see that the writer of the second testimonial, Mrs Mavis McKay, was his dead patient Ina's daughter.

'Dear Morag,

It was nice to hear from you on the phone yesterday. I wish it was a happier thing you had phoned about. But I am pleased to write and support Dr Douglas Barker. You did not give me details but I do understand that he is in trouble and you wanted to know what my experience of him had been like. As you know he looked after my mother (Ina Wylie) when she was ill in hospital last year. He was not involved at the beginning and she had been diagnosed with depression because of the death of my father. It was Dr Barker who was the first one to speak to my mother and me properly and he found out that it had nothing to do with my father. My mother had cancer and it was Dr Barker who found out about that too and got her the proper treatment. He is a very caring doctor and he went to visit her in the infirmary after she stopped being his patient. He phoned me after she died and asked if he could come to the funeral and he was crying when we spoke to him after it at the crematorium.

So he was the best doctor my mother saw and she saw quite a few. That is really all I can say but I hope it is helpful. I hope you are well yourself. As I said on the phone we all miss my mum but we are getting on with things.

With my sincere best wishes,
Mrs Mavis McKay.'

The next letter Barker looked at was from Bill Wiseman.

'To whom it may concern Private and confidential
Re: Dr Douglas Hamish Barker,
Senior House Officer training in Psychiatry.

In the context of current General Medical Council inquiries into allegations of Serious Professional Misconduct by the above named medical practitioner, I have been asked to provide reflections upon his work and his character.

Dr Barker came to our team in February of this year. Unusually, he had completed only six months of his psychiatric training—doctors coming to psychotherapy tend to have more experience—and thus I was especially delighted to note his balanced good sense and his maturity. He demonstrated sensitivity and insight in his approach to patients on our ward, most of whom had complex difficulties and needs. He is extravert and straightforward, and he quickly became a popular member of our team. He impresses as a young man who is honest and trustworthy; he is the type of person in whom one would happily entrust a personal confidence. This was a general perspective on Dr Barker in our unit, not only my own observation.

It is worth drawing attention to the fact that he is an accurate and fastidious note keeper. I anticipate that the Council will have paid close attention to his detailed recordings relating to the case that has given rise to the current inquiry, and I would underline that I have every faith in the accuracy and reliability of Dr Barker's written case records.

I am aware that this testimonial will not be required by the Council unless Dr Barker is found to be guilty of the charges against him, and thus I hope and anticipate that my reflections will prove to be redundant. Should members of the panel read these comments, therefore, then I would suggest that a grave miscarriage of justice has taken place, and that the utmost leniency should be exercised in determining the fate of this competent and trustworthy young doctor.

Signed,
Dr William J Wiseman,
Consultant Psychotherapist.'

The last testimonial was from Billy Franks.

'Dear Morag,

I understand that you will be passing on this letter about Dr Douglas Barker to the Medical Counsel in London. Please do that. I am very happy to speak up for him.

You did not want to discuss with me what the case is all about. But it gets discussed round the hospital. We know that a crazy woman is accusing him of having sex with her. He would not do that. No way.

You were wanting my personal opinion about Dr Douglas Barker because you knew that I knew him pretty well as one of his patients. He was on the ward a year ago when I was in and I got to know him then and he has been my own doctor for the last few months. This is a man you can trust, not like a lot of the doctors I have seen over the years. Others should be answering to the Medical Counsel but not him. You can speak to him and he listens. He does not look down on you. I have been ill off and on for a long time and I have seen a lot of psychiatrists but he is the first one who has got me taking my pills every day. And he fixed me up with work that is helping me. I think I am starting to turn things around and it is all credit to him. So I am pleased to speak up for him and if the doctors doing his trial think he did it then they are completely daft. Much dafter than I have ever been.

All the best to you and him,

Sincerely,

William (Billy) Franks.'

Douglas read each testimonial several times. Although he recognised that the context predisposed people to describe him in a positive light, he was touched by what had been written. Vince Green had been right; the letters did cheer him up.

He decided to have a three course meal—crisps, sandwich, crisps—and to drink a can of beer with each course. He had just opened his first packet of crisps when there was a loud knock at the door. To Douglas's amazement, it was Chris who walked in past him.

"Ye've got some beer in. Ye wir expectin' me."

"Far from it," said Douglas. "What on earth are you doing here?"

"Moral support fir the immoral. So how's it been goin'?"

"Sorry, Chris, but I can't tell you. I've started giving my evidence and there's this weird thing called *purdah*. Because

I'm in the middle, I can't speak to anyone about the case until after I'm finished."

"What? That's bizarre, is it no'? I've come doon tae keep ye off the drink, tae make sure ye're coherent when ye give yir evidence tomorrow. But ye've started drinkin' already and ye cannae speak about it?"

"I'm afraid not. I'm not allowed to speak to anyone."

"But we could go oot fir a quiet pint and talk about football or Freud, or somethin', eh?"

"No, we can't do that either. I've got to be socially isolated. But it was very nice of you to come down. Nearly as nice as that testimonial of yours. I've just read it. I didn't know you thought so well of me."

"Morag wis twistin' my arm tae come up wi' somethin' nice," said Chris, while extracting a crumpled envelope from his back pocket, "but what you got wis a copy o' my first draft. I've brought ye the one that actually went off tae the GMC."

"Yeah, well thanks anyway," said Douglas. "I'm really sorry you've had a wasted journey."

"Wasted? Who knows? I'll go out and about tonight. And if ye get finished tomorrow, I can chum ye back on the train. And I'll be there bright and early at the GMC, tae get intae the spectators' bit tae hear ye tryin' tae talk yir way oot o' it. But right, I get it," said Chris, raising his palm to Douglas and backing towards the door, "ye can say no more. So I'll leave ye tae yir nutritious tea and bugger off tae the bright lights o' London town."

After watching Chris stride purposefully down the corridor, Douglas started his first can of beer while saying "Cheers, Chris" to himself, and then opened the second draft of his testimonial.

'Dear GMC,

Re: Dr Douglas Barker

I have been asked, as his flatmate, to give a view about this man's character.

It would be fair to say that he is one of the most irritating people I have met. He is thoughtless and untidy. He gives unwanted advice when it has not been asked for, and seems to regard himself as an expert on most things, notably psychotherapy, women and drinking. As far as I know, the only one of these things he is good at is the last named.

He enjoys passing wind in company, especially in an enclosed space. He thinks of himself as a sportsman, but knows nothing about football, and can be easily beaten at golf. If he often seems entirely senseless, then this may not be all his fault, since he is so tall that not much blood will get up to his brain.

On the topic of his drinking, he seems to be unaware of its extent, even if he does find reason to criticise the consumption of other moderate drinkers he knows. His drinking is linked to his womanising, and he probably drinks so much that he gets lapses of memory. It seems quite likely to me that he has had sexual relationships with lots of his patients, probably of both genders, and even if he thinks he hasn't done this, then he has forgotten it due to alcohol induced amnesias.

I cannot see him changing and anticipate that you will throw the book at him.

Yours in hope,
Dr Christopher Dunn
P.S. Good luck you big useless bastard.'

****

Douglas spent much of the night trying to anticipate what Miss Shapiro might ask during the continuation of her cross examination and to rehearse possible answers. He had found her interrogation so unpredictable, however, that he started to imagine bizarre scenarios in which he was quizzed about his sexual history and his childhood. When he did fall asleep, he dreamt that he was responding to questions about toilet training while standing naked in the witness box.

In the cold light of day, as he prepared to give evidence again, his brain felt entirely scrambled. Vince Green had tried to give him supportive advice, the only part of which Douglas retained was to 'relax and be yourself', and his legs felt distant and rubbery as he took the stand.

"Please resume your questioning of Dr Barker, Miss Shapiro," said Professor Nelson rather unnecessarily, since she was already advancing towards Douglas.

With hands on hips, she stood staring at him for what felt like several minutes. Douglas tried to look past her into the middle distance.

"Good morning, doctor," she said finally. "Do you consider yourself to be an eminent person?"

"Me, eminent? No."

"Indeed, doctor, senior house officers in psychiatry are scarcely eminent people, are they?" she continued.

"No, they're not."

"I must have misunderstood then. You explained to us yesterday that so-called *erotomania* is when someone develops a delusion about an eminent person. And yet, as you have just confirmed, you are *not* eminent. So, surely, you would have to rethink your diagnosis."

"The person is not necessarily all that eminent. It often happens to doctors."

"I see," said Miss Shapiro, with her back to him, "so you are not *necessarily* eminent. But a bit eminent, maybe? Eminent enough for it to be much more likely that vulnerable female patients might comply with your sexual advances?"

"Objection," shouted Simpson Stone.

"Yes, Miss Shapiro," said Professor Nelson, "that is a quantum leap."

"Very well, I shall go in another direction," said Miss Shapiro. "Even if most directions may lead to similar conclusions about Dr Barker. I am sure we all recall yesterday's vivid evidence from consultant psychiatrist, Dr Edwin Burlington. We will have noted, *en passant*, that Dr Barker felt sufficiently eminent to contradict his consultant on matters relating to both patients and service planning, but I shall not focus on that. No. I shall return to Dr Barker's prurient sexual behaviour. How often, doctor," she asked, turning towards him, "could you be found in your office during an average working week without your trousers on?"

"Never," said Barker. "That was a one off. I was changing to play golf."

"While a patient was in your office?"

"No. She wasn't. She burst in."

"And she was an attractive patient?"

"Quite attractive. Yes."

"And what was her occupation, doctor?"

"A call girl, I think. She wasn't my patient."

"You thought correctly. She was indeed a *call girl*, she was a *prostitute*. And she *just happened* to burst into your office during the one and only time that you were there without your trousers?"

"That's what happened," said Douglas.

"Do I look naive to you, doctor? Do you take me—and do you take the panel here—for fools? Do you think we can accept this *utterly extraordinary* coincidence?"

"I'm telling you that's what happened. That's all I can say!" asserted Douglas, realising that he was nearly shouting.

"That is all you can say," repeated Miss Shapiro, as she walked back toward her team.

On cue, one of them handed her a sheet of paper. She walked back to Douglas.

"And what have you to say about this, doctor?" she demanded, waving the sheet in his face.

"What is it, please, Miss Shapiro?" the chairman asked with a little impatience.

"It is the Burns poem he wrote for Miss Campbell," said Miss Shapiro.

"Objection!" said Simpson Stone and Vince Green in unison.

"Is it your writing, Dr Barker?" Miss Shapiro demanded.

"It looks like it but I didn't write it," said Douglas.

"It is your writing, but you didn't write it, and yet Lucy Campbell gave it to us as evidence? Please explain."

"I can't explain," said Douglas forlornly. "I don't know how she got it."

Miss Shapiro turned to the panel and stretched out her arms with a look of theatrical incomprehension.

"Dr Barker denies the charges against him," she said, "and expects us to believe the *truly incredible coincidence* which he says gave rise to his being found undressed in his office with an attractive prostitute. And he expects us to believe that *somehow* his patient had seen a birthmark on his buttock, and that *somehow* she was in possession of a love poem in his handwriting that he did not write. *And yet,* he

299

seems to think that we should accept his innocence. *I think not!* And here, chairman, sir, I shall rest my case."

Miss Shapiro paused long enough to make eye contact with each panel member before returning to her seat.

"Do the panel members have questions for Dr Barker?" asked Professor Nelson.

School teacher Philip Jones raised his forefinger.

"Dr Barker," he said, "I did ask Dr Burlington, and I'd like to ask you. How did the two of you get on?"

"Not all that well," said Douglas.

"I thought that was plain from his testimony," said Mr Jones. "And perhaps his view of the events in your office with the young lady might have been coloured by that?"

"Yes, I think that's possible," said Douglas, with a small grateful smile.

"If there are no other points," said the chairman, "you can stand down, Dr Barker, and we shall have time to hear another witness before morning coffee."

As he turned to leave the witness stand, Douglas saw Jim Horsefall in the doorway of the chamber, incongruously giving Douglas a grin and a double thumbs up of encouragement.

As Jim was being sworn in, Douglas thought he was looking less eccentric than usual. He was wearing much larger spectacles, and perhaps this helped to make his head look less oversized.

Simpson Stone established that Jim had been the senior registrar on the ward, and asked his view about the relationship between Douglas and Dr Burlington.

"It was strained," said Jim. "The problem seemed to start with a disagreement about a patient, and it developed from there."

"And what was the nature of this disagreement?"

"Dr Burlington had concluded that an elderly female patient was grieving for her dead husband. Dr Barker—and I shared his view—thought she was clinically depressed. Dr Barker investigated the lady and found that she had bowel cancer. Dr Burlington did not take this well and he blamed Dr Barker for not discovering it earlier."

"And what would you have to say about Dr Burlington's attitude on this matter?"

"It was unreasonable. Dr Barker should have been praised rather than blamed," said Jim.

"So by the time of the incident witnessed by Dr Burlington in Dr Barker's office, their relationship was deteriorating. And this may have coloured Dr Burlington's perspective?"

"Indeed. It may well have done," Jim agreed.

"And you are familiar with the details of this incident?"

"Oh yes. It was widely discussed in the ward."

"Perhaps you could summarise these discussions for us," Simpson Stone requested.

"Certainly. The patient in question had come up on the train from the midlands. She was hypomanic, disinhibited. She had a habit of going into doctors' offices uninvited. She came into mine twice. She returned to the ward after going into Dr Barker's office and told everyone how funny it was that he had been changing his trousers."

"She specifically mentioned that Dr Barker had been *changing his trousers*. So he had not taken them off for her benefit?"

"Oh no."

"You sound very sure of that?" said Simpson Stone.

301

"I am," said Jim. "It was widely discussed, as I said. And it was my job to cover Dr Barker's clinical work when he went away to his lecture course. He was supposed to be going to lectures that afternoon. It was an open secret that he sometimes dodged his classes to play golf. I used to watch him and his friend leave from my office window."

"And you saw him on the afternoon in question?"

"Yes. His golfing partner was waiting at Dr Barker's car."

"And how could you be sure that they were going off to play golf, Dr Horsefall?"

"His friend had his golf clubs with him. And Dr Barker has these very distinctive golf trousers. You wouldn't wear them for anything else."

"And he was wearing them that day?"

"He was indeed," Jim confirmed, "when he went out to his car."

Simpson Stone folded his arms, paused and smiled.

"So, I shall attempt to summarise your views, Dr Horsefall," he said. "It seems clear that you had no doubt at all that Dr Barker was indeed changing into his golfing trousers when the patient came uninvited into his office, and that no sexual motive whatsoever for this incident could be inferred?"

"That would be an accurate summary," said Jim.

"No further questions from me, chairman," said Simpson Stone, with a slight bow of his head in the direction of the panel.

"Miss Shapiro? Any questions?" asked Professor Nelson.

Miss Shapiro looked decidedly less smug.

"The matter of why a doctor might take off his trousers in his office seems conjectural to me," she said, "but it is not a point I shall pursue further. I am concerned, however, that you have cast aspersions upon the evidence, and upon the motives, of consultant psychiatrist Dr Edwin Burlington. Do you still work with him, doctor?"

"This is my last week in that post," said Jim.

"Your inference seemed to be that you do not respect your consultant's judgement. Is this what you are saying?"

"To be frank with you," said Jim, looking at her squarely, "that is exactly what I am saying. In my view, the objectivity of Dr Burlington's judgement is open to question across a wide range of issues."

"Come, come, doctor, surely that is a most inappropriate comment," said Miss Shapiro crossly.

"Not in my view," said Jim. "Dr Burlington is arrogant and conceited, and he cannot tolerate people who disagree with him, especially if it happens to be a junior psychiatrist."

Miss Shapiro turned round, with her back to Jim Horsefall, and said to the panel:

"This is *insupportable*! I sense a strong whiff of conspiracy between the witness and the accused—"

"Objection!" shouted Simpson Stone.

"Quite so," Professor Nelson agreed. "That comment was entirely out of order. The witness is under oath. Do you have any other appropriate questions, Miss Shapiro?"

Miss Shapiro frowned, shook her head and walked back to her team with pursed lips.

The panel had no points to raise with Jim Horsefall, and the chairman announced that they would break for coffee. As Jim left the chamber, Douglas suppressed an impulse to run over and hug him.

"I thought he'd be good," said Vince Green.

"He was brilliant!" said Douglas.

"We spoke again to Pauline Brown this morning. I think she'll be helpful too. Simpson and I feel very optimistic. Enjoy your coffee, Douglas," said Vince.

****

Douglas was relaxing slightly in the small tea room until Miss Shapiro and her two associates came in. They gave him what felt like a rehearsed, synchronised scowl, and he retreated, carrying his coffee back into the chamber.

He wondered if Vince's confidence had been misplaced as Pauline was ushered towards the witness stand. She was wearing a black suit with a skirt that looked too short and revealing. She appeared flustered, and her characteristic blush was already evident.

Simpson Stone sensed Pauline's apprehension, and he went slowly through questions about her qualifications and her nursing career to date. He ascertained that Pauline had worked with Douglas in both of his psychiatric posts.

"It is fortuitous, Miss Brown," said Simpson Stone, "that you and Dr Barker have, in a sense, followed each other professionally for the last year. I think we have almost heard enough about the incident when Dr Barker was found in his office without his trousers. But perhaps, very briefly, you could tell us about that?"

Pauline was sufficiently relaxed to smile towards Douglas.

"I wasn't on duty that day," she said, "but I heard all about it. Dr Barker was changing into his golf outfit when the manic patient burst in on him."

"You have no doubts about this?"

"That's what everyone on the ward told me."

"Thank you, Miss Brown."

Simpson Stone paused to gaze pointedly at the opposition counsel before continuing.

"Let us move on to discuss the patient whose complaint is the principal reason we are here today. You looked after Lucy Campbell when she was in hospital?"

"I was her primary nurse while she was in the ward."

"And what impression did you form of her?"

"Is it OK to be completely honest?" asked Pauline uneasily. "She was a patient."

"You are under oath, Miss Brown. There is an obligation upon you to be completely honest," Mr Stone said.

Pauline looked relieved.

"I thought she had a severe personality disorder. She was a man hater, but out of nowhere she decided that Dr Barker was in love with her. She developed a fantasy that they had a relationship."

"She developed a *fantasy out of nowhere* about a relationship with Dr Barker, you say?"

"That's right."

"You may be aware of Lucy Campbell's allegations that she and Dr Barker had a sexual relationship. She alleges that he seduced her. She further alleges that he conducted an intimate physical examination in his office. Can you tell me how you respond to those claims?"

"They're ridiculous," said Pauline. "She was saying that on the ward. Before she left she was screaming about it. But everyone knew it was ridiculous."

"Ridiculous, thank you. And yesterday, Miss Campbell spoke very softly," mused Simpson Stone. "I find it interesting that she screamed."

"She could certainly scream," said Pauline.

"And generally, Miss Brown, did you find Lucy Campbell to be credible? Could you believe what she said?"

"We do always try to believe our patients," said Pauline. "But she was unusual. You couldn't really believe a word she said. In my opinion, that is."

"It's your opinion I was seeking. And I thank you for your balanced view, delivered from the position of having worked with both Lucy Campbell and Dr Barker. It is very helpful for us to record your opinion that her account of the relationship between them, as Dr Barker testified, was *ridiculous,* a *complete fantasy.* Thank you, Miss Brown, I have no further questions."

Miss Shapiro was already on her feet before an invitation came from the chair. She advanced on Pauline.

"How can you help patients when you do not believe them, Staff Nurse?" demanded Miss Shapiro.

"It makes it difficult," said Pauline defensively.

"It would indeed make it difficult. It seems to me like a *very bad habit.* Would you agree?"

"It's not a habit," said Pauline. "Lucy was unusual."

"And I suppose it would be unusual for a nurse not to believe a doctor, would you say?"

"Yes, that would be unusual."

"But here, perhaps, we are dealing with the unusual. You seem to have chosen to believe Dr Barker and to disbelieve Lucy Campbell. As a nurse might do."

Miss Shapiro appeared to go for a reflective stroll in a circle, absently pausing to pick up a sheet of paper from her team's desk as she passed.

"But in this *unusual* case," she continued, "there are two strands of evidence of which you may be unaware. And these strands of evidence point strongly towards Lucy Campbell's honesty and towards Douglas Barker's guilt."

Miss Shapiro handed Pauline the sheet of paper and said: "Please read this out."

"My love is like a red, red rose

That's newly sprung in June," Pauline recited.

"Thank you. This was given to the inquiry by Lucy Campbell. She said that Dr Barker wrote it for her. Is that plausible?"

"It looks like his writing," said Pauline, glancing at Douglas.

"So you agree that he wrote this love poem for Lucy Campbell, then Miss Brown?" asked Miss Shapiro airily.

"No. I didn't say that. It must be a forgery," said Pauline calmly.

Miss Shapiro seemed genuinely surprised.

"A *forgery*?" she asked. "How could it possibly be a *forgery*?"

"I don't think it would have been difficult for her to get a sample of Dr Barker's writing," Pauline told her. "The table the nurses use is out in the ward corridor. Dr Barker would write things, leave us notes on the nurses' desk. She could easily have got hold of one of his notes. He does have unusual writing. She could have copied it from that."

As Pauline spoke, Miss Shapiro's frown had been deepening.

"But why would she do that, Miss Brown?" she demanded.

"To prove her point about Dr Barker. That's the kind of person she is," said Pauline.

"This seems to me to be an *utterly extraordinary* allegation!" Miss Shapiro exclaimed. "I trust the panel will share my huge scepticism about this outlandish theory, this speculative accusation."

"We shall decide in our own time, Miss Shapiro," interjected the chairman, "without your comments on the witnesses' views. Please proceed with questions, not statements."

"Very well," said Miss Shapiro brusquely, "I shall move on to the other piece of strong corroborative evidence. In your experience, Miss Brown, do junior psychiatrists, in the course of their routine duties, reveal their buttocks to their patients?"

"No. Of course not," said Pauline.

"It would be, to use your term, *unusual*? To say the very least?"

"I can't see how it would happen," said Pauline, looking bemused.

"So if a patient saw a doctor's buttocks, Staff Nurse, it is likely that this would be in the course of a sexual relationship, rather than during an interview, or during a session of psychotherapy?"

"I suppose it would be," Pauline agreed.

"So if Lucy Campbell gave an accurate description of Dr Barker's buttocks, then you might wish to reconsider your certainty that they did not have a sexual relationship?" Miss Shapiro demanded.

Pauline looked imploringly towards the chairman.

"I don't understand the question," she said.

"During Miss Campbell's evidence," Professor Nelson explained, "she described a particular aspect of Dr Barker's buttocks. A characteristic aspect."

Pauline blushed even more deeply.

"Oh. The birthmark thing," she said.

"Well, yes," said Professor Norman. "It is not my role to question you but perhaps you could tell us what you know about this."

"It's a sort of joke, around the hospital," said Pauline hesitantly. "Dr Barker is, eh, popular with the nurses. One of them, em, saw it, the Australia thing, and called him 'Ozbum' and the name stuck. Some of the patients on the ward found out too. We all—the women that is—sort of had a bit of a laugh about it," she concluded, looking warily towards Douglas.

"Thank you for sharing this with the inquiry, Miss Brown," said Professor Nelson, smiling for the first time that Douglas recalled. "Any further questions, Miss Shapiro?"

Miss Shapiro's fury was evident. She wheeled towards Pauline.

"You are determined to dig Dr Barker out of a hole, are you not? Tell me, perhaps you are in love with him yourself?"

Pauline's consternation was cut short by Simpson Stone's 'Objection!' and by Professor Nelson.

"That is enough, Miss Shapiro. We shall adjourn the inquiry for lunch and during that time we shall consider our verdict."

Douglas grinned gratefully at Pauline as she departed from the chamber, and then saw that his legal team were grinning too.

"What fun that was!" exclaimed Simpson Stone. "Did you see Eva Shapiro? I thought she was going to explode!"

"She was a picture," Vince agreed. "I think you can relax, Douglas. I was watching the panel while Dr Horsefall and Pauline were testifying. The verdict was written all over their faces."

"It was as clear as that, Vincent?" asked Simpson Stone. "Excellent!"

"Douglas," said Vince, "let us shepherd you through to a quiet spot where you can eat a hearty lunch and await the outcome. The press may well be milling around wanting more photographs of 'Dr Ozbum' for tomorrow's papers."

****

Douglas sat in the small room Vince Green had found for him. It was well stocked with books and magazines, and he tried to distract himself by reading an article in The Cricketer about Sri Lanka. Vince told him that he would be 'going over things' during the lunch break with Simpson Stone.

"Just in case we're entirely wrong and they reach a guilty verdict—and I see that as a chance in a million—we need to mug up on Simpson's plea in mitigation. That includes your testimonials. They were good, weren't they?"

"They were," agreed Douglas. "They were nice."

He was searching among the books for an atlas, hoping to discover the location of Sri Lanka, when Vince returned. "We're going back in, Douglas. That was a very quick. Makes us even more optimistic. Come on then, once more into the breach."

Vince sounded excited, and he propelled Douglas at speed back into the chamber, where the panel were already in their seats.

Professor Nelson cleared his throat loudly.

"Dr Douglas Hamish Barker," he said, "please stand."

Douglas rose, gripping the edge of the table.

"We have studied and listened to the evidence in this case," Professor Nelson continued, "in relation to the charges against you. We have concluded that this evidence is insufficient to support or sustain these charges, and thus we have agreed that you should be found Not Guilty of Serious Professional Misconduct."

Douglas heard a muffled "Yes!" from the public gallery. Professor Nelson looked at him with a trace of a smile.

"I hope you have not found this to be too arduous an experience, Dr Barker," Professor Nelson added. "The Inquiry is now closed."

Douglas's sweaty palm was seized by Vince Green, while Simpson Stone clapped him on the back with surprising vigour. Douglas was limp with relief.

"You guys have been great," he said.

"It has been a pleasure to represent you," said Simpson Stone, returning to more formal barrister mode.

"We've seen some unsavoury doctors pass this way, so it's been good to work with you," said Vince.

"Yes, you've been more savoury than many," said Simpson Stone.

"Your fans are trying to attract you," said Vince, pointing to the public gallery.

Douglas looked up to see Chris pumping his fists. Pauline gave him a wave while Jim Horsefall repeated his exuberant thumbs up. Chris mimed that they should meet downstairs.

He found Chris, Pauline and Jim near the front door. There were congratulatory handshakes from the men. Douglas gave Pauline a slightly uncertain hug, and she reached up to kiss him on the cheek.

"Were these guys no' great witnesses? How much did ye pay them?" asked Chris.

"I can buy them a drink. Maybe you too. Shall we find a pub?"

"Nah," said Chris, "let's find a taxi and get out o' here. We can make it fir the three o'clock train."

****

They caught the train with time to spare, and found seats at a table in a carriage which was, as Chris pointed out, conveniently close to the bar. Jim and Pauline took the window seats, and Douglas sat next to Pauline.

"Before we start celebratin', I thought we might have a wee glance at these," said Chris, as he extracted a bundle of newspapers from his bag.

"As ye'll see," he continued, "there's some fine photos in this morning's papers of someone ye might know, and some classy journalism about his misdeeds."

"Alleged misdeeds, if you don't mind," said Douglas.

Chris picked up the top paper from the pile.

"Ye can look at all o' them, but this is my favourite. As usual, The Sun covers it best," he said as he held up the paper.

The headline read: 'Doc Fears Bum Rap'.

"And see this photo o' the accused guzzlin' a sandwich in a park? It says, 'Barker relaxes during sex trial'. I'm sure ye'll want tae read it all, but the article kicks off wi': 'A weird birthmark on his buttock may have sealed the fate of a Scottish doc accused of rampant sex with a patient.' Aye, 'Doc Fears Bum Rap' right enough! It must have kept ye awake last night."

"I didn't sleep all that well, even if I wasn't seeing the situation in those exact terms," said Douglas.

The train was picking up speed as it reached the outskirts of London.

"You guys read about the sex doc and I'll see if I can find some beers," said Chris.

"You're a rabbit in the headlights in The Times photo," said Jim, showing it to Douglas.

"That was coming back from lunch," said Douglas. "I do look like I'm shitting it."

"This is from The Express," said Pauline. "'The press gallery had been cleared during the evidence of the attractive young patient. But Barker admitted to a birthmark on his buttock that she had described. The doctor's consultant, an eminent psychiatrist, had earlier confirmed that he caught Barker without his trousers cavorting with another female patient'. And they finish with: 'At the end of the first day of the hearing, prospects looked bleak for the young psychiatrist'."

"And they felt bleak," said Douglas.

Chris returned, carrying cans of beer, and he removed more from the pockets of his jacket.

"They only had these wee British Rail sized cans," he said. "So I thought I would buy a few tae keep us goin'. I hope lager's OK fir you, Pauline."

"It's fine," she said. "I'll drink anything."

Douglas was staring at the newspaper on the table in front of Pauline.

"I'm not good at faces," he said, "but I've just recognised her in that photo. 'Miss C, unemployed barmaid,' it says. Christ! Why have I not seen it before? She's the lass I had a wee liaison with on my first night in psychiatry. I thought she looked familiar."

"So you did have sex with Lucy?" asked Pauline.

"Last August. Before she was a patient. Just one night."

"Aye," said Chris, "your womanisin' comin' back tae haunt ye, eh? It's little wonder ye can't remember all their faces."

"I have a disability. Facial agnosia. If I see people out of context, I can't recognise them unless I know them well," said Douglas.

"So it makes a bit more sense," said Jim. "She was a woman perceiving herself to be spurned. And she thought you knew who she was, when you didn't. I'm Jim Horsefall, by the way."

"Ha, ha. But yes, it does make more sense," said Douglas, followed by a long exhalation.

They sat quietly for a while. Chris broke the silence.

"So the lassie, Lucy, she complains because ye've shagged her, and she thinks ye've misused her and because she's no' right in the head. Nasty—but maybe fair enough," he said. "It's Burlington that gets me. He had actually *written* tae the GMC about ye. And see him in the Daily Mail here,"

314

he said, stabbing a photograph with his finger, "did ye ever see a man more up his own arse?"

"That point was made by Jim this morning," said Douglas.

"And very well made," said Chris. "Ye're a brave bugger, Jim."

"No, not really," said Jim.

"You are!" said Douglas. "Saying what you said could be a real career wrecker. We've seen what Burlington can do when he bears a grudge."

"It needed to be said, though, by somebody," said Pauline.

"It did, and it might as well have been me. I don't usually detest people, but I can make an exception for Edwin Burlington," said Jim. "This has not been a happy year working with him. He undermines you and he disparages you. Sometimes to prove himself right, but sometimes just for the fun of it. He's a genuine, class A bastard!"

"But he's a bastard that could now be out to get you, too," said Douglas.

"He could try," said Jim, "but I don't think he will. I'm off to Melbourne in October—a consultant job. I told you this morning, Pauline, but you guys probably don't know."

"No, I didn't know, well done," said Douglas.

"It was just confirmed last week," said Jim.

"And ye're pleased?" asked Chris. "That's where ye were actually wantin' tae go?"

"It certainly is," said Jim. "How much sun have you seen this summer? And what about last winter? The thing that clinched it was being stranded in my car in Wales, covered in snow, stuck overnight in the middle of January. I planned to go somewhere sunny that night."

"Well, it's Scotland's loss, Jim," said Douglas as he stood up. "I'm going for more beer. How many did you manage to carry, Chris?"

"Ten," said Chris.

"I'll beat that," said Douglas.

When he returned with twelve cans of beer in his arms and crammed into his pockets, debate was continuing about the merits of Scotland and Australia.

"When ye wir away," said Chris, "we decided it wis you that should be goin' tae Australia. They would make ye a citizen right away if ye just showed them yir bum."

"Ha, ha," said Douglas as he opened a can of beer. "Cheers, Jim. Here's to a happy life in Australia."

They clinked cans and drank to the success of Jim's emigration.

"I could've sunk like a stone today, without you, Jim. And without you too, of course, Pauline," said Douglas. "And now you're off to Australia. I never said it to you, but the very first day I met you, I thought you were a bit of an idiot. And now you've saved my bacon."

"You thought I was an idiot? Why was that?" asked Jim.

"You maybe wouldn't remember. It was my first day. You and me, and Dick went for coffee, and the two of you prattled on about the collective unconscious and returning to the womb in some weird play you'd seen."

"I do remember," said Jim. "I'd never seen the play."

"*What?*" exclaimed Douglas. "But you were chatting all that rubbish with Dick."

"I'd maybe seen a review, but I was just winding him up," said Jim. "Seeing what crap he might come out with next."

Douglas laughed uproariously.

"You dark horse!" he shouted. "You dark *Horsefall*!"

"Douglas," said Pauline, "you're shouting. We'll get thrown off the train."

"Sorry," said Douglas contritely. "But come to that, Pauline, you're a bit of a dark horse yourself. I thought you were quiet and shy, and you stood up and said all that stuff today."

"I don't think of myself as quiet and shy," said Pauline.

"Not like you tae misjudge a woman," said Chris.

"And as for you," said Douglas, "you might like to take the piss, but I've got a letter, signed by Dr Christopher Dunn, telling the GMC all the nice things you *really* think about me. 'He is an extremely ethical doctor'. Stuff like that. It'll be framed and up on the wall in the flat before you know it."

"Aye. And then 'Doc Fears Bum Rap' will be up right next tae it," said Chris.

"You two are a bit of a double act, aren't you? And Chris mentioned you'll be working together in August," said Pauline.

"Are we? I hadn't heard about next month's jobs when I went down south," said Douglas.

"Aye well," said Chris, "they probably left your name off the list till the last minute, thinkin' ye'd be struck off and lookin' fir a job as a bouncer. Nah, we're both goin' tae psychogeriatrics."

"You'll like it," said Jim, who had looked as if he were dozing. "I liked it. Nice old people with real illnesses. Not much neurosis or personality disorders."

"I'm hopin' tae see Dr Barker's psychotherapy skills in action wi' the dementia patients. Maybe they'll all recover when he tells them they're forgettin' things because they're repressin' memories about incest," said Chris.

By the time the train was coming into Newcastle, Jim was asleep, his head knocking gently against the window. Douglas opened another can of beer which frothed violently and sprayed over Chris. A few droplets hit Jim's face, causing him to open his eyes blearily.

"Hey, I'm reporting you tae the GMC, ye clumsy arse!" shouted Chris, wiping his jacket.

"Clumsy Ozbum," said Jim as he fell back to sleep.

"Sorry folks. I didn't get you too, did I, Pauline?" asked Douglas.

"No, I'm the only one sober enough to dodge," she told him.

"Well, ye'll need tae drink quicker, then," said Chris, as he stood up. "I'm off tae the toilet. I'll get some more cans on my way back."

"I have to tell you," said Douglas, turning to Pauline, "that it's very good I didn't spoil your nice outfit. It's sexy. And I thought it was *too* sexy when I saw you this morning. Tottering on your big heels across to that witness box thing. But you knocked them dead, didn't you?"

"I'll take that as a compliment."

"It was compliments. It *is* compliments. I'm saying you looked great. But what about the thing? Eh? The Ozbum thing. How come I never heard about that? Hey, half of my can was missing, you know. It's finished. He's got it on his jacket. I need another one."

"He'll be back soon with some more," said Pauline, handing him her beer, "and you can drink this in the meantime."

"Cheers," said Douglas. "But don't change the subject. What about Ozbum? How come you never said? How come I never heard?"

"Well, Douglas," said Pauline quietly in his ear, "nobody did actually call you that. But I thought it would go down well. And I think it did."

Douglas sat back drunkenly and gazed at her with an open mouth.

"What are you two whisperin' about?" asked Chris as he returned to the table. "I thought just six cans would do us the rest o' the way."

"Slow down, boys," advised Pauline. "You'll regret it tomorrow."

"It's a time fir celebrations. No' fir regrets," said Chris.

"I regret it," said Douglas. "I regret changing my trousers and going to play golf with you or all this would never have happened. In fact, it's all been your fault."

"Ye regret it because I thrashed ye that day. Ye're always a bad loser," Chris told him.

"I need to get revenge. We haven't played for weeks and weeks and months. But might not be fit tomorrow. For golf," said Douglas.

"Or for much else," added Pauline.

"What about Thursday? Day after tomorrow. It's my birthday. Thursday. I could destroy you at golf on Thursday," said Douglas.

"I've told ye a million times," said Chris. "The only reason I think there might be some good inside Barker somewhere is because my dear old mother has the same birthday that you do too. The 29th. Right? So I'm off through to see her wi' a cake on Thursday. And flowers. Pauline'll play ye at golf."

"I've never played," she said to Douglas, blushing slightly. "But I'm sure we could find something fun to do together on your birthday."